The Luminous Face

By Carolyn Wells

Originally published in 1921

The Luminous Face

© 2013 Resurrected Press
www.ResurrectedPress.com

Published by Resurrected Press

This classic book was handcrafted by Resurrected Press. Resurrected Press is dedicated to bringing high quality classic books back to the readers who enjoy them. These are not scanned versions of the originals, but, rather, quality checked and edited books meant to be enjoyed!

Please visit ResurrectedPress.com to view our entire catalogue!

ISBN 13: 978-1-937022-64-8

Printed in the United States of America

RESURRECTED PRESS CLASSIC MYSTERY CATALOGUE

Journeys into Mystery
Travel and Mystery in a More Elegant Time

The Edwardian Detectives
Literary Sleuths of the Edwardian Era

Gems of Mystery
Lost Jewels from a More Elegant Age

Anne Austin
One Drop of Blood
The Black Pigeon
Murder at Bridge

E. C. Bentley
Trent's Last Case: The Woman in Black

Ernest Bramah
Max Carrados Resurrected:
The Detective Stories of Max Carrados

Agatha Christie
The Secret Adversary
The Mysterious Affair at Styles

Octavus Roy Cohen
Midnight

Freeman Wills Croft
The Ponson Case
The Pit Prop Syndicate

J. S. Fletcher
The Herapath Property
The Rayner-Slade Amalgamation
The Chestermarke Instinct
The Paradise Mystery
Dead Men's Money
The Middle of Things
Ravensdene Court
Scarhaven Keep
The Orange-Yellow Diamond
The Middle Temple Murder
The Tallyrand Maxim
The Borough Treasurer
In the Mayor's Parlour
The Saftey Pin

R. Austin Freeman
The Mystery of 31 New Inn from the Dr. Thorndyke Series
John Thorndyke's Cases from the Dr. Thorndyke Series
The Red Thumb Mark from The Dr. Thorndyke Series
The Eye of Osiris from The Dr. Thorndyke Series
A Silent Witness from the Dr. John Thorndyke Series
The Cat's Eye from the Dr. John Thorndyke Series
Helen Vardon's Confession: A Dr. John Thorndyke Story
As a Thief in the Night: A Dr. John Thorndyke Story
Mr. Pottermack's Oversight: A Dr. John Thorndyke Story
Dr. Thorndyke Intervenes: A Dr. John Thorndyke Story
The Singing Bone: The Adventures of Dr. Thorndyke
The Stoneware Monkey: A Dr. John Thorndyke Story
The Great Portrait Mystery, and Other Stories: A Collection of Dr. John Thorndyke and Other Stories
The Penrose Mystery: A Dr. John Thorndyke Story
The Uttermost Farthing: A Savant's Vendetta

Arthur Griffiths
The Passenger From Calais
The Rome Express

Fergus Hume
The Mystery of a Hansom Cab
The Green Mummy
The Silent House
The Secret Passage

Edgar Jepson
The Loudwater Mystery

A. E. W. Mason
At the Villa Rose

A. A. Milne
The Red House Mystery

Baroness Emma Orczy
The Old Man in the Corner

Edgar Allan Poe
The Detective Stories of Edgar Allan Poe

Arthur J. Rees
The Hampstead Mystery
The Shrieking Pit
The Hand In The Dark
The Moon Rock
The Mystery of the Downs

Mary Roberts Rinehart
Sight Unseen and The Confession

Dorothy L. Sayers

Whose Body?

Sir William Magnay
The Hunt Ball Mystery

Mabel and Paul Thorne
The Sheridan Road Mystery

Louis Tracy
The Strange Case of Mortimer Fenley
The Albert Gate Mystery
The Bartlett Mystery
The Postmaster's Daughter
The House of Peril
The Sandling Case: What Would You Have Done?

Charles Edmonds Walk
The Paternoster Ruby

John R. Watson
The Mystery of the Downs
The Hampstead Mystery

Edgar Wallace
The Daffodil Mystery
The Crimson Circle

Carolyn Wells
Vicky Van
The Man Who Fell Through the Earth
In the Onyx Lobby
Raspberry Jam
The Clue
The Room with the Tassels
The Vanishing of Betty Varian
The Mystery Girl
The White Alley
The Curved Blades

FOREWORD

By the time that Carolyn Wells *wrote The Luminous Face* she was already an old hand at writing mysteries, having written over a dozen since turning her hand to the genre in 1909 with The Clue. Originally a poet and humorist, she had developed a unique style that ran counter to most of the detective fiction of the period. Rather than concentrating her narrative on the details of evidence and the power of inductive reasoning displayed by the master detective, she was much more concerned with the domestic and psychological effects that a crime had upon those that were suspects.

The interplay between the various characters as one by one they come under suspicion was a hallmark of her mysteries. The master detective, usually Fleming Stone, or as in the case of *The Luminous Face*, Pennington Wise, often don't turn up until the last few chapters, well after the various clues and alibis have all been discovered and explored by the family and close associates of the murder victim. It is the suspects themselves who undertake the majority of the task of detection. What is important, is not so much who is guilty, but how friends and lovers react when the evidence seems to point to those closest to them. Do they refuse to believe the worst, or do they prove false?

Along with this interplay, Wells often examined the conventions and attitudes of the subjects of her mysteries who mostly come from the wealthy upper middle class of the East Coast. The changing role of women in particular was often an underlying theme of her works, and the dynamics between husband and wife, father and daughter, both before and after the crisis created by a crime play a major part of the story. The dozen years of her career as a mystery writer was an important one for women, with questions of suffrage, education, and employment opportunities all in the public eye.

This is not to say that Wells was not concerned with the finer points of the detective fiction. Her characters often discuss various theoretical aspects of detection and whether real life crimes can be solved as neatly as they are in fiction. In the first chapter of *The Luminous Face* there is an extended discussion of the role of establishing a motive in the successful solving of a case. Wells took this examination one step further, writing a book, *The Technique of the Mystery Story*, one of the first works to look at the subject critically.

The Luminous Face begins conventionally enough as a locked room murder, the victim, Robert Gleason, is found dead in his apartment with two gunshot wounds and a revolver lying by his side, an apparent suicide . Yet from the begin facts seem to conflict with that verdict. The victim had phoned his doctor saying that he had been shot, yet an examination reveals that the first shot had been fatal. There are plenty of suspects, his sister and her step-daughter who stand to benefit from his will, her step-son who was in debt, the artist Barry, who was his romantic rival, Pollard, who expressed a dislike of the victim and claimed he would kill him, his chorus-girl ex-girlfriend, all of whom have suspicion fall on them. But confronted with conflicting and possibly false clues and unwilling witnesses the police remain baffled. Only when the private detective Pennington Wise and his mysterious assistant Zizi are called in, is the puzzle solved, and then only by noticing the most inconsequential clue.

Carolyn Wells was an important figure in the evolution of detective fiction, and in the end, quite a successful one, authoring some seventy mysteries over three decades from 1909 to 1942. It is therefore with great pleasure, that Resurrected Press presents this new edition of *The Luminous Face*.

About the Author

Carolyn Wells, June 18, 1862 March 26, 1942 was an American writer and poet. She was best known for her books of poetry and humor until around 1910 she read one of Anna Katherine Green's mysteries and took up the genre. Many of her mysteries featured the detective Fleming Stone. She was married to Hadwin Houghton, heir to the Houghton-Mifflin publishing company. She was a collector of poetry by other authors, and, upon her death, she bequeathed her collection of the works of Walt Witman to the Library of Congress.

Greg Fowlkes
Editor-In-Chief
Resurrected Press
www.ResurrectedPress.com

Table of Contents

CHAPTER 1: DOCTOR FELL

"A bit thick, I call it," Pollard looked round the group; "here's Mellen been dead six weeks now, and the mystery of his taking-off still unsolved."

"And always will be," Doctor Davenport nodded. "Mighty few murders are brought home to the villains who commit them."

"Oh, I don't know," drawled Phil Barry, an artist, whose dress and demeanor coincided with the popular idea of his class. "I've no head for statistics," he went on, idly drawing caricatures on the margin of his evening paper as he talked, "but I think they say that only one-tenth of one per cent, of the murderers in this great and glorious country of ours are ever discovered."

"Your head for statistics is defective, as you admit," Doctor Davenport said, his tone scornful; "but percentages mean little in these matters. The greater part of the murders committed are not brought prominently before public notice. It's only when the victim is rich or influential, or the circumstances of some especial interest that a murder occupies the front pages of the newspapers."

"Old Mellen's been on those same front pages for several weeks—off and on, that is," Pollard insisted; "of course, he was a well-known man and his exit was dramatic. But all the same, they ought to have caught his murderer—or slayer, as the papers call him."

"Him?" asked Barry, remembering the details of the case.

"Impersonal pronoun," Pollard returned, "and probably a man anyway. 'Cherchez la femme,' is the trite advice, and always sounds well, but really, a woman seldom has nerve enough for the fatal deed."

"That's right," Davenport agreed. "I know lots of women who have all the intent of murder in their hearts, but who never could pull it off."

"A good thing, too," Barry observed. "I'd hate to think any woman I know capable of murder! Ugh!" His long, delicate white hand waved away the distasteful idea with a gesture that seemed to dismiss it entirely.

There were not many in the Club lounge, the group of men had it mostly to themselves, and as the afternoon dusk grew deeper and the lights were turned on, several more went away, and finally Fred Lane rose to go.

"Frightfully interesting, you fellows," he said, "but it's after five, and I've a date. Anybody I can drop anywhere?"

"Me, please," accepted Dean Monroe. "That is, if you're going my way. I want to go downtown."

"Was going up," returned Lane, "but delighted to change my route. Come along, Monroe."

But Monroe had heard a chance word from Doctor Davenport that arrested his attention, and he sat still.

"Guess I won't go quite yet—thanks all the same," he nodded at Lane, and lighted a fresh cigarette.

Dean Monroe was a younger man than the others, an artist, but not yet in the class with Barry. His square, firm-set jaw, and his Wedgwood blue eyes gave his face a look of power and determination quite in contrast with Philip Barry's pale, sensitive countenance. Yet the two were friends—chums, almost, and though differing in their views on art, each respected the other's opinions.

"Have it your own way," Lane returned, indifferently, and went off.

"Crime detection is not the simple process many suppose," Davenport was saying, and Monroe gave his whole attention. "So much depends on chance."

"Now, Doctor," Monroe objected, "I hold it's one of the most exact sciences, and—"

Davenport looked at him, as an old dog might look at an impertinent kitten.

"Being an exact science doesn't interfere with dependence on chance," he growled; "also, young man, are you sure you know what an exact science is?"

"Yeppy," Monroe defended himself, as the others smiled a little. "It's—why, it's a science that's exact—isn't it?"

His gay smile disarmed his opponent, and Davenport, mounted on his hobby, went on: "You may have skill, intuition, deductive powers and all that, but to discover a criminal, the prime element is chance. Now, in the Mellen case, the chances were all against the detectives from the first. They didn't get there till the evidences were, or might have been destroyed. They couldn't find Mrs Gresham, the most important witness until after she had had time to prepare her string of falsehoods. Oh, well, you know how the case was messed up, and now, there's not a chance in a hundred of the truth ever being known."

"Does chance play any part in your profession, Doctor?" asked Monroe, with the expectation of flooring him.

"You bet it does!" was the reply. "Why, be I never so careful in my diagnosis or treatment, a chance deviation from my orders on the part of patient or attendant, a chance draught of wind, or upset nerves—oh, Lord, yes! as the Good Book says, 'Time and Chance happeneth to us all.' And no line of work is more precarious than establishing a theory or running down a clew in a murder case. For the criminal, ever on the alert, has all the odds on his side, and can block or divert the detective's course at will."

Doctor Ely Davenport was, without being pompous, a man who was at all times conscious of his own personality and sure of his own importance. He was important, too, being one of the most highly thought of doctors in New York City, and his self-esteem, if a trifle annoying, was founded on his real worth.

He often said that his profession brought him in contact with the souls of men and women quite as much as with their bodies, and he was fond of theorizing what human nature might do or not do in crucial moments.

The detection of crime he held to be a matter requiring the highest intelligence and rarest skill.

"Detection!" he exclaimed, in the course of the present conversation, "why detection is as hard to work out as the Fourth Dimension! As difficult to understand as the Einstein theory."

"Oh, come now, Doctor," Pollard said, smiling, "that's going a bit too far. I admit, though, it requires a superior brain. But any real work does. However, I say, first catch your motive."

"That's it," broke in Monroe, eagerly. "It all depends on the motive!"

"The crime does," Davenport assented, drily, "but not the detection. You youngsters don't know what you're talking about—you'd better shut up."

"We know a lot," returned Monroe, unabashed. "Youth is no barrier to knowledge these days. And I hold that the clever detective seeks first the motive. You can't have a murder without a motive, any more than an omelette without eggs."

"True, oh, Solomon," granted the doctor. "But the motive may be known only to the murderer, and not to be discovered by any effort of the investigator."

"Then the murder mystery remains unsolved," returned Monroe, promptly.

"Your saying so doesn't make it so, you know," drawled Phil Barry, in his impertinent way. "Now, to me it would seem that a nice lot of circumstantial evidence, and a few good clews would expedite matters just as well as a knowledge of the villain's motive."

"Circumstantial evidence!" scoffed Monroe.

"Sure," rejoined Barry; "Give me a smoking revolver with initials on it, a dropped handkerchief, monogrammed, of course, half a broken cuff-link, and a few fingerprints, and I care not who knows the motive. And if you can add a piece—no, a fragment of tweed, clutched in the victim's rigid hand—why—I'll not ask for wine!"

"What rubbish you all talk," said Pollard, smiling superciliously; "don't you see these things all count? If you have motive you don't need evidence, and —. That is, if both motive and evidence are the real thing."

"There are only three motives," Monroe informed. "Love, hate and money."

"You've got all the jargon by heart, little one," and Pollard grinned at him. "Been reading some new Detective Fiction?"

"I'm always doing that," Monroe stated, "but I hold that a detective who can't tell which of those three is the motive, isn't worth his salt."

"Salt is one commodity that has remained fairly inexpensive," said Barry, speaking slowly, and with his eyes on his cigarette, from which he was carefully amputating the ash, "and a detective who could truly diagnose motive is not to be sneezed at. Besides, revenge is often a reason."

"That comes under the head of hate," promptly responded Monroe. "The three motives include all the gamut of human emotion, and some of their ramifications will include every murder motive that ever existed."

"Fear?" quietly suggested Doctor Davenport.

"Part of hate," said Monroe, but he was challenged by Pollard.

"Not necessarily. A man may fear a person whom he does not hate at all. But there's another motive, that doesn't quite fit your classification, Monroe."

Before the inevitable question could be put another man joined the group.

"Hello, folks," said Robert Gleason, as he sat down; "hope I don't intrude—and all that. What you talking about?"

"Murder," said Barry. "Murder as a Fine Art, you know."

"Don't like the subject. Let's change it. Talk about the ladies, or something pleasant, you know. Eh?"

"Or Shakespeare and the musical glasses," said Pollard.

"No musical glasses, nowadays," bewailed Gleason. "No more clink the canakin, clink. It's drink to me only with thine eyes. Hence, the preponderance of women and song in our lives, since the third of the trio is gone."

Gleason was the sort of Westerner usually described as breezy. He was on intimate terms with everybody, whether everybody reciprocated or not. Not a large man, not a young man, he possessed a restless vitality, a wiry energy that gave him an effect of youth. About forty, he was nearer the age of Doctor Davenport than the others, who were all in their earliest thirties.

Nobody liked Gleason much, yet no one really disliked him. He was a bit forward, a little intrusive, but it was clear to be seen that those mannerisms were due to ignorance and not to any intent to be objectionable. He was put up at the Club by a friend, and had never really overstepped his privileges, though it was observable that his ways were not club ways.

"Yep, the Ladies—God bless 'em!" he went on. "What could be a better subject for gentlemen's discussion? No personalities, of course; that goes without saying."

"Then why say it?" murmured Pollard, without looking at the speaker.

"That's so! Why, indeed?" was the genial response. "Now, you know, out in Seattle, where I hail from, there's more—oh, what do you call it, sociability like, among men. I go into a club there and everybody sings out something gay; I come in here, and you all shut up like clams."

"You objected to the subject we were discussing," began Monroe, indignantly, but Barry interrupted, with a wave of his hand, "The effete East, my dear Gleason.

Doubtless you've heard that expression? Yes, you would. Well, it's our renowned effeteness that prevents our falling on your neck more effusively."

"Guying me?" asked Gleason, with a quiet smile. "You see, boys, before I went to Seattle, I was born in New England. I can take a little chaff."

"You're going to tell us of your ancestry?" said Pollard, and though his words were polite his tone held a trace of sarcastic intent.

Gleason turned a sudden look on him.

"I might, if you really want me to," he said, slowly. "I might give you the story of my life from my infancy, spent in Coggs' Hollow, New Hampshire, to the present day, when I may call myself one of the leading citizens of Seattle, Wash."

"What or whom do you lead?" asked Pollard, and again the only trace of unpleasantness was a slight inflection in his really fine voice.

"I lead the procession," and Gleason smiled, as one who positively refuses to take offense whether meant or not. "But, I can tell you I don't lead it here in New York! Your pace is rather swift for me! I'm having a good time and all that, but soon, it's me for the wildness and woolliness of the good old West again! Why, looky here, I'm living in a hole in the wall—yes, sir, a hole in the wall!"

"I like that!" laughed Doctor Davenport. "Why, man, you're in that apartment of McIlvaine's—one of the best put-ups in town."

"Yes, so Mac said," Gleason exploded. "Why, out home, we'd call that a coop. But what could I do? This old town of yours, spilling over full, couldn't fix me out at any hotel, so when my friend offered his palatial home, I took it—and—"

"You'd be surprised at the result!" Barry broke in. "That's because you're a Western millionaire, Mr Gleason. Now we poor, struggling young artists think that apartment you're in, one of the finest diggings around Washington Square."

"But, man, there's no service!" Gleason went on, complainingly. "Not even a hall porter! Nobody to announce a caller!"

"Well, you have that more efficient service, the—"

"Yes! the contraption that lets a caller push a button and have the door open in his face!"

"Isn't that just what he wants?" said Barry, laughing outright at Gleason's disgusted look. "Then, you see, Friend Caller walks upstairs, and there you are!"

"Yes, — upstairs. Not even an elevator!"

"But your friends don't need one," expostulated Davenport. "You're only one flight up. You don't seem to realize how lucky you are to get that place, in these days of housing problems!"

"Oh, well, 'tis not so deep as a well, nor so wide as a church door, but it will serve," said Gleason, with one of his sudden, pleasant smiles.

"I see your point, though, Mr Gleason," said Dean Monroe. "And if I were a plutocrat from Seattle, sojourning in this busy mart, I confess I, too, should like a little more of the dazzling light in my halls than you get down there. I know the place, used to go there to see McIlvaine. And while it's a decent size, and jolly well furnished, I can see how you'd prefer more gilt on your ginger bread."

"I do, and I'd have it, too, if I were staying here much longer. But I'm going to settle up things soon now, and go back to home, sweet home."

"How did you, a New Englander, chance to make Seattle your home?" asked Monroe, always of a curious bent.

"Had a chance to go out there and get rich. You see, Coggs' Hollow, as one might gather from its name, was a small hamlet. I lived there till I was twenty-five, then, getting a chance to go West and blow up with the country, I did. Glad of it, too. Now, I'm going back there, and—I hope to take with me a specimen of your fair feminine. Yes, sir, I hope and expect to take along, under my wing, one of these little moppy-haired, brief-skirted lassies, that will grace my Seattle home something fine!"

"Does she know it yet?" drawled Barry and Gleason stared at him.

"She isn't quite sure of it, but I am!" he returned with a comical air of determination.

"You know her pretty well, then," chaffed Barry.

"You bet I do! I ought to. She's my sister's stepdaughter."

"Phyllis Lindsay!" cried Barry, involuntarily speaking the name.

"The same," said Gleason, smiling; "and as I'm due there for dinner, I'll be toddling now to make myself fine for the event."

With a general beaming smile of good nature that included all the group, Gleason went away.

For a few moments no one spoke, and then Monroe began, "As I was saying, there are only three motives for murder—and I stick to that. But you were about to say, Pollard—?"

"I was about to say that you have omitted the most frequent and most impelling motive. It doesn't always result in the fatal stroke, but as a motive, it can't be beat."

"Go on—what is it?"

"Just plain dislike."

"Oh, hate," said Monroe.

"Not at all. Hate implies a reason, a grievance. But I mean an ineradicable, and unreasonable dislike—why, simply a case of:

'I do not like you, Doctor Fell,
The reason why I cannot tell;
But this I know and know full well,
I do not like you, Doctor Fell.'

One Tom Brown wrote that, and it's a bit of truth, all right!"

"One Martial said it before your friend Brown," informed Doctor Davenport. "He wrote:

'Non amo, te, Sabidi, nec possum dicere quore; Hoc tantum possum dicere, non amo te.'

Which is, being translated for the benefit of you unlettered ones, 'I do not love thee, Sabidius, nor can I say why; this only can I say, I do not love thee.' There's a French version, also."

"Never mind, Doc," Pollard interrupted, "we don't want your erudition, but your opinion. You say you know psychology as well as physiology; will you agree that a strong motive for murder might be just that unreasonable dislike—that distaste of seeing a certain person around?"

"No, not a strong motive," said Davenport, after a short pause for thought. "A slight motive, perhaps, by which I mean a fleeting impulse."

"No," persisted Pollard, "an impelling—a compelling motive. Why, there's Gleason now. I can't bear that man. Yet I scarcely know him. I've met him but a few times— had little or no personal conversation with him—yet I dislike him. Not detest or hate or despise—merely dislike him. And, some day I'm going to kill him."

"Going to kill all the folks you dislike?" asked Barry, indifferently.

"Maybe. If I dislike them enough. But that Gleason offends my taste. I can't stand him about. So, as I say, I'm going to kill him. And I hold that the impulse that drives me to the deed is the strongest murder motive a man can have."

"Don't talk rubbish, Manning," and young Monroe gave him a frightened glance, as if he thought Pollard in earnest.

"It isn't altogether rubbish," said Doctor Davenport, as he rose to go, "there's a grain of truth in Pollard's contention. A rooted dislike of another is a bad thing to have in your system. Have it cut out, Pollard."

"You didn't mean it, did you, Manning?"

Monroe spoke diffidently, almost shyly, with a scared glance at Pollard.

The latter turned and looked at him with a smile. Then, glaring ferociously, he growled, "Of course I did! And if you get yourself disliked, I'll kill you, too! —"

They all laughed at Monroe's frightened jump, as Pollard Booh'd into his face, and Doctor Davenport said, "Look out, Pollard, don't scare our young friend into fits! And, remember, Monroe, 'Threatened men live long?' I've my car—anybody want a lift anywhere?"

"Take me, will you?" said Dean Monroe, and willingly enough, Doctor Davenport carried the younger man off in his car.

"You oughtn't to do it, Pol, you know," Barry gently remonstrated. "Poor little Monroe thinks you're a gory villain, and he'll mull over your fool remarks till he's crazy—more crazy than he is already."

"Let him," said Pollard, smiling indifferently. "I only spoke the truth—as to that motive, I mean. Don't you want to kill that Gleason every time you see him?"

"You make him seem like a cat—with nine or more lives! How — you kill a man every time you see him? It isn't done!"

The two men left the Club together, and walked briskly down Fifth Avenue.

"Going to the Lindsays' to-night, of course?" asked Barry, as they reached Forty-fifth Street, where he turned off.

"Yes. You?"

"Yes. See you later, then. You gather that Gleason has annexed the pretty Phyllis?"

"Looks like it, doesn't it? I suppose the announcement will be made to-night at the dinner or the dance."

"Suppose so. How I hate to see it that way. I'm in love with that little beauty myself."

"Who isn't?" returned Pollard, smiling, and then Barry turned off in his own street, and Pollard went on down toward his home, a small hotel on West Fortieth.

Held up for a few moments by the great tide of traffic at Forty-second Street, he glanced at his wrist watch and found it was ten minutes after six. And then, a taxicab passed him, and in it he saw Phyllis Lindsay. She did not see him, however, so, the traffic signal being given, he went on his way.

CHAPTER 2: THE TELEPHONE CALL

Every hour of every twenty-four is filled with amazing occurrences and startling episodes. Astonishing incidents and even more startling coincidences are happening every minute of every sixty minutes, but the fact that those most interested are unaware of these deeds is what makes the great cases of mystery.

Only an omniscient eye that could see all the activities of the few hours following the events just related could pierce the veil of doubt and uncertainty that overhung the ensuing tragedy.

The first human being to receive news of it was Miss Hester Jordan.

This capable and efficient young woman was the office nurse of Doctor Davenport, and her position was no sinecure.

Of a highly nervous temperament, she yet managed to preserve the proper calm and poise that nurses should always show, except when, at the end of a long, hard day, she became mentally and physically exhausted.

Though supposed to be off duty at six o'clock, her relief was frequently late in arriving and in this instance had not yet put in an appearance, though it was half past the hour.

Wearily, Miss Jordan answered telephone calls, striving to keep her tired voice pleasant and amiable.

"No," she would answer the anxious speakers, "Doctor Davenport is not in." "Yes, I expect him soon." "Can you leave a message?" "Yes, I will tell him." "He will surely be in by seven." "No, he left no message for you." "No, I don't know exactly where he is." "Yes, I will let you know."

Replies of this sort, over and over, strained her nerves to their furthest tension, and when at six-forty the telephone bell jangled again she took the receiver from its hook with what was almost a jerk.

"Hello," she said, unable to keep utter exasperation out of her voice.

But instead of a summons from some impatient patient, she heard a faint voice say, "Come, Doctor—oh, come quick—I'm—I'm done for—shot—"

There were more incoherent words, but Nurse Jordan couldn't catch them.

"Who are you?" she cried, alert now. "Who is speaking?"

"Gleason," came back the faint voice. "Wash'—t'n Square—come—can't you come quick—"

She could get no more. The voice ceased, and only blank silence met her frantic queries.

She hung up her receiver, and a sudden realization of the situation came to her. She seemed to see the scene— somebody shot—somebody telephoning that he was shot—somebody's voice getting weaker and ceasing to sound at all—the picture was too much for her tired brain, and she buried her face in her hands and sobbed hysterically from sheer nervous excitement.

Only for a moment did she give way. Nurse Jordan's training and personality was not to be conquered by a sudden shock of any sort.

Pulling herself together, she set to work to find the doctor.

This meant telephoning to two or three places where she knew there was a chance of locating him.

And at the third call she found him at Mrs Ballard's, and, though still shaken and quivering, she controlled her voice and told him distinctly of the tragic telephone call she had taken.

"Gleason!" cried the Doctor, "Washington Square? What number?"

But Nurse Jordan didn't know, and Doctor Davenport had to call up somebody to inquire.

He tried Mrs Lindsay, who was Gleason's sister, but her wire was busy and after an impatient moment, Davenport called Pollard, at his hotel.

"Here," he cried, handing the receiver to a staring butler, "take this and when the gentleman answers, ask him the address of Robert Gleason. Tell him Doctor Davenport's inquiring."

He then returned to the prescription he had been writing, and gave it to Mrs Ballard, who was indignant at having her interview with her doctor intruded upon.

"I'll call to-morrow," he soothed her; "you'll be better in the morning. Let fish alone, and stick to simple diet for a few days. Get that address, Jenkins?"

"Yes, sir," and the butler gave him a slip of paper.

"H'm—near Washington Square, not on it," he murmured, looking at the written number, and then he ran down the Ballard front steps, and jumping into his waiting car, gave his chauffeur Gleason's address.

"Wonder what's up?" he thought, as his car rolled down Fifth Avenue. "Accident, I suppose. Jordan is always on edge this time of night. Have to take her excitement with a grain of salt."

But when he reached the house, and pushed the button that indicated McIlvaine's apartment, there was no response from the closed street door.

He rang again, long and insistently, then, still getting no encouragement, he pushed another button.

The door gave a grudging grunt, and, unwillingly, as it seemed, moved slowly inward.

Doctor Davenport was half way up the first flight of stairs, when a woman's head appeared through a doorway.

"What do you want?" she inquired, a little crisply.

"Mr McIlvaine's apartment."

"That's it, opposite," she returned, more affable as she caught sight of the good-looking man. "Mr Gleason's in there now."

"Yes, he's the man I want. Thank you, madame."

She still stood, watching, as he rang the doorbell of the designated apartment.

There was no answer, nor any sound from inside. The doctor looked apprehensively at the door.

"Your key wouldn't let me in, I suppose," he said, turning back to the now frankly curious spectator.

"Oh, Lord, no! We don't have interchangeable keys! He's out, I expect. He's mostly out."

"But I want to get into his place—"

"You do! And he not there! You a friend of his?"

"Why—yes; I'm his doctor—and I'm afraid he's ill."

"Oh—that. But look here—if you're his doctor, why didn't you know which was his place? You're pretty slick, mister, but it's a bit fishy—I think."

She half withdrew back into her own doorway, but curiosity still detained her, and, too, Doctor Davenport's demeanor impressed her as being quite all right.

"Nothing wrong—is there?" she whispered, coming across the small hall, and peering into the doctor's face.

"Oh, no—I think not. But he may be helpless, and I must get in. I've never been here before, but I've been called by him just now. I — get in. Where's the janitor?"

"Where, indeed? If you can find him, I'll bless you forever. I've wanted him all day."

"Isn't he on duty?"

"He doesn't know the meaning of duty. It's something he's never on."

She smiled at him, and noticing her for the first time, Davenport saw that she was handsome, in a careless, rather blatant way.

Her ash-blonde hair was loosely pinned up, and her dress—negligee or tea-gown—was fussy with lace, and not quite immaculate.

Her wide, light blue eyes returned his scrutiny, and for an instant each studied the other.

"There is something wrong," she nodded, at last, "What you going to do, Doctor?"

"I'm going to get in. I've wasted precious time already." He ran down the stairs and opening the front door summoned his chauffeur.

"Come up here, Chris," he ordered, and the two returned together.

"Can we break in that door?" he said, ignoring the woman now.

"My husband'll help," she volunteered, but Chris was already delivering effective blows.

However, the lock held, and turning to her, Doctor Davenport said, "Do ask your husband to help us, please. I assure you it's an emergency. I'm Doctor Ely Davenport."

"Come here, Jim," she obeyed orders. "This is Doctor Davenport."

"I've heard of you," said a big, commonplace looking man, appearing. "I'm Mansfield. What's up?"

"I have reason to think Mr Gleason is very ill. He just telephoned for me. I must get in. These old doors are strongly built, so I'd like your help."

Mansfield looked at him sharply, and seeming satisfied, put his shoulder to the door.

United effort succeeded, and the three men entered, the woman hanging back in fear.

Gleason lay on the floor, in a crumpled heap, and the first glance proclaimed him dead.

Stooping quickly, Doctor Davenport felt for his heart, and shook his head as he rose again to his feet.

"He's dead," he said, quietly. "Shot through the temple. Suicide, apparently, as the door was locked on the inside. Better take your wife away, Mr Mansfield. She'll be getting hysterical."

"No, I won't," declared the lady referred to, but she was quite evidently pulling herself together. "Let me come in."

"No," forbade Davenport. "You've no call in here. Go back home, both of you. I shall send for the police and wait till they come."

But the doctor hesitated as he was about to touch the telephone.

The matter was mysterious. "Suicide, of course," he ruminated, as he remembered the message received by Nurse Jordan. "Shot himself, then, still living, cried to me for help. Wish I knew exactly what he said to Jordan. But, anyway, I'm not going to disturb things—there may be trouble ahead. Guess I'll leave the telephone alone—and everything else."

"Sit right here, Chris," he said, "and don't move or stir. Look around all you like—note anything and everything that strikes you. I'll be back soon."

Closing the broken door behind him, he went to the Mansfield's apartment and asked to use their telephone. On this, he called the police, while the two listened eagerly.

"Why did he do it?" broke out Mrs Mansfield, as the receiver was hung up. "Oh, Doctor, tell us something about it! I'm eaten alive with curiosity."

Her big blue eyes shone with excitement, which her husband tried to suppress.

"Now, be quiet, Dottie," he said, laying a hand on her shoulder.

"I won't be quiet," and she shook off the hand. "Here's a great big mystery right in my own house—on my own floor—and you say, 'be quiet!' I've got a right to know all about it, and I'm going to! I'm going up now, to tell Mrs Conway!"

Her husband held her back forcibly, but Doctor Davenport said, "Of course, it must become known, and if Mrs Mansfield enjoys spreading the news, I suppose she has a right to do so. No one may enter the Gleason rooms, though—understand that."

"Go on, then, Dottie," Mansfield said; "maybe you'd better."

"She's very excitable," he sighed, as his wife ran up the stairs.

"She's better off, unburdening her news, than being thwarted," said the doctor, indifferently. "Let her do what she likes. What can you tell me, Mr Mansfield, of your neighbor, Gleason?"

"Not much, Doctor. He kept to himself, as far as the people in this house were concerned. We didn't know him socially—no one in the house did—and though he said good-day, if we met in the halls, it was with a short and unsocial manner."

"Nobody actively disliked him?"

"Nobody knew him well enough for that—unless— well, no, I may say none of us knew him."

"Yet you hesitated," the doctor looked at him keenly; "why did you?"

"A mere passing thought—better left unspoken."

"All right, Mr Mansfield—perhaps you are wise. But, if asked to, you'd better speak your thought to the police."

"Oh, sure. I'm a law-abiding citizen—I hope. Will they be here soon?"

"Nothing happens soon in matters like this. It's delay, linger and wait on the part of everybody. I'm bothered— I've important affairs on hand—but here I must stick, till the arm of the law gets ready to strike."

Davenport returned to Gleason's apartment, where the stolid Chris kept guard.

"Well?" said the doctor, glancing at his man.

"Looks like a suicide to me, sir. Looks like he shot himself—there's the revolver—I haven't touched it. And then he fell over all in a heap."

"It seems he telephoned after he shot—"

"He did? How could he?"

"Look again at his position. Near the desk, on which the telephone sits. He might have shot, and then—"

"Not that shot in his temple!"

"No; but there may be another. I haven't looked carefully yet. Ah, yes—see, Chris, here's another bullet hole, in his left shoulder. Say, he fired that shot, then, getting cold feet, called off the suicide idea and telephoned for me. Then, getting desperate again, fired a second shot through his temple, which, of course, did for him—oh, a fanciful tale, I know—but, you see, the detective work isn't up to me. When the police come they'll look after that and I can go."

But the police, arriving, were very much interested in this theory of Doctor Davenport's.

Prescott, an alert young detective, who came with the inspector especially interested the physician by his keen-witted and clearly put questions.

"Did you know this man?" he asked among his first queries.

"Yes," returned Davenport, "but not well. I've never been here before. He's Robert Gleason, a very rich man, from Seattle. Staying here this winter, in this apartment which belongs to McIlvaine, a friend of Gleason's."

"Where's McIlvaine?"

"In California. Gleason took over the place, furnished and all, for the winter months."

"Any relatives?"

"Yes"; Davenport hated to drag in the Lindsays, but it had to be done. "His sister, Mrs Lindsay, lives in upper Park Avenue."

"Have you called her up?"

"No; I thought wiser to do nothing, until you people came. Also, I'm a very busy man, and outside my actual duty here, I can't afford to spend much time."

"I see. Then the sister is the only relative in New York?"

"I think so. There are two Lindsay children, but they're not hers. She married a widower."

"I see. And the address?"

Doctor Davenport gave it, and then started to go.

"Wait a minute, please," urged Prescott. "Had the dead man any friends, that you know of?"

"Oh, yes. Many of them. He was put up at the Camberwell Club, by McIlvaine himself. And he had many friends among the members."

"Names?"

Doctor Davenport thought quickly, and decided to give no names of the group that had been with Gleason that same afternoon.

He gave the names of three other Club members, and sending Chris down ahead, again endeavored to depart himself.

Again Prescott detained him.

"Sorry, Doc," he said, pleasantly, "but you're here now, and something tells me it'll be hard to get hold of you again, once I lose you. Inspector Gale, here, is putting through the necessary red tape and all that, and he'll see to notifying relatives and friends, and he'll take charge of the premises—but—well, I've a hunch, this isn't a suicide."

"What, murder?" cried the doctor, his quick acceptance of the suggestion proving the thought had been in his own mind.

"Well, you never can tell. And I want to get all the sidelight on the case I can. Was Mr Gleason happy—and all that?"

"Yes; so far as I know. I tell you I was not an intimate—scarcely enough to be called a friend—merely an acquaintance."

"I see. Had the man any enemies?"

The direct glance that accompanied these words discomfited Davenport a little.

"Why do you ask me that?" he said, shortly. "How should I know?"

"Oh, it's a thing anybody might know—even a mere acquaintance. And your desperate hurry to get away makes me think you don't take kindly to this catechism."

"Rubbish! I'm a busy man—a doctor sometimes is. I've numerous and important engagements for the evening. Now, if that's incriminating, make the most of it!"

"Fie, fie, don't get peeved! Now, tell me once again, what the injured man said to your nurse and I'll let you go."

"I don't know the exact words. I've not seen her. But he called my office, said he was shot, and for me to come right here and quickly. That's all I know of the message. Now as to my report—it's that the man received two shots—whether by his own hand or another's. One, in his left shoulder—and another—the fatal one—through his temple, producing instant death. You can get me at any time—if necessary. But I don't want to be hauled over here, or summoned to headquarters to repeat these facts. I'll send a typed report, and I'll do anything in reason— but I know how you detectives mull over things, and how your slow processes eat up time—which though it seems of little account to you, is mighty valuable to me."

"Yes, sir—yes, sir. Now if you'll speak to Inspector Gale a minute, you can go."

Grunting an assent, Davenport waited for the Inspector to finish writing a bit of memorandum on which he was busily engaged.

The doctor was sitting in a big easy chair, and as he squirmed impatiently, he felt something soft beneath his heavy frame.

Feeling about the chair cushions, he found it was fur, and a fleeting thought that he had sat on a cat passed through his mind.

A second later he knew it was a fur strip, probably a neck piece, doubtless belonging to some woman.

Now, the doctor had a very soft place in his heart for the feminine sex in general, and his mind leaped to the idea of this fur, left there by some indiscreet girl visitor, and the possibility of its getting the doubtless innocent young lady into a moil of trouble.

Also, he had a dim, indistinct notion that he recognized the fur, at which he had stolen a furtive look.

At any rate, unseen by the Inspector or either of his two colleagues present, Davenport adroitly slipped the small fur collar into his capacious overcoat pocket, and sat, looking as innocent of duplicity as a canary-fed cat.

"Now, Doctor," and Inspector Gale frowned importantly, "this may be a simple case of suicide, and again it may not. So, I want your opinion as to whether it is possible that both those shots were fired by Mr Gleason himself."

"Quite possible, Inspector, and, it seems to me, decidedly probable, as I cannot see how the victim could have telephoned, with a murderer in the room."

"That's apparently true, but we have to think of even the remotest possibilities. If the murderer—granting there was one—had been merely intending to frighten his victim, maybe a robber, he might have been—and if after that call for help, the intruder finished off his victim—oh, well, all these ideas must be looked into, you know. The case is not entirely clear to me."

"Nor to me," returned Davenport, "but I cannot feel that I can help you in your deductions. Answering your questions, I say it would have been quite possible for Mr Gleason to have fired those two shots himself. You see the first one hit his left shoulder, leaving his right arm available to fire the second shot."

"Why did he merely maim himself first?"

"Heavens, man! I don't know. Missed aim, perhaps— or, just shooting for practice! Such questions make me mad! If you want any more medical statements, say so—if not, for goodness' sake, let me go!"

"For goodness' sake, let him go," repeated Prescott, and Dr Davenport went.

"Some mess," Prescott said, after the doctor's angry footsteps tramped down the stairs.

CHAPTER 3: THE LINDSAYS

"You're sure no one in this building knew Mr Gleason any better than you two did?" Prescott asked of the Mansfields, as he put them through a course of questioning.

"Oh, no," Mrs Mansfield informed him, volubly, "and we didn't know him much, but being on the same floor—there are only two apartments on each floor, we saw him once in a while, going in or out, and he would bow distantly, and mumble 'good-morning,' but that's all."

"You heard no noise from his apartment, during the last hour?"

"No; but I wasn't noticing. It's across the hall, you know, and the walls are thick in these old houses."

"Was he going out, do you think?" asked Jim Mansfield, thoughtfully. "He always went out to dinner."

"Probably he was, then. It's evident he was dressing—he was in his shirtsleeves—his day shirt—and his evening clothes were laid out on the bed."

"When did it happen?"

"As nearly as I can make out, he telephoned for the doctor about quarter before seven. He must have expired shortly after. As I figure it—oh, well, the medical examiner is in there now, and I don't want to discuss the details until he gets through his examination. It's an interesting case, but I'm only out for side evidence. What about Gleason's visitors? Did he have many?"

"No," offered Mrs Mansfield, "but he had some. I've heard—well, people go in there, and he was mighty glad to see them, judging by the gay laughter and chatter."

"Oh—lady friends?"

Mrs Mansfield smiled, but her husband said quickly, "Shut up, Dottie! You talk too much! You'll get us involved in this case, and make a lot of trouble. He had callers occasionally, Mr Prescott, but we never knew who they were and we've no call to remark on them."

"Well, I give you the call. Don't you see, man, your information may be vitally necessary—"

Here Prescott was recalled to the Gleason apartment.

The medical examiner had concluded his task. He agreed with Doctor Davenport that the shots could have been fired by Gleason himself, though, but for the locked door, he should have thought them the acts of another person. The presence of powder stains proved that the shots were fired at close range, but not necessarily by the dead man himself.

Still, the door being locked on the inside, it looked like suicide.

"No," Prescott disagreed, "that doesn't cut any ice. You see, it's a spring catch. It fastens itself when closed. If an intruder was here and went out again, closing that door behind him, it would have locked itself."

"That's right," assented Gale. "So, it may be suicide or murder. But we'll find out which. We've hardly begun to investigate yet. Now, we must let his sister know."

"It's pretty awful to spring it on her over the telephone," demurred Prescott, as Gale started for the desk.

"Got to be done," Inspector Gale declared, "I mean we've got to tell somebody who knew him. How about those men at the Club?"

"That's better," consented Prescott. "Just call the Camberwell Club, and get any one of those Davenport mentioned. But, I say, Gale, use the Mansfields' telephone. I'm saving up this one for fingerprint work."

"Oh, you and your fingerprint work!" Gale grumbled. "You attach too much importance to that, Prescott."

"All right, but you let the telephone alone. And the revolver, too. Why, I wouldn't have those touched for anything! I'll get them photographed to-morrow. Shall I call the Club?"

"Yes," grunted Gale, and Prescott went back to the opposite apartment.

"Sorry to trouble you people," he said, with his winning smile, "but if you object, say so, and I'll run out to a drug store."

"None around here," vouchsafed Mansfield, looking a little annoyed at the intrusion, however. "Isn't there a telephone in the Gleason rooms?"

"Yes; but I don't want to use that." Prescott had already taken up the Mansfield receiver. "Please let me have this one," and a bright smile at Dottie Mansfield made her his ally.

Getting the Club, Prescott asked for the names Davenport had supplied. Only one man was available, and Mr Harper was finally connected.

"What is it?" he asked, curtly.

"Mr Robert Gleason has been found dead in his home," Prescott stated; "and as you're said to be a friend of his, I'm asking you to inform his sister, or—"

"Indeed I won't! Why should I be asked to do such an unpleasant errand? I've merely a nodding acquaintance with Mr Gleason. Dead, you say? Apoplexy?"

"No; shot."

"Good God! Murdered?"

"We don't know. Murder or suicide. I'm Detective Prescott. I want you to tell his sister, or advise me how best to break the news to her. She's Mrs Lindsay—"

"Yes, yes—I know. Well, now, let me see. Dead! Why, the man was here this afternoon."

"Yes; apparently he returned home safely, and while dressing for dinner, either shot himself or was shot by some one else."

"Never shot himself in the world! Robert Gleason? No, never shot himself. Well, let me see—let me see. Suppose you call up some closer friend of his. Really, I knew him but slightly."

"All right. Who was his nearest friend?"

"Humph—I don't know. He wasn't long on intimate friends!"

"Little liked?"

"I wouldn't say that—but close friends, now—let me see; he was talking this afternoon with a bunch—Doctor Davenport, Phil Barry, Dean Monroe, Manning Pollard— oh, yes, Fred Lane. And maybe others. But I know I saw him in the group I've just mentioned. Call up Davenport."

"Tell me the next best one to call."

"Barry—but wait—they had a quarrel recently. Try Lane or Pollard."

"Addresses?"

These were given and as soon as he could get connection, Prescott called Pollard.

But he was out, and Philip Barry was also.

"Can't expect to get anybody at the dinner hour," Prescott said, and looked at his watch. "After eight, already. One more throw, and then I make straight for the sister."

Fred Lane proved available.

"No!" he exclaimed at the news Prescott told. "You don't mean it! Why I was talking with him yesterday. And only to-night I heard—Oh, I say," he pulled himself together. "Tell me the details. Can I do anything?"

"You sure can. Break it to Mrs Lindsay, Gleason's sister."

"Oh, not that! Don't ask me to. I'm—I'm no good at that sort of thing. I say—let me off it. Get somebody else—"

"I've been trying to, and I can't. If you won't do it, I'll have to call up the lady and tell her myself—or go there."

"That's it. Go there. And, I say, get her son—her stepson, you know—young Lindsay. He's not related to Gleason—and so—"

"That's it! Fine idea. I'll see the young man. What's his name?"

"Louis Lindsay. There's a girl, too. Miss Phyllis. She's more of a man than her brother—oh, not a masculine type at all—I don't mean that, but she's a whole lot stronger character than the chappie. It might be better to tell her. But do as you like."

"Thank you for the information, Mr Lane. Good-by."

"Oh, wait a minute. Do you think Gleason killed himself?"

"Dunno yet. Lots of things to be looked into. I don't think it will be a difficult case to handle, yet it has its queer points. Did you say you heard something—"

"Oh, no—no."

"Out with it, man. Better tell anything you know."

"Don't know anything. You going to the Lindsays' now?"

"Yes, I think so."

"Well, there's a dinner party on there. A big one—followed by a dance. I mean it was to have been followed by a dance. Your news will change their plans!"

"You're rather unconcerned yourself! Didn't you like Gleason?"

"Not overly. Yet he was a big man in many ways. But, come now, wasn't he bumped off?"

"By whom?"

"I'm not saying. But while you're at the Lindsays', look out Dean Monroe—and ask him what he knows about it!"

"Dean Monroe! The artist?"

"Yes. Oh, he isn't the criminal—if there *is* a criminal. But maybe he can give you a tip. I'm mighty interested. How can I hear the result of your investigations?"

"Guess it'll be in the morning papers. Anyway, I may want to see you."

"All right; call me up or call on me whenever you like. I'm interested—a whole lot!"

"Guess I'd better go right to the Lindsay house," Prescott said, going back to the Gleason apartment. "There's a big party on there, and it ought to be stopped. It's an awkward situation. You see, Mrs Lindsay,

Gleason's sister, has two step-children—they're having the party, as I make it out. But they've got to be told."

"Yes," agreed Gale; "go along, Prescott. And you'd better have somebody with you."

"Not at first. Let me handle it alone, and I can call Briggs if I want him."

"Go on, then. The sooner we start something the better. I incline more and more to the murder theory, but if the sister thinks there was any reason for suicide— well, run along, Prescott."

Prescott ran along, and reached the Lindsay home, on upper Park Avenue, shortly after nine o'clock.

He was admitted by a smiling maid, and he asked for Mr Lindsay.

"He's still at dinner," she returned, doubtfully, glancing at Prescott's informal dress. "Can you come some other time?"

"No; the matter is urgent. You must ask him to leave the table and come to me here."

His manner was imperative, and the maid went on her errand.

In a moment Louis Lindsay came to Prescott, where the detective waited, in the reception hall.

"What is it, my man?" said Lindsay, looking superciliously at his visitor. "I can't see you now."

"Just a moment, Mr Lindsay. Listen, please."

Noting the grave face and serious voice of the speaker, young Lindsay seemed to become panic-stricken.

"What is it?" he said, in a gasping whisper. "Oh, what *is* it?"

"Why do you look like that?" Prescott said quickly. "What do you *think* it is?"

"I don't know—I'm sure! Tell me!"

The boy, for he was little more than a boy, was ghastly white, his hands trembled and his lips quivered. He took hold of a chair back to steady himself, and Prescott, remembering what he had been told of Miss

Lindsay, was tempted to ask for her. But he somehow felt he must go on with this scene.

"It's about your uncle—or rather your step-uncle—Mr Gleason."

Lindsay slumped into a chair, and raised his wild, staring black eyes to Prescott's face.

"Go on," he muttered; "what about him?"

"Didn't you expect him here to-night?"

"Yes—yes—and he didn't come—what is it? Has anything happened? What has happened? Who did it?"

"Who did what?" Prescott flung the words at him, in a fierce low tone. "What do you know? Out with it!"

His menacing air quite finished the young man, and he buried his face in his hands, sobbing convulsively.

A slight rustle was heard, and a lovely vision appeared in the doorway.

"What is going on?" said a clear young voice. "Louis, what is the matter?"

Phyllis Lindsay faced the stranger as she put her query.

The sight nearly dazzled Prescott, for Miss Lindsay was at her best that night.

She was a little thing, with soft dark hair, bundled about her ears, soft, dark eyes, that were now challenging Prescott sternly, and a slim, dainty little figure, robed in sequin-dripping gauze, from which her soft neck and shoulders rose like a flower from its sheath.

"Who are you?" she asked, not rudely, but with her eyes wide in dismay. "What are you doing to my brother?"

"Miss Lindsay?" and Prescott bowed politely. "I bring distressing news. Your uncle—that is, Mr Robert Gleason, is—has—well, perhaps frankness is best—he is dead."

"Robert Gleason!" Phyllis turned as pale as her brother, but preserved her calm. "Tell me—tell me all about it."

She, too, placed her little hand on a chair, as if the grip of something solid helped, and turned her anxious eyes to Prescott.

"I thought better to tell you young people," he began, "and let you tell your mother—Mr Gleason's sister."

"Yes; I will tell her," said Phyllis, with dignity. "Go on, Mr—"

"Prescott," he supplied. "The facts in brief are these. Mr Gleason called up Doctor Davenport on the telephone, and asked the doctor to come to him, as he was—well, hurt. When the doctor reached there, Mr Gleason was dead."

"What killed him?" Phyllis spoke very quietly, and looked Prescott straight in the face. Yet the alert eyes of the detective saw her fingers clench more tightly on the chair, and noticed her red lips lose a little color as they set themselves in a firm line.

He thought her even more beautiful thus, than when she had first arrived, smiling.

"The Medical Examiner is not quite sure, Miss Lindsay. It may be that he took his own life—or it may be—"

"That he was—murdered," she said, her gaze never wavering from Prescott's face.

It was a bit disconcerting, and the detective oddly felt himself at a disadvantage. Yet he went on, inexorably.

"Yes; either deduction is possible."

"How—how was he killed?"

At last her calm gave way a little. The tremor of her voice as she asked this question proved her not so self-controlled as she had seemed.

"He was shot." Prescott watched both brother and sister as he spoke. But Louis still kept his face hidden in his hands, and Phyllis was once more perfectly calm.

"What with?" she went on.

"His own revolver. It was found close beside the body, and so as I said, it might have been—"

"Yes, I know what you said." Phyllis interrupted him impatiently, as if deeming repetition of the theories unnecessary. "How shall we tell Millicent?"

"Mrs Lindsay?" asked Prescott respectfully.

"Yes; we have never called her mother, of course." She looked at Louis. "Go to your rooms, if you wish, Buddy," she said, kindly, and Prescott marveled at this slight, dainty young thing taking the situation into her own hands.

"No, I'll stand by," Louis muttered, as he rose slowly. "What shall we do? Call her out here?"

"That would do," said Prescott, "or take her to some other room. The guests must be told—and the party—"

"The party broken up and the guests sent home—" Phyllis declared. "But first, let's tell Millicent. She'll be terribly upset."

At Phyllis' dictation, Prescott and young Lindsay went into the little library. Like the other rooms this was beflowered for the party and scant of furniture, for dancing purposes. The Lindsay apartment was a fine one, yet not over large, and sounds of conversation and light laughter came from the dining room. Phyllis quickly brought Mrs Lindsay from the dinner table, and they joined the men.

As the girl had predicted, her stepmother was greatly shocked and her nerves utterly upset by Prescott's story.

The detective said little after outlining the facts, but listened closely while these members of the family talked. Though there on the ungracious errand of breaking the sad news, he was also eagerly anxious to learn any hints as to the solution of the mystery.

"Oh, of course, he never killed himself!" declared the dead man's sister. "Why should he? He had everything life can offer to live for. He was rich, talented, and engaged to Phyllis, whom he adored—worshipped! How can any one think he would kill himself?"

"But the evidence is uncertain," Prescott began; "you see—"

"Of course the evidence is uncertain," Phyllis broke in. "It always is uncertain! You detectives don't know evidence when you see it! Or you read it wrongly and make false deductions!"

"Why, Phyllis," remonstrated her brother, "don't talk like that! You may—" he hesitated a long time, "you may make trouble," he concluded, lamely.

"Trouble, how?" Prescott caught him up.

"Don't you say another word, Louis," Phyllis ordered him. "You keep still. Millicent, you go to your room, and let Martha look after you. Louis, you either go to your room—or, if you stay here, don't babble. Mind, now! Mr Prescott, we must tell the guests. Come with me and we will tell those at the table. They will go home, and those who come later can be told at the door and sent away."

"Very well, Miss Lindsay," Prescott replied, feeling that here was a strength of character he had never seen equaled in such a mere slip of a girl!

They went to the dining room, and without preamble, Phyllis said:

"Listen, people. I've very bad news. Mr Gleason—Robert Gleason—has just been found dead in his home. He was shot—" Her voice, steady till this moment, suddenly broke down, and as her eyes filled with tears, Philip Barry, who had already risen, hastened to her side.

There was a general commotion, the ladies rising now, and with scared faces, whispering to one another.

"Wait a moment," Prescott spoke, as some seemed about to leave; "I must ask you all if you know anything of importance concerning the movements of Mr Gleason this afternoon or evening. I am a detective, the case is a little mysterious, and it may be necessary to question some of you. Will any one volunteer information?"

Nobody did so, and Prescott, steeling himself against the entreaties of Phyllis that all be allowed to depart, asked several of their knowledge of the man.

Most of these declared they were unacquainted with Mr Gleason's whereabouts on that day, and some denied knowing the man at all. These were allowed to go, and at last, Prescott found himself surrounded by the men who knew Gleason and who had seen him that very day.

These included Barry, Pollard and Monroe, of the group that had talked together at the Club in the afternoon, and one or two others who had seen Gleason during the day.

Each was questioned as to the probability, in his opinion, of Robert Gleason having shot himself.

"I can't make a decision," Philip Barry said; "to my mind, Gleason would be quite capable of doing any crazy or impulsive thing. He may have had a fit of depression, he sometimes did, and feeling extra blue, may have wanted to end it all. But, also it's quite on the cards that somebody did for him."

"Why do you say that, Mr Barry?" asked the detective.

"Because you asked me for my opinion," was the retort. "That's it. I would believe anything of Gleason. I'm not knocking him—but he was a freak—eccentric, you know—"

"Oh, not quite that," Dean Monroe spoke very seriously. "Mr Gleason was a Westerner, and had different ideas from some of ours, but he was a good sort—"

"Good sort!" scoffed Barry. "I'd like to know what you call a bad sort, then!"

"Hush, Phil," Phyllis said, quietly. "Don't talk like that of a man who is dead."

"Forgive me, Phyllis, I forgot myself. Well, Mr Prescott, I can only say you'll have to solve your mystery on the evidence you find; for I assure you Mr Gleason would fit into almost any theory."

Prescott questioned Dean Monroe next, remembering what Lane had told him over the telephone.

But, though interested, Monroe told nothing definitely suggestive, and at last Prescott said, directly, "Do you know anything, Mr Monroe, that makes you suspect that Mr Gleason might have been killed by an intruder?"

"Why—why, no," stammered the young artist, quite palpably prevaricating.

"I think you do, and I must remind you that I have a right to demand the truth."

"Well, then," Monroe looked positively frightened, "then—I say, Manning, maybe it'll be better for me to speak out—I heard somebody say to-day, that he meant to—to kill Gleason."

"Indeed," and Prescott, accustomed as he was to surprises, stared wonderingly at the speaker. "And who said that?"

But Monroe obstinately shook his head and spoke no word.

Philip Barry raised his head with a jerk and looked straight at Manning Pollard.

Pollard's face was white, and his voice not quite steady, but he stated, "I said it."

"Why?" asked Prescott, simply.

"Oh—oh, because—I—I don't—didn't like Gleason."

"And so you killed him?"

"I haven't said so."

"I'm asking you."

"And I'm not obliged to incriminate myself, am I?" Pollard looked at him coldly.

"Where were you between six and seven this evening?"

"I refuse to tell," Pollard answered, with a belligerent look, and Prescott nodded his head, with a satisfied smile.

CHAPTER 4: POLLARD'S THREAT

"Of course, you know, Mr Pollard," Prescott said, "you are incriminating yourself by your refusal to answer my question. No one is as yet under suspicion of crime—indeed, it is not certain that a crime has been committed—but it is my duty to learn all I can of the circumstances of the case, and I must ask you what you meant by a threat to kill Mr Gleason."

"It wasn't exactly a threat," Pollard returned, speaking slowly, and looked decidedly uncomfortable; "it was merely a—a statement."

"A statement that you would like to—to see him dead?"

"Well, yes, practically that."

"Why?"

"Because I didn't like the man. I took a dislike to him the first time I saw him, and I never got over it."

"But that's not reason enough to kill a man."

"I haven't said I killed him. But I hold it is reason enough. I hold that an utter detestation of seeing a person around, a positive irritation at his mere presence, is a stronger motive for murder than the more obvious ones of jealousy or greed."

"You weren't jealous of Mr Gleason?"

Pollard started, the detective had scored that time.

But he replied, quietly. "Not jealous, no."

"Envious?"

"Your questions are a bit intrusive, but I think I may safely say many men were envious of Mr Gleason."

"On what grounds?"

"Oh, he was wealthy, important and of a happy, satisfied disposition. Truly an enviable person."

Pollard's manner was indifferent and his tone light and flippant. Prescott a judge of human nature and an expert detective, concluded the man was sparring for time, or trying to camouflage his guilt with an effect of careless unconcern in the matter.

"I think, Mr Pollard," he said, seriously, "I shall have to insist on knowing your whereabouts at the time of Mr Gleason's death."

"And I refuse to tell you. But, look here, Mr Prescott, as I understand it, Mr Gleason was found dead in his room, with the door fastened. How do you argue from that a murderer at all? How could he get out and lock the door behind him? Where was the key?"

"Spring catch," Prescott returned, shortly. "Snapped shut as he closed the door."

"Oh, come now, Pollard," said Philip Barry, "say where you were at that time. Six to seven, was it? Why, Pol, you were walking down Fifth Avenue with me. We left the Club together."

"Did we?" said Pollard. His face was inscrutable. It seemed as if he had made up his mind that no information should be gathered from his words or manner. Prescott, watching him closely thought he had never seen such a strange man, and decided that he was the criminal he sought, and a mighty clever one at that.

Manning Pollard was tall and large, and of fine presence. He would not be called handsome, but he had a well-shaped head, well set on his broad shoulders. His special charm was his smile, which, though rare, was spontaneous and illuminated his face with a real radiance whenever he saw fit to favor his auditors. However, his expression was usually calm and thoughtful, while occasionally it became supercilious and even cynical.

When displeased, Pollard was impossible. He shut up like a clam and preserved a stony silence or blurted out some caustic, almost rude speech.

"Yes, we did," went on Barry, eagerly. "And I left you at Forty-fourth Street."

"Did you?" said Pollard, in the same colorless voice.

Now Philip Barry had little love for Manning Pollard. To begin with, they were both in love with the same girl, and—as either of them would have agreed—there was no use in going further than that.

Moreover, they were of widely different temperament. Barry was all artist; dreamy, impractical, full of enthusiasms and a bit visionary. Pollard was a hard-headed business man, successful, rich and influential, but not by any means universally liked, by reason of his sarcastic and cynical outlook. Yet he was polite and courteous of demeanor, and his imperturbable calm and unshakable poise gave him an air of superiority that could not be gainsaid.

Up to a few months ago the two men had been chums—were still—but the advent of Phyllis Lindsay into their circle had made a difference.

For, though many men admired the little beauty, Pollard and Barry were the most favored and each felt an ever-increasing hope that he might win her.

Then along had come Robert Gleason, the brother of Phyllis' stepmother. He was at the Lindsay home continually, and by some means or for some reason he had persuaded the girl to marry him. At least, he implied that at the Club in the afternoon, and both Pollard and Barry had been greatly disturbed thereby.

But others were also greatly disturbed and the news, which had flown like wildfire, had caused panic in the breasts of several who were to attend the dinner or the dance.

Then had come the dinner, and the unexplained absence of Gleason. They had telephoned his place twice, but could get no response, Phyllis told the detective in the course of his questioning.

"H'm," Prescott listened; "at what time did you call him up, Miss Lindsay?"

"Why, about seven o'clock, I think. I was dressing for dinner, and I happened to think of something I wanted to ask Mr Gleason, and I called his number. But nobody answered, so I concluded to wait till he arrived to ask him."

"And the next time? You called him twice?"

"Yes; the next time was when dinner was ready—about eight. He wasn't here, and I thought it so strange—I—telephoned—"

"Yourself?" asked Prescott, quickly, scenting unexpected information.

"No—I—I asked one of the guests to do it."

"Which one?"

"Me." Pollard smiled at Phyllis. "Miss Lindsay asked me to telephone to Mr Gleason, and I did, but no one answered the call."

The speaker turned his calm eyes to Prescott, and met the detective's suspicious gaze.

"You're sure you called, Mr Pollard," Prescott asked, his tone plainly indicating his own doubt.

"I have said so," Pollard replied, and let his own glance wander indifferently aside.

"Well, I don't believe you!" Prescott was angered at Pollard's quite evident lack of interest in his inquiries, and he now spoke sharply. "I believe, Mr Pollard, that you know more than you have told regarding this matter, and unless you see fit to become more communicative, I shall have to resort to outside inquiry as to your own movements this evening, prior to your arrival here."

"That is your privilege," Pollard said, with an exaggerated politeness.

"It is my duty also," Prescott retorted, "and I shall begin right now. You say you left Mr Pollard on Fifth Avenue, Mr Barry?"

"Yes," was the reply.

"At what time?"

"About six o'clock."

"It was ten minutes past," Pollard volunteered, still with the air of superior knowledge that exasperated Prescott almost beyond bounds.

"Did any one present see Mr Pollard between that time and his arrival here for dinner?" Prescott looked about the room.

No one responded, and the detective said, curtly:

"Where do you live, Mr Pollard?"

"At the Hotel Crosby, Fortieth Street, near Fifth Avenue," and this time Pollard gave his questioner one of his best smiles, which had the effect of embarrassing him greatly.

But with determination, he took up the telephone and called the hotel.

"Ask for the doorman," said Pollard, helpfully.

Prescott did, and learned that Mr Pollard was out. "Had he been in?" "Yes, he had come in soon after six o'clock, and had left again, later, in a taxicab."

Nothing more definite could be learned, and Prescott hung up the receiver, conscious only of a great desire to get down to the hotel and ask questions before Pollard could get there himself.

But first, he must look into other matters, and he turned his attention to the guests who sat round, all looking decidedly uncomfortable and some very much scared.

"Now look here, Mr Prescott," said Pollard, with the air of one humoring a spoiled child, "you have your duty to do—we all comprehend that. But can't you satisfy yourself regarding the innocence of most of these men and women, and let them go home? I assume there will be no dance this evening, and the troublesome circumstance of sending away the guests who are yet expected will be about all Miss Lindsay—and her brother," he added, with a sudden remembrance of the unhelpful Louis—"can cope with. I will await your pleasure, as you seem to have picked me out for suspicion, but do get through with these others."

Angry at this good advice, coming from the man he was questioning, and embarrassed because it was really good advice, Prescott began, a little sulkily, to take the names and addresses of many of them, and inform them they were free to leave. He detained any he thought might be useful to him, and among them he held Barry and Dean Monroe.

This matter took some time, especially as Prescott was twice interrupted by telephone.

Mrs Lindsay and Louis had retired to their rooms, and Phyllis, at the helm of the situation, proved herself a staunch and capable upholder of the dignity of the Lindsay family.

"Send away all you can, please, Mr Prescott," she requested. "Mr Pollard is right; I have my hands full. I will give the doorman, who is from the caterer's, instructions to explain the situation and admit none of the evening guests. But, I daresay some intimate friends will insist on coming in. Shall I allow it?"

"Better not, Miss Lindsay. You see, there's no use giving the thing more publicity than you have to. The reporters will come, of course. Will you see them?"

"Oh, goodness, no! Let some of the men do that. Mr Pollard, won't you?"

"I'd prefer Mr Monroe should," interrupted Prescott, and winced under Pollard's smile.

"Oh, Manning," said Dean Monroe, "why do you act like that! You make people suspect you, whether they want to or not."

"Suspect all you like, Dean," came the quiet reply; "if I'm innocent, suspicion can't hurt me. If I'm guilty, I ought to be suspected."

"You did say you intended to kill Gleason," Monroe repeated, staring at Pollard. "It's queer he should be killed right afterward."

"Mighty queer," agreed Pollard. "But are you sure he was murdered?"

"Yes," said Prescott. "Inspector Gale told me over the telephone just now, that further investigation proves it is a murder case. I think, Mr Pollard, I'll ask you to go with me right now to your hotel. I want to check up your story."

"But I haven't told you any story," said Pollard.

"Well, then," Prescott shrugged impatiently, "I'll check up the story you didn't tell! Come along. Anybody got a car I can borrow?"

Nobody had, as the guests had all expected to remain the whole evening. So Prescott called a taxicab, and soon the two started for Pollard's hotel.

"You're a queer guy," the detective said, the semi-darkness in the cab giving him greater freedom of speech.

"As how?" asked Pollard, quietly.

"Well, first, saying you proposed to kill a man."

"I'm not unique. I've often heard people say, 'I'd like to kill him!' or 'I wish he was dead!'"

"Yes, but they don't mean it."

"How do you know I meant it?"

"I don't, for sure, but I'm going to find out. If you haven't got an air-tight alibi—it's going to be trouble for yours!"

"I haven't any alibi. Guilty people prepare alibis."

"That's all right. You're cute enough to fix an alibi that don't look to be fixed! But I'll see through it. Here we are. Come along."

"A little less dictating, please, Mr Prescott. Remember, I'm not under arrest."

"Not yet—but soon!" was the retort as the two men entered the small, but exclusive, hotel where Manning Pollard made his home.

The doorman bowed, pleasantly, but not obsequiously, and Prescott went straight to the desk.

"I want to learn," he said, straightforwardly, "all you can tell me of the movements of Mr Pollard tonight between six and seven o'clock."

The clerk at the desk smiled at Pollard and gazed inquiringly at the other.

"Better tell him, Simpson," said Pollard; "he's a detective, and he's a right to ask. I'm under a cloud—I think I may call it that—and he's going to—well, clear me."

Pollard's smile flashed out, and the desk clerk, in his turn, smiled at the investigator.

"Go ahead, sir," he agreed, "what do you want to know?"

"What time did Mr Pollard come in this afternoon?"

"What time, Henry?" the clerk asked the doorman.

"'Bout quarter past six," was the reply. "I come on at six, and I'd been here a bit before Mr Pollard came along."

"What did he do?" went on Prescott, a little less certain of his convictions.

"Went up in the elevator."

"Same elevator boy on now?"

"Yes, sir. The car's up. Be down in a minute."

It was; and the elevator boy related that he had taken Mr Pollard up as soon as he came into the hotel.

"Went right to his room, did he?"

"Yes, sir." The woolly-headed one rolled his eyes in enjoyment of his sudden importance. "I knows he did, kase I watched after him."

"Why did you look after him?"

"No reason, p'tikler. Only kase he's such a fine gentleman. I most allus looks at him march down the hall. He marches like a—a platoon."

"He does? And he marched straight to his room?"

"Yessuh."

"When did you bring him down again?"

"'Bout an hour later, all dressed up in his glad raggses. Just like he is now."

"Just so. Now, during that hour do you know that Mr Pollard didn't leave his room? Didn't go down stairs again?"

"Not in my car, he didn't. And he always uses my car."

"Ask the other boy." Prescott gave this order shortly. The scene was getting on his nerves. Pollard, quiet, calm, but superior. The clerk, ready to enjoy the detective's discomfiture, if he failed to prove the point he was evidently trying hard to make. Black Bob, the elevator boy, his white teeth all in evidence, and his admiration for Pollard equally plain to be seen. And even the telephone girl, smirking from her switchboard nearby.

All of these were in sympathy with Pollard, and Prescott felt himself a rank outsider. But he persevered.

Joe, the other elevator boy, declared he had not carried Mr Pollard up or down that evening, and the clerk said there were but two cars.

"Go on, Mr Prescott," Pollard adjured him. "I have prepared no air-tight alibi."

"Did any one here see Mr Pollard in his room," the detective asked in desperation, and to his surprise a bellhop piped out, "I did."

"You did!" and Prescott turned to him. "How did you happen to do so?"

"He rang, and I went up there, and he gave me a letter to mail for him. It was a wide letter, too wide to go in the chute."

"Did you mail it?"

"I put it with the stuff for the postman to take. He hasn't been round yet."

"Get the letter."

The bellhop did so, while the others looked on.

It was a large, square envelope addressed to a business firm downtown.

"Your writing, Mr Pollard?" said Prescott, not knowing, in fact, just what to say.

"Yes," said Pollard, glancing at it. "Open it, if you want to. It's not private business."

"No; I don't want to. It looks very much as if you were in your room during the hour between six and seven."

"It does have that appearance," said Pollard, "but I make no claims."

"He telephoned twice," vouchsafed the girl at the switchboard.

"He did!" Prescott wheeled on her.

"Once not very long after he came in—maybe fifteen or twenty minutes after."

"To whom?"

"To a Cleaning Establishment. I remember, because I couldn't get them—the shop was closed. And then, he telephoned again for a taxi, when he was ready to go out."

"At what time?"

"About half-past seven—or maybe a little earlier."

"Earlier," said the doorman, who had drawn near again. "Not more'n twenty past. I put him in the taxi myself. And it wasn't as late as half past."

"Where did he drive to?"

"I don't know. He 'most always gives the driver a slip of paper with the numbers on it—'specially if he's going to more than one address. He did this tonight."

"Where's that taxi man?" asked Prescott, feeling his last prop being pulled from under him.

"He's outside now," said the doorman. "He's waiting for a man upstairs."

"Call him in."

The taxi driver looked at Pollard, nodded respectfully, and replied to Prescott's queries by saying that Mr Pollard did give him a memorandum of the places he wanted to go to, and that they were, first, the Hotel Astor, where he went in for a moment, and came back with some theater tickets which he was putting in his pocket.

"How do you know he had theater tickets?"

"Well, he had a little pink envelope, and he often does get tickets there. Next, he stopped at Bard's, the Florist's, and brought out a small square box with him, and next I took him up to a house on Park Avenue, and he stayed there, and I came back."

"All right, Mr Pollard, my duty is done." The detective looked a respectful apology. "But I had to find out all this. And remember you did make a surprising statement."

"Surprising to you, perhaps. But my friends, who know my eccentricities, weren't surprised at it."

"No? Well, if it's your habit to threaten to kill people you don't like—"

"I'd rather you didn't call it a threat. To my mind, a threat is spoken to the intended victim."

"I don't know," Prescott gazed thoughtfully at the speaker. "Can't you threaten—"

"But I didn't threaten. I merely said I should kill Gleason some day. It's too late, now, to make good my promise, and you've satisfied yourself—or, haven't you?—that I didn't do it?"

"Yes, I'm satisfied. You couldn't be here at home and in a taxicab doing errands, between six-fifteen and seven-forty-five, and have any chance to get away long enough to get yourself down to Washington Square and do up that murder business, too."

"It does look that way," Pollard agreed. "You've checked me up pretty thoroughly. Now do you want me any further? For, though I'm as good-natured and patient as the average man, I *have* something else to do with my time when you're through with me."

"Of course, of course. But, I say, Mr Pollard, can you give me a hint which way to look?"

"Sorry, but I can't."

The two had drawn aside from the hotel desk, and were by themselves in an alcove of the lobby. Prescott, eagerly trying to learn something further from his vindicated suspect—Pollard, calm and polite, but quite evidently wishing to get away about his business.

"You don't suspect anybody?"

"No; you see I knew Mr Gleason but slightly. I didn't like him, but I assure you I didn't kill him. And I don't know who did."

CHAPTER 5: MRS MANSFIELD'S STORY

"Distrust the obvious, Prescott," said Belknap, didactically. "It is the astute detective's weak point that he cannot see beyond the apparent—the evident—the obvious."

"Oh, yes," Prescott sniffed; "distrust the obvious is as hackneyed a phrase as *Cherchez la femme!* and about as useful in our every day work. You make a noise like a Detective Story."

"And they're the Big Noise, nowadays," Belknap returned, unruffled.

"All the same," and Prescott spoke doggedly, "when a guy says he's going to kill somebody, and that somebody is found croaked a few hours later, seems to me—"

"Seems to me, your guy is the last person in the world to suspect. It's the obvious—"

"Yes, an obvious that I sorta hate to distrust!"

"Nonsense! And you've disposed of Pollard anyway, haven't you."

"Yes, I have. Half a dozen people were in touch with him all through the time of the murder. He's out of it."

Prescott looked as disheartened as he felt.

"And you've wasted good time tracking him down, when you might have been investigating the evidence while it was fresh! I'm disappointed in you, Prescott; you oughtn't to have fallen for a steer like that."

Belknap was the Assistant District Attorney, and the Gleason case seemed to him important and absorbing. In his office the morning after the murder, he was getting all the information Prescott could give him, and he was really disgusted with the detective for having followed up the wild goose chase of Manning Pollard's impulsive speech about the Western millionaire.

Belknap was an earnest, honest investigator, not so much brilliant by deduction as clear-sighted, hard-headed and practical.

He distrusted the obvious, not so much because of the hackneyed aphorism as because his own experience had proved to him that nine times out of ten, or oftener, the obvious was wrong. It must be looked into, of course, but not to the exclusion of other evidence or the neglect of other lines of investigation. And now, he felt, the trail had cooled somewhat, and valuable clews might be lost because of Prescott's conviction of Pollard's guilt.

Belknap was of a higher mentality than Pollard, and he also was a man of more education and refinement. He was especially interested on this case, for the Lindsays were an exclusive family and kept themselves out of the limelight of publicity.

But there were rumors that the lovely daughter was a harum-scarum, that the son of the house was addicted to bright lights and high stakes, and that the still young stepmother was quite as fond of social life as her two charges.

But never were their names seen on the society columns or in the gossip papers and now, Belknap reflected, they could be approached by reporters.

Indeed, he saw himself admitted to that hitherto inaccessible home, and in imagination he was already preening himself for the occasion.

But Belknap was methodical, and he was preparing to go at once to the Gleason apartment, to begin his line of investigation.

"How does Mrs Lindsay act?" he allowed himself to ask as he and Prescott started for Washington Square.

"Oh, I don't know," returned Prescott; "about like you'd expect a sister to act. She was fond of her brother, I take it, but—well, I didn't see much of her; still, I've a vague impression that she's revengeful—anxious to find and punish the murderer—that struck me more than her grief."

"You can't tell. She may be sorrowing deeply, and also be desirous of avenging her brother's death. No question of suicide?"

"Not now, no. There was at first. But an autopsy showed the second shot was fired first."

"What do you mean?"

"The one they thought was second was first. It seems the first shot—through the temple—killed Gleason. And then, for some unexplained reason, the slayer fired again, through the dead man's shoulder."

"Whatever for? And how do they know?"

"Oh, the doctors could tell, by the blood coagulation or something. As to why it was done, I've no idea. What's the obvious—I want to distrust it."

"Don't be too funny, Prescott. This is a big case. Not only because of the prominence of the people involved, but it's pretty mysterious, I think. We ought to get something out of the other people in the house."

"Not a chance. I tried it."

Belknap said nothing, but a close observer might have thought his silence not altogether an assent to Prescott's corollary.

"In fact," Prescott went on, "I believe you'll find your murderer among Gleason's own bunch. Not the people in the house he lived in. You see that place was wished on him by a friend, and Gleason hated it. I got this from those men who know him. Miss Lindsay agreed to it. Gleason meant to move out—only took it because it was represented to him as a bijou apartment, and he thought it was a luxurious little nest—and, it isn't. As you can now see for yourself."

At the house, Prescott pushed the button below McIlvaine's card, and after a moment the door clicked, and grudgingly, as it seemed, moved itself a little, and Prescott pushed it open.

"That's the way the murderer got in," he said positively.

"Maybe not," demurred Belknap. "Maybe he came in with Gleason."

"Oh, maybe he came in at the window, or down the chimney!" exclaimed Prescott shortly; "you can't admit the obvious ever, can you?"

Belknap chuckled at the other's quick temper, and they went upstairs.

They found Policeman Kelly in charge, and he greeted them gladly.

"Get busy," he said, genially. "Sure, there's enough to engage your attention."

Belknap, beyond a word of greeting, ignored the officer, and took a swift, comprehensive survey of the place.

It was a large front room, apparently library and cutting room. A bedroom was back of it and a bath room behind that. An old house, quite evidently remodeled for bachelor or small family apartments.

Though up to date as to plumbing, lighting and decoration, the window and door frames proclaimed it an old building. The furniture was over ornate, and the pictures and ornaments a bit flamboyant. But it was a comfortable enough place, and the personal belongings of the dead Gleason were scattered about and gave a homey appearance. A silver framed photograph of Mrs Lindsay was on a table, and on another were two more portraits of less distinguished-looking ladies.

"That's Ivy Hayes, the movie star," Kelly said, as Belknap looked at one picture.

"I know it," the attorney said, so shortly that Kelly lapsed into silence.

"Nothing been disturbed?" Belknap asked presently, and receiving a negative answer went on observing.

Kelly winked at Prescott, with an expression that said, "I like 'em more sociable, myself!" and Prescott nodded acquiescence.

But at last Belknap began to talk.

"Dressing for dinner, they tell me," he said.

"Yes," said Prescott, eagerly, "I was here right away, quick, you know. They took the body to the Funeral Rooms, early this morning. But he was in his shirt sleeves—day shirt—"

"Yes, here are all his evening clothes on the bed in the next room. Was he going to the Lindsay dinner?"

"Yes, he was. I believe he said it was to be the occasion of the announcement of his engagement to Miss Lindsay—"

"Does she say that?"

"She does not! She denies it."

"Then you'd better keep still. You have no gumption, Prescott. Don't you see you mustn't say those things?"

"Oh, bother! let up on knocking me, and get down to business. Don't touch the telephone or revolver. I've had them photographed for fingerprints."

"Yes, that's good." Belknap was getting more genial. "Anybody been through his papers?"

"No; Lane is his lawyer, Fred Lane. He's coming here to-day to look over them."

"All right." Belknap was already absorbed in the loose papers scattered on the desk. "Several notes from ladies."

"Yes, I noticed them. Old Gleason had a few friends in the chorus, I judge. But, unless they have any bearing on the case, there's no call to exploit 'em, eh?"

"No, of course not. Nor any reason to mention them to the Lindsays."

"They'll know all there is to know. You can't fool 'em. Miss Phyllis is as wide-awake as they come, and the Mrs is nobody's fool. The boy, I don't think much of. Say, aren't you going up there? Don't you want to see them?"

"Later, yes. But me for the other tenants here, first. Here's where Gleason lay, was it? Near the telephone table—look here, if the first shot did for him, how could he telephone to the doctor that he was wounded?"

"Oh, I don't know! I don't believe that dope about the doctors knowing which shot came first. And, as you say, it couldn't have been the fatal one first, or how could he

have phoned? Anyway he could only have called the
doctor if it was a suicide. You don't think, do you, that the
murderer would stand by and let him call up!"

"Scarcely. That's why I haven't given up the idea that
it was a suicide."

"Never mind, Oscar, you will. Why, that man was too
happy to kill himself. His friends all say so. No, he was
shot, all right, but the two shots make a mystery that I
can't get yet."

Belknap frowned deeply, and thought for a few
moments.

"Great mistake," he said at last, "to reason from
insufficient data."

"Another of your 'familiar quotations,'" chaffed
Prescott.

"Another good rule," retorted the attorney, and went
out in the hall.

Prescott followed and together they went to the
Mansfields' apartment.

"We've been thinking it over," Mrs Mansfield said,
after she had admitted her callers and taken them to her
living room, "and my husband and I feel we ought to tell
all we know."

"You certainly ought to," Belknap assured her.

"Well," the blonde head nodded mysteriously, "that
man, Gleason, he was a gay old bird."

"Just what do you mean, Mrs Mansfield? Speak
plainly," adjured Belknap.

"Oh, well," she shrugged her shoulders pettishly, for
she was the sort of woman who loved innuendo better
than statement. "I don't know the girls, of course, I'm not
in that class of society, but he did have gay looking girls
coming to his apartment now and then."

"Every day?" Belknap looked at her sharply.

"Oh, my land, no, not every day. Just now and then?"

"Every other day?"

"No," pettishly.

"Maybe once a week?"

"Maybe."

"Maybe, you saw one, once—"

Mrs Mansfield laughed out.

"That's it, Mr Belknap," she said. "How you do pin me down. Well, all I can swear to is one time I did see a fly little piece of baggage go in at his door."

"Day or night?"

"Daytime." Mrs Mansfield spoke aggrievedly, as if all the zest had been taken out of her news.

"Humph! And she might have been his lawyer's stenographer, with an important paper."

"She might not!" Mrs Mansfield declined to lose her last shred of excitement. "Stenographers are flippy enough, Lord knows! But this little snipjack, now, she was a real little vamp!"

"You don't know her?"

"My land! I guess I don't! I'm a respectable married woman—"

"And probably she is a respectable unmarried woman—"

"Coming to see a man in his apartment?"

"Well, until we know the circumstances we can't judge her. I say, Prescott, get that photograph, will you. You know, the—"

"I know," and Prescott went back across the hall. He returned with the picture of the girl Kelly had called Ivy Hayes.

"This the lady?"

"That's the one," said Mrs Mansfield, drawing away from it, "but she's no lady."

"Oh, come, now, you don't know her. She's a little moving picture actress. She may have had business with Mr Gleason."

"She may have!" and the disdainful lady sniffed. "But it's none of *my* business, and I don't care to discuss her."

"You say you saw her go in there, yesterday?"

"Good land, no! I didn't say yesterday! I said, one day."

"All right, I'm glad you told us about it. It might mean something and it might not."

"Of course, it means something!" Mrs Mansfield didn't want her news scorned as naught. "An actress calling on a man like that—of course it means something!"

"If it does we'll find it out," Belknap said. "You don't think this little thing shot Gleason, do you?"

"I don't know why she couldn't. Little women have done such deeds."

"So they have. Now, you've nothing more to tell us?"

But though Mrs Mansfield said quite a bit more, she had really nothing more to tell them that they wanted to hear, and they got away, though with some difficulty, for the lady was of a garrulous type.

To the floor above Belknap went, Prescott returning to the Gleason rooms to look about.

The apartment above McIlvaine's was occupied by a spinster named Adams who was, as the attorney deduced, from New England.

This good lady was even more disgusted than Mrs Mansfield with the whole matter of Gleason, his life and death. More especially the last for, it seemed to her, no one had a right to die a violent death under the same roof with refined and conservative people.

"Why, he was a loud-voiced man," declared Miss Adams, as if pronouncing the last and worst word of opprobrium.

"Ah, you heard him from up here?"

"Sometimes, yes. He had chums visit him, and they would laugh and talk so loudly, I couldn't help hearing them."

"Could you distinguish what they said?"

"No; not words. But I could hear well enough to know whether he was merry or angry—for, I assure you, sometimes he was the latter."

"Did you hear anything from that apartment yesterday?"

"Oh, yes, I heard the two shots."

"You did! What did you do?"

"Nothing. What should I do? As a matter of fact I didn't think they were shots. I thought them tire explosions or some noise in the street. But after I knew about the murder, I realized that I had heard the fatal shot."

"Yet you said nothing to anybody?"

"Man alive, what could I say? I had nothing to do with Mr Gleason or his murder—"

"But your duty as a citizen—"

"Look here, what do you mean? Where was any duty? You people—you police people knew the shots were fired, didn't you? Then why should I inform anybody that they were? And that's all I knew—or know about them. They were fired. I heard them. No more."

The sharp-featured, sharp-tongued old maid sat bolt upright in her chair, and glared at Belknap. Her hair was drawn up in a tight knot, after the fashion of New England spinsters, and Belknap wondered what it was about her appearance that seemed so strange.

Then he realized it was her exposed ears! He had not seen a woman with bared ears for so long that it looked most peculiar to him.

For the rest, Miss Adams was angular, even gaunt, and apparently of a decided and forceful nature. And her testimony might be valuable.

"Your knowledge is of importance," he said, gravely. "To be sure we know the shots were fired, but a witness is always of interest. What time was it that you heard the shots?"

"I've no idea," she returned, carelessly. "Oh, I know, in the story books, the witness always knows, because he was just going to keep an engagement—or, setting his watch, or something. But I don't know at all."

"You are quite conversant with detective stories, though!"

"Yes. I read them, since they're getting so popular. Anything more you want to ask?"

"Yes, please. I want to try to fix the time of those shots."

"And I tell you I can't do it. Look here, did you meet any one you know, on the street yesterday afternoon?"

"Why, yes, I did—I met two or three."

"All right. Mention one."

"Well—a Mr Hartley."

"All right, what time did you meet him?"

"I don't know exactly—"

"About?"

"Oh, about half-past four or five—no, it was later—"

"There!" triumphantly. "It is not easy to state the time, when you paid no special attention to the occurrence."

"You've proved your point, Miss Adams!" Belknap exclaimed, looking at her with new interest. "I wish you *had* noted the time—you would have done so accurately."

"Yes, I should have. But I didn't. Now, when I tell you that's all I know about the whole matter, will you go away and leave me in peace?"

"No; Miss Adams, I won't!"

"Why not?" and to Belknap's satisfaction she turned a shade paler.

"Because, I am sure you do know more. You are too cute to be so ignorant. Your smartness has overreached itself. You're trying to disarm me by the appearance of absolute frankness, and you almost did so—but—I've—well, I've got a hunch that you know something else."

"I swear I don't," and Miss Adams set her thin lips in a tight, straight line. "You go away."

"I'm going, I've much to do. But I warn you I shall return. You know something, Miss Adams, something of importance, but I do not think you are yourself implicated. Moreover, what you know frightens you a little, and you don't want to tell it. Now, if I can get all the information I want, without yours, well and good. If not, I shall come back for yours. And don't try running away—for you won't get far!"

"Are—are you going to have me watched!" she gasped.

"No—not quite that. But if you attempt flight, we may have to follow you."

As a matter of fact, the astute Belknap had sized up the old maid pretty carefully, and was convinced that what little she knew was unimportant to him, though it doubtless seemed vital to her. Also, he had no time just now, to persuade or wheedle her, and he feared frightening her would do little good. So, he concluded to wait and see what else he could find out, before seeing her again. A woman on the floor above could easily know something definite, yet somehow Miss Adams did not impress him as doing so.

He went downstairs, and looking in the door, said, "Come on, Prescott, let's go up to the Lindsays' and start out right."

"All right. Wait a minute, come in here, will you? We've got word from the photographer, and there are no fingerprints on the revolver or on the telephone except Gleason's own."

"What! Suicide? No, not possible, if the fatal shot was fired first."

"It was. I just called up Doctor Davenport, and he hedged at first, but then he acknowledged it was true. The shot in the shoulder was fired after the man was already dead. Now, what do you make of that! Why, in heaven's name shoot a dead man?"

Belknap looked thoughtful. "It's a deep game somebody's playing," he said. "We've got our work cut out for us. Come along, let's get busy. Guard everything mighty carefully, Kelly. Don't let anybody in, but people who belong. Our criminal is a slick one, and no obvious measures go, this time. No fingerprints! Some expert, that murderer!"

CHAPTER 6: THE FUR COLLAR

Prescott, absorbed in the fingerprint matter, went off to see about it, leaving Belknap to take up the trail alone.

The attorney concluded to go first to Pollard's, and note for himself the attitude of the man who had threatened Gleason's life.

He found Manning Pollard in his rooms at the little hotel, and was greeted with courtesy, though with no great cordiality.

"Come in, Mr Belknap," Pollard said, "I can give you a short interview, but I've a piece of important work on hand."

"I'll stay only a few minutes," the other said, ingratiatingly, "but I'd like your help. I know all about that remark of yours concerning your dislike of Mr Gleason. That's past history—though I may say it will become famous."

"But why?" broke in Pollard, frowning a little. "You must admit there are lots of people who feel like that—"

"I know, but they don't put it into words. Just as there are lots of people who would steal if they were sure they'd not be caught. But they don't, as a rule, advertise this."

"All right, go ahead. You don't suspect me of the murder?"

Pollard's frank glance seemed to compel an honest reply, and Belknap said, "I don't—but only because it has been proved that it was impossible for you to have been in the vicinity of Gleason's place at that time."

"You couldn't have much more positive proof, I suppose," and Pollard smiled. "All right, then, what can I do for you?"

"Tell me whom you suspect." Belknap shot out the words, in an effort to catch Pollard off his guard, for it was the attorney's belief that the clubman knew more of the matter than he had told.

"You give me a difficult question, Mr Belknap," Pollard said, in a serious tone. "I daresay everybody has vague suspicions floating through his brain, but to put them in words is—well, might it not start inquiry in a wrong direction and do ultimate harm?"

"It might, if spoken to the public, but to the investigators of the case, I think it is your duty to tell all you know."

"Oh, I don't *know* anything. Not anything. I assure you. But if I were to express an opinion or make a surmise, I should say look for some incident in Mr Gleason's private life. I know enough of his character and temperament to feel sure that he had friends among people outside the social pale, and it seems to me there's the direction in which to look. It's really no secret that Mr Gleason entertained the sort of young ladies who are usually classed under the general title of 'chorus girls' whether they are in the chorus or not. Look that way, I imagine, and you will, at least, find food for thought."

"You don't know of any particular girl in whom he was interested?"

Pollard stared at him. "I do not. I knew Mr Gleason but slightly. I know nothing of his private affairs, and, as I told you, even the surmise I made is based merely on the man's general characteristics. I have heard him refer to the girls I spoke of, but only in general conversation, and seldom at that. Please understand, I was not only no friend of Robert Gleason, but scarcely an acquaintance. I never met him more than three or four times."

"Yet you took a positive dislike to him."

"I did. I frequently take dislikes at first sight. Or, I am attracted at first sight. Mine is not a unique nature, Mr Belknap. Many people like or dislike a stranger at first meeting."

"But they don't threaten to kill them."

Pollard reached the end of his patience. "Mr Belknap," he said, "I'm tired of having that remark of mine quoted at me. If it had not chanced that Gleason was killed yesterday, that speech would never have been remembered. I do not deny the remark; I do not deny that it was spoken in earnest. But I do deny that I killed Robert Gleason. Now, if you still suspect me, go to work and bring the crime home to me, if not, let up on your insinuations!"

"All right, I will. I don't believe for a minute that you had a hand in it—but I hoped you knew something more definite than you've told me. And, maybe you do. If for instance, you had suspicion of any friend of yours, or an acquaintance, you would, doubtless, try to throw me off the track, and point my attention to Mr Gleason's little lady friends."

Pollard looked at his visitor with fresh interest. "You're cleverer than I thought," he said, frankly. "I don't mind telling you that if I did suspect a friend, the first thing I should do, would be to try to throw the police off his track."

"Have you no sense of justice—or duty to the state?"

"Quite as much as most people, only I don't pretend to more than I have—as most people do. Nine men out of ten would protect a friend, only they wouldn't be so open-mouthed about it."

"That's so; and in a way I'm glad you are so frank. Now, if I come to suspect any friend of yours, I shall return to you and get some information—from the things you *don't* say!"

"Good for you, Mr Belknap. I like your shrewdness. And, truly, if the time comes when I can help, without running a friend's head into the noose, I'll do it."

"And now, I'm going up to the Lindsay house."

"I believe I'll go with you. I may be of some help to them."

"I thought you were so terribly busy!"

Pollard smiled. "I am. But, my business is a movable feast. I'm a writer, you know."

"Yes, I know your two books."

"And I'm just getting out another. I write essays for the magazines, and when I get enough, I bunch 'em up and call it a book."

"And the reviewers call it a good book," Belknap complimented.

"Some of them do. But, I'm my own master—if I neglect my work it hurts no one but myself, and nothing but my own bank account. And so, I'll give up doing a bit of writing I planned for this morning, and go up to the Lindsays' with you. If I can do anything for them, in any way, I'll be glad."

The Lindsay apartment wore the air common to homes where death has entered, yet not to one of the actual household. The shades were partly drawn and a few shaded lamps were lighted. A silent maid admitted the callers and they were shown into the living room where a group of people sat.

The three Lindsays were there, also Doctor Davenport, who had been prescribing for Mrs Lindsay.

"You're all right," he was telling her, "just keep quiet and—"

"But, Doctor," her shrill voice responded, "how can I keep quiet, when I'm so excited? My nerves are on edge—I'm frightened—I can't sleep or eat or rest—"

"The medicine I prescribed will help all that; now, just obey my orders and do the best you can to keep cool and calm."

"Let me help you," and Manning Pollard took the seat next Millicent; "sometimes the mere presence of an unexcitable person helps frazzled nerves."

"You're surely that," and Mrs Lindsay smiled a welcome. "I never saw any one less excitable than you are. Do help to calm me."

She laid her hand in Pollard's and sank back in her chair, already quieted by his silent sympathy.

"Wait a minute, Doctor," Belknap said, as Davenport was about to leave. "I'm asking a few questions, and I want you to tell me as to those two shots that killed Mr Gleason. You don't mind being present, Mrs Lindsay?"

"Indeed, no. I want to be. I want to know every bit of evidence, every clew to the murderer of my brother! I am not excited over the investigation, I only get nervous when I think you will not avenge the crime!"

"We're trying our best," returned Belknap. "What is your theory, Doctor Davenport?"

"I haven't any," and the doctor looked slightly embarrassed.

"Well," Belknap thought to himself, "all these people act queer! Are they all shielding the same person? Is it the precious son of the house?"

"I don't believe in laymen having theories," Davenport went on. "Those are for the police to form and then to prove." He spoke shortly, but in an even time, as one who was sure of what he wanted to say.

"All right," agreed Belknap, "and to form and prove our theories, we must get all the evidence we can. Now, Doctor, as to those shots."

The doctor became all the professional man again. "There's no doubt as to the facts," he replied, straightforwardly; "the fatal shot was most certainly fired first, and the shot in the shoulder some minutes later— after the man had been dead at least several minutes."

"How do you, then, explain Mr Gleason's ability to telephone a message that he was shot?"

"I don't explain it—nor can I conceive of any explanation. It's the strangest thing I ever heard of!"

"It is strange," Belknap mused, "but there must be some explanation. For he did telephone. Your nurse took the message?"

"She did. And she is a most reliable woman. Whatever she reported as to that message, you may depend on as absolute truth. Nurse Jordan has been with me many years, and she is most punctilious in the repetition of messages."

"Mightn't he have telephoned after the first shot," Pollard said, his air more that of one thinking aloud, than of one propounding a theory, "and then with a spasmodic gesture or something, have fired the second shot by accident?"

"The second shot was fired after the man was dead," repeated Doctor Davenport, positively.

"Then there was a murderer," Belknap said, "which fact we have decided upon anyway. And an unusually clever murderer, too."

"But I can't see it," Millicent Lindsay said, speaking in a low moaning voice. "Why would anybody shoot my brother after he had already killed him? I can't see any theory that would explain that."

"Nor I," declared the doctor. "It's the queerest thing I ever knew."

"Leave that point for the moment," Belknap advised, "if we get other facts they may throw light on that. Do any of you think that Mr Gleason," he glanced furtively at Mrs Lindsay to see if he might go on, "was acquainted with—with young ladies—"

"Not in our set?" cried Louis; "he most assuredly was. Now you're getting on the right tack! You don't mind this talk, Millicent?"

"No; go on," returned Mrs Lindsay. "I want to know the truth. And, of course, my brother was no saint. Moreover, if he chose to entertain chorus girls or that sort of people he had a perfect right to do so. I'm not surprised or shocked at anything of that kind. But if they were in any way responsible for his death, I want to know it. Do you know anything definite, Louis?"

"No," was the reply, but the youth went white.

Belknap studied his face, feeling sure that to go white was not absolutely unusual with the young man. He was apparently anaemic, unstrung, and very emotional. His lips twitched, and he curled and uncurled his fingers.

As a matter of fact, Belknap was looking toward Louis as a possible suspect. Though, as yet, he had no reason for such a suspicion.

"I do," said Phyllis Lindsay, speaking for the first time during this discussion. "I know he was intimate with some moving picture actresses. He had their photographs in his rooms."

"When were you there last?" asked Belknap suddenly.

"I don't know—about a week ago, I think. I called in one day to see a new picture Mr Gleason had just bought."

Her face was slightly flushed, but she was cool and composed of manner. Belknap despaired of getting any real information here.

Doctor Davenport looked at Phyllis.

"Did you leave anything there?" he asked abruptly.

"Leave anything?" she repeated.

"Yes," impatiently. "Any of your belongings—wearing apparel?"

"Why, no," the girl smiled. "I didn't."

"Sure?"

"Of course, I'm sure. Unless I dropped a handkerchief, maybe. I'm forever losing those."

"You didn't leave a fur collar?"

"Of course I didn't! My fur collars are too valuable not to keep track of."

"Then," and Doctor Davenport drew from his bag a small fur neckpiece. "Then, I guess it's my duty to show up this. It's a thing," he looked a bit embarrassed, "I picked up in Gleason's room when I first went there last night. I thought it was yours, Phyllis, and I brought it to you."

"Well, of all performances!" exclaimed Belknap, astonished.

"Oh, come now," and Davenport smiled, "I meant to give it up sooner, but I forgot it. I only thought, if it should be Phyllis', she'd rather know about it—"

"All right, as long as I have it now," and Belknap
reached for the fur with an air of authority. "This may be
the clew that will lead us straight to the murderer—or
murderess."

"It may," agreed the doctor, "and it may set you off on
the wrong track, hounding some poor little innocent girl!"

"Is it a valuable piece?" and Belknap held it out
toward Phyllis.

"I don't want to touch it," she shrank back. "Please
don't make me."

"Let me see it," said Millicent reaching out a hand.
"I'll soon tell you."

After a moment's scrutiny she said, "It's a fairly good
fur, and it's the latest style; what they call a choker. It's
new this season, but not worth more than thirty or forty
dollars."

"It might belong to 'most anybody, then," mused
Belknap.

"Yes," said Millicent, "but you see by the label inside,
it came from a shop patronized more by bargain hunters
than by an exclusive class of customers."

"Pointing to the less aristocratic type," Belknap
nodded. "Well, we must trace the owner of the collar.
Where was it, Doctor?"

"In a chair in the room," said Davenport, looking as
sheepish as a censured schoolboy. "I was a fool I suppose,
to take it, but I thought if it belonged to Miss Lindsay, it
might lead to a lot of unpleasant notoriety for her—"

"All right, all right," Belknap shut off his apologies.
"Now to find an owner for the fur. Any suggestions?"

He looked around the group, with a general survey,
but really scanning Louis' face, in hopes the boy might
show some sign of recognition.

But it was from Pollard that the advice came,
"Advertise."

"Just what I planned to do," Belknap said: "I'll take
the fur and advertise for its owner. An adroitly worded
advertisement ought to bring results."

There was little more conversation of importance, the attorney merely taking some notes of certain data he desired, and learning of the arrangements for the funeral which was to take place next day at the Funeral Rooms.

"I probably shan't see you again, Mrs Lindsay, until after I hear from the advertisement," Belknap told her.

"Oh, come to see me whenever you have any fresh evidence or any news," she urged him. "After the funeral, may be too late. Follow up all trails—spare no effort. I may be a peculiar person, Mr Belknap, but I can't help it. I never thought I was of a revengeful nature, but I think it is a righteous indignation that I have now. And I will do anything, spend any amount to find the murderer of my brother."

"You are his heir?" Belknap asked, casually.

"I have not inquired into that as yet," was the reply, spoken rather coldly. "I don't even know whether my brother left a will or not. Mr Lane is his lawyer."

"My question was not prompted by idle curiosity," Belknap assured her, "but it is of importance to know who will benefit financially by the death of this rich man."

"If he left no will," Mrs Lindsay informed him, "I am the only heir. If he left a will, I've no idea as to its contents."

"I must inquire of Lane, then; though doubtless he will see you on the matter very soon."

Belknap departed and first thing he did was to put an advertisement in the Lost and Found columns of several evening papers.

And the next afternoon his zeal was rewarded.

He had instructed the owner of the collar to call at a small shop on a side street, which had no apparent connection with Mr Robert Gleason or his affairs.

By arrangement with the proprietor, Belknap himself was behind the counter and greeted the sweetly smiling young woman who came for the fur.

"Are you sure it's yours?" Belknap asked the fashionably dressed little person.

"No; are you?" she replied, saucily. "But I can describe mine."

"Go ahead, then."

"It's a soft, gray fur, squirrel it's called. And it has *a* label inside with the name of the store where it was bought."

"Yes? And the store is—?"

"Cheapman's Department Store." She smiled triumphantly. "Guess you'll have to give up the goods!"

"It looks that way," Belknap smiled. "Now where did you lose it?"

"Haven't the least idea. Somewhere between starting out from home and getting back there."

"Day before yesterday?"

"Yep. I went to a whole lot of places—"

"Mention some. You see, the store you speak of sells a good many fur collars, so it all depends on where you left yours."

The girl's face fell. "Oh, come now," she said, "s'pose I don't want to tell?"

"Then I shall think you're putting up a game on me, and trying to get a fur collar that doesn't belong to you."

"Oh, well, it doesn't. But it does belong to a friend of mine—and I'm after it for her."

"And she doesn't want to admit where she lost it?"

"I don't know why she wouldn't. But you see, I don't know all the places she went to, and—"

"Look here, Miss—you'll have to give your name, you know."

By this time the girl looked decidedly frightened. "I don't want to," she said, almost crying. "Let the old fur go—I don't want it! I wish I'd kept out of this!"

"Tell me who sent you here, and you can keep out of it."

The girl brightened decidedly, and looked at Belknap.

"Honest," she said; "if I tell you who sent me, can I go home?"

"Certainly you may. I've no right to detain you."

"All right, then, it was Mary Morton."

"Address?"

She gave a street number in the Longacre district, and hurried away almost before Belknap finished writing it down.

Thanking and remunerating the shopkeeper for the use of his premises, Belknap went directly to the address he had obtained.

"Like as not she'll be out," he thought, "but if she is, I'll go again. I'll bet it's one of Gleason's lady friends, and though I've no idea she shot him—yet, she might have. Anyway, I'll get a line on his gay acquaintances. It's bound to be the owner of the collar, for her friend described it exactly, and gave the right maker's name."

Reaching the address given him, Belknap felt a sudden qualm of suspicion. It did not look at all like a boarding house, theatrical or any other kind. In fact it was a shop where electrical goods were sold.

"Upstairs, I s'pose," Gleason mused, and went in.

But nobody at that number could tell him anything of Miss Mary Morton. No one had ever heard of her, and Belknap was confronted with the sudden conviction that he had been made a fool of!

"Idiot! Dunderhead!" he called himself, angrily, as he left the place. "I am an ass, I declare! That little snip jack took me in completely, with her honest gray eyes! Well, let me see; I've a start. That girl described that fur too accurately not to be the owner herself, and I'll track her down again yet. It can't be a hard job. I'll see her picture in some theatrical office or somewhere."

But it was a hard blow, and Belknap felt pretty sore at Prescott's jeers when he learned the story.

"Anyway, it's given us a way to turn," said Belknap. "We've got the fur."

"Yes," grinned Prescott, wickedly, "we've got the fur, and that's as fur as we have got!"

CHAPTER 7: BARRY'S SUSPECT

After the funeral of Robert Gleason, Lane, his lawyer, went to the Lindsay home, for the purpose of reading to the family the will of his late client.

There was no one present except the three Lindsays and Doctor Davenport. The physician was keeping watch over Millicent Lindsay, for her volatile nature and nervous condition made him fear a breakdown.

But Millicent was quiet and composed, only an occasional quiver of her lip or trembling of her fingers betrayed her agitation.

Phyllis' eyes were bright with repressed excitement, but she, too, preserved her poise.

Louis, however, was in a high state of nervous tension. He was jumpy and erratic of speech and gesture, and again, he would relapse into a sulky mood and become perversely silent.

The little party gathered in the library and Lane read the will of Robert Gleason.

The terms were simple. Except for bequests to some personal friends and some charities, the fortune was equally divided between Millicent, his sister, and Phyllis, her stepdaughter.

No mention whatever was made of Louis, and the young man burst forth into a torrent of angry invective.

"Hush, Louis," Doctor Davenport said, sternly; "such talk can do you no good, and it is a disgrace to yourself to speak so of the dead!"

"I don't care," Louis stormed, "why did he leave a lot to Phyllis, and nothing to me? I'm no relative of his, but neither is Phyl!"

"But he was very much in love with Miss Lindsay," Lane explained the situation, "and as he had no expectation of this immediate death, he hoped to make her his wife. But, he told me this when I drew up his will—he provided for Miss Lindsay in case of premature death or accident to himself. I feel sure he hoped to win Miss Lindsay's promise to be his wife—if he had not already done so."

"He had not!" exclaimed Phyllis, but she looked thoughtful rather than indignant at the idea.

"If he found that he could not do so," Lane went on, "he planned to change his will. It was, I think, tentative, and dependent on the course of his wooing."

"Never mind all that," said Phyllis, speaking slowly and a little hesitantly; "the will is valid and final, is it not?"

"Certainly," returned Lane, but he gave her a searching glance.

"Then half the money is mine, and half Millicent's," Phyllis went on, still with that thoughtful manner. "Don't worry, Buddy, I'll give you part of my share." She looked at her brother with fond affection.

"I suppose it's all right," Millicent said, her glance at Phyllis a little resentful. "It would have been quite all right, if Phyllis had meant to marry my brother—but she had no such intention!"

"You don't know—" began the girl.

"I do know," declared Millicent. "And what's more, if you had any hand in his murder—"

"Oh, hush!" cried Fred Lane, shocked even more at Millicent's look than at her words.

"I won't hush! I'm going to find out who killed my brother! He was the only human being whom I loved. These step-children mean nothing to me—although we have always lived harmoniously enough. Now, if Phyllis is innocent, that's all there is about it. But her innocence must be proved!"

Phyllis gave her stepmother a kindly, pitying glance.

"Now, Millicent," she said, "you're excited and nervous, and you don't know what you're saying. Go and lie down, dear—"

"'Go and lie down, dear!'" Millicent mocked her, eyes flashing and her voice hard. "Yes, that's just what you'd say, of course! You fear investigation! No one would dream of suspecting you—unless they knew what I know! and you say—'go and lie down!' Indeed, I *won't* go and lie down! Now, look here, Phyllis Lindsay, you knew what was in that will of my brother's! I didn't—but you did!"

"No, I didn't, Millicent—"

"You did! You led my brother on—and on—letting him think you would marry him—then, when he'd made a will in your favor, you killed him to get the money! That's what you did! And I'll prove it—if it costs me all my share of my poor brother's fortune!"

She collapsed then, and sat, huddled in the big chair, shaking with sobs.

Without a word, Doctor Davenport went to her, assisted her to rise, and, summoning a maid to help him, took Millicent Lindsay away to her own room.

"What ails her, anyway?" Louis growled, looking at Phyllis, curiously.

"Oh, she's like that when she gets a tantrum," the girl responded, looking worried. "She's really good friends with me, but if she takes a notion she turns against me, and she can't think of anything bad enough to say to me."

"I don't like her present attitude," Lane said, abruptly. "She may make a lot of trouble for you, Miss Lindsay. *Did* you know of contents of the will?"

"No," she returned, but she did not look at the lawyer. If, he mused, she were telling an untruth, she would, doubtless, look just like that.

"Are you sure?" he followed up.

"Of course, I'm sure!" she flung up her head and looked at him. Her dark eyes were not flashing, but smoldering with a deep fire of indignation. "How dare you question my statements!"

"Now, Phyl," said her brother, "be careful what you say. Millicent has it in her power to do you a bad turn, and she's willing to do it if she thinks you're mixed up in her brother's case. Do you know *anything* about it, old girl?"

Phyllis gave him a look of reproach, but he went on.

"Now don't eat me up with your eyes, Sis. When I ask if you know anything about the thing, I don't mean did you kill Robert Gleason! Of course, I know better than that! But—oh, well, don't you think, Lane, that Millicent can make trouble for us?"

"Us?" and the lawyer raised his eyebrows. "Where do you come in, Lindsay?"

"Oh," with an impatient shrug, "Phyl's troubles are mine, of course. And seems to me, Millicent has a very annoying bee in her bonnet."

"Easy enough to settle the matter," Lane said, briefly. "Where were you, Miss Lindsay, when the—the tragedy took place?"

"Why, I don't know," Phyllis replied. "Here—at home—I think."

But a sudden flood of scarlet suffused her face, and she was quite evidently preserving her composure by a strong effort.

The small, slight figure, sitting in a tall-backed chair was a picture of itself. Phyllis' bright coloring, her deep, glowing eyes, scarlet lips and rose-flushed cheeks were accented by the plain black gown she wore and her graceful little hands moved eloquently as she talked, and then fluttered to rest on the carved arms of the great chair.

"Sure?"

"Stop saying 'sure?' to me!" Phyllis spoke shortly, and then gave a good-natured laugh. "Of course, I'm not sure, Mr Lane. I'll have to think back. I haven't a—what do they call it—an alibi, but all the same I didn't kill—"

"Don't say that," Lane interrupted her, "nobody for a minute supposes you killed anybody. Mrs Lindsay herself doesn't. It's hysteria that makes her say so. But, she *can* make trouble. And, so, I want you to think carefully, and have your evidence ready. Where were you last Tuesday at about half-past six or seven o'clock?"

Phyllis thought. "Here, I think," she reiterated. "I was out—and I came home and dressed for the dinner party."

"What was the dinner hour?"

"Eight."

"And you were dressing—how long?"

"Oh, I don't know—an hour, probably."

"That leaves some time yet to be accounted for. Where were you just before you came home?"

"Look here, Mr Lane," Phyllis' eyes flashed now, "I won't be quizzed like that! If I'm suspected of a crime—"

"You aren't," Lane repeated, "but if Mrs Lindsay accuses you of a crime, you must be prepared to defend yourself."

"Wait till she does, then," said Phyllis, curtly, and lapsed into silence.

But Louis looked disturbed.

"What can Millicent do, Lane?" he asked. "She can't make up any yarn that will implicate my sister, can she?"

"Oh, no; probably not. All she can do, is to show that Miss Lindsay knew what she would inherit, and, therefore, can be said to have a motive for the—"

"Rot! As if Phyllis would shoot a man to get his money!" But Louis Lindsay's looks belied his words. While showing no doubt or distrust of his sister, he had all the appearance of a man deeply anxious or alarmed at his thoughts. "And, besides, Phyl knew nothing about the will—did you, Sis?"

Phyllis looked at him without replying, for a moment, then she said, "Hush, Louis; don't keep up the subject. I'm going straight to Millicent—and if she's able to talk to me, I'll find out what she means."

Phyllis left the room, and his business over, Lane went away from the house.

As he walked along the street, he mused deeply on the matter.

Of course, Phyllis was in no way concerned in the crime—but Lane couldn't help thinking she knew something about it—or something bearing on it. What could it be? How could that delicate, exclusive girl be in any way mixed up with the deed done down in Washington Square?

Lane made his way to the Club. He knew he'd find a lot of his friends there at this hour, and he wanted to hear their talk.

He was not surprised to find a group of his intimates discussing the Gleason case.

"Now the funeral's over," Dean Monroe was saying, "the detectives can get busy, and do some real work."

"They can get busy," Manning Pollard agreed, "but can they do any real work? I mean, any successful, decisive work?"

"You mean, discover the murderer," Lane said, joining in the talk at once, as he took his seat among them.

"Not a hard job, to my mind," Dean Monroe said, slowing inhaling his cigarette's smoke. "*Cherchez la chorus girl.*"

"Oh, I don't know—" said Pollard.

"Well, I know!" Monroe came back quickly. "Oh, I don't mean I know—but who else could it have been? You may say Pollard, here, because he announced his intention of killing Gleason. But we all know Pol's little smarty ways. He didn't even defend himself, because, secure in his innocence, he let the old detectives themselves find and prove his alibi! A silly grandstand play, I call it!"

Pollard smiled. "It was silly, I daresay, but if I had eagerly defended myself, they might have thought me guilty. So, why not let them find out the truth for themselves? But, as to the chorus kiddies—I doubt if the bravest of them would have the nerve to shoot a man. Remember they're only babies."

"Not all of them," offered Barry.

"Oh, well, those who have arrived at years of wisdom are not the ones Gleason favored," Pollard said. "However, there's a possibility that some man—some bold, bad man may have done it for the sake of a girl."

"Then he must be found through the discovery of the girl," declared Lane. "And with that fur piece to work on, it's a funny thing if they can't get the lady."

"It would be coincidence, I think," Pollard said, seriously. "I don't know much about real detective work, but it seems to me, if I found a fur collar at the scene of the crime, the owner of that would be the last person I'd look for."

"You give the collar too much importance, Monroe, and you, Pollard, give it too little," Lane spoke in his most judicial manner. "I'm no detective myself, but I am a lawyer, and I modestly claim a sort of knowledge of criminal doings. The fur collar is a clew. It must be investigated. It may lead to the truth and it may not."

"Hear, hear!" cried Barry. "What wisdom! Oh, what sagacity! It may and it may not! Lane, you're a wizard at deduction!"

They all laughed, but Fred Lane was in no way dismayed.

"All right, you fellows," he said; "but which of you can make any better prognostication? Come now, here are four of us; let's make a bet—or, no, that's hardly decent—let's each express an opinion regarding the murderer of Robert Gleason, and see who comes nearest to the truth."

"Sure we'll ever know the truth?" asked Monroe.

"Well, if we don't there's no harm done. Go ahead, and let it be understood that these are merely thoughts—private opinions and absolutely confidential."

"All right," agreed Dean Monroe, "I'll speak my mind first. I'm all for the chorus girl—and when I say chorus girl, I use the term generically. She may be a Movie Star or a Vaudeville artist. But some chicken of the stage, is my vote. Yet I don't claim but she did the deed herself—it may well have been her stalwart gentleman friend, who was jealous of the rich man's friendship with his girl. There's my opinion."

"Good enough, too," appraised Lane. "Moreover, you've got the fur collar in evidence. You may be right. You next, Pollard?"

"I'm inclined to think it was somebody from Gleason's Seattle home. Seems to me there must have been people out there who felt as I did about the man—who really wanted him out of the world; and, too, they may have had some definite grievance—some conventional motive— what are they? Love, hate, money?"

"Revenge is one."

"All the same, revenge and hate. Well, doesn't it seem more like a wild Westerner to come there and shoot up his man than for a New Yorker to do it? I don't take much stock in the chorus girl theory."

"Wait a bit, Pol," put in Barry. "Seattle isn't wild and woolly and cowboyish and bandittish! It's as civilized as our own fair city, and as little given to deeds of violence as New York itself!"

"Your logic is overwhelming," Pollard laughed. "Ought to have been a lawyer instead of an artist, Barry! But I stick to my guns—which are the guns of the Westerners who knew Gleason—the inhabitants of Seattle and environs. I may be all wrong, but it seems the most plausible theory to me. Perhaps I'm prejudiced, but I think Seattle is mighty well rid of its leading citizen."

"Hush up, Manning," reproved Monroe; "your foolish threat was bad enough when the man was alive, it's horrid to knock him now he's dead."

"That's so—I'll shut up. But Lane asked for my opinion, and now he's got it."

"Yours, Barry?" asked Lane, without comment on Pollard's.

"I don't want to express mine," said Philip Barry, with such a serious look that nobody smiled. "You see, I have a dreadful suspicion of—of some one I know—we all know."

"Me?" asked Pollard, cheerfully.

"No"; Barry grinned at him. "You're just plain idiot! But, truly, haven't any of you thought of some one in—in our set?"

Apparently no one had, for each man present looked blankly inquiring.

"Oh, I'm not going to put it into words," and Barry gave a shrug of his shoulders. Slightly built, his dark, intense face showing his artistic temperament, Philip Barry had a strong will and a high temper.

Moreover, unlike his type, he had a desperate tenacity of opinion, and once convinced of a thing would stick to it through thick and thin.

"Just because an idea came into my head," he went on, "is no reason I should give it voice. I might do an innocent man a desperate injustice."

"As you like, Barry," Lane said, "but to my way of thinking, if you have such an idea it's your duty to give it voice. If your man's innocent it can't harm him. If he's guilty he ought to be suspected. And, among us four, your views are an inviolable secret, unless justice requires them to be told."

"Well," Barry began, reluctantly, "who first heard of this murder?"

"Doctor Davenport," said Monroe, quickly. "His nurse telephoned from the office—"

"Did the nurse tell you that?" Barry shot at him.

"Why, no, of course not. I haven't seen the nurse."

"Has anybody?"

"I don't know. I suppose the police have."

"You suppose! Well, they haven't. I found that out. No, the police have not thought it worth while to check up Doctor Davenport's story of his nurse's message to him. They take it as he told it. It was nine chances out of ten they would do so. I say, fellows, don't you remember that conversation we had about murder that afternoon—last Tuesday afternoon?"

"I do," answered Pollard. "It was then that I made my famous speech."

"Yes; and that was remembered because it was unconventional and damn-foolishness besides. But Doctor Davenport's speeches, though of far greater importance, are all forgotten."

"I haven't forgotten them," said Pollard, thoughtfully. "He said the detection of crime depended largely on chance."

"Yes, and he minimized the chances."

"But, good Lord, Barry, you're not hinting—"

"I'm hinting nothing," said Barry, speaking decidedly now, "I'm reminding you what Davenport said; I'm reminding you of his whole attitude toward the matter of murder; I'm reminding you of his psychological mind, and that it might have been swayed in the direction of crime; I'm reminding you that Pollard's fool remark about killing Gleason might have started a train of thought in the doctor's mind—"

"Making me accessory before the fact!" suggested Pollard.

"Unconsciously, yes, maybe. Well, there it is. You asked me for my guess. You have it. It isn't a suspicion, it isn't even a theory—it's merely a guess—but it's at least a possible one."

"Barry, you're batty!" Dean Monroe declared. "Us artists get that way sometimes." He beamed round upon the group. "Don't mind Phil. He'll come out all right. And for heaven's sake, fellows, forget what he has said."

Monroe was always looking out for his fellow artist and friend.

Barry's impulsiveness had often been checked or steadied by Monroe's better judgment and clearer thought. And now, Monroe was truly distressed at Barry's speech.

"But where's the motive?" Lane was asking, interested in this new suggestion, and determined to look into it.

"That I don't know," said Barry. "I've no idea what his motive could have been. But, for my part, I don't believe in hunting the motive first. A motive for murder is far more likely to be a secret than to be something that anybody can deduce or guess."

"Guessing is foolishness," Pollard remarked, "but don't you all remember that Davenport mentioned fear as a common motive. I recollect he did, and while I don't for one minute incline to Barry's suggestion, yet I can admit the possibility of fear."

"You mean Doc was afraid of Gleason? Why?" Lane spoke sharply.

"I don't know why. I don't know that he *was* afraid—of Gleason or anybody else. But I do say that he might have been—there are a hundred reasons why a man may be secretly afraid of another man. Who knows the secrets of his neighbor's heart? I'm making no claim, educing no theory, but it's at least a fact that Davenport did speak of fear as a motive. Now, I merely say, if you're going to suspect him, you may as well use that tip. That's all."

Pollard smoked on in silence, and each of the four thought over this new idea.

"It's shocking, that's what it is, shocking!" exclaimed Dean Monroe, at last. "I'm ashamed of you all, ashamed of myself, for harboring this thought for a minute. Forget it, everybody."

"Not so fast, Dean," Barry rebuked him. "Any thought has a right to expression—at the right time and place. I've given you this suggestion for what it's worth. I've nothing to base a suspicion on—except that the first man to hear of a crime or to go to the spot is a fair topic to think about."

"But a doctor—called there!" Monroe went on, "You might as well suspect the police themselves!"

"Yes, if they gave us a surprising story of a man killed by a shot and *afterward* telephoning for help."

"That story is fishy," admitted Lane.

"You bet it is," assented Barry. "I can't *see* that telephoning business at all!"

CHAPTER 8: MISS ADAMS' STORY

In the offices of the District Attorney, Lane discussed the case with Belknap. Without giving names or making any definite accusations, the lawyer asked the Assistant District Attorney what he thought of Dr Davenport's story.

"True on the face of it," replied Belknap, promptly.

"Yes," Lane reminded him, "because it has not occurred to you to think otherwise about it. But, how can you explain that telephoning?"

"It can't be explained, so far as we know about it now. But, look here, if Doctor Davenport killed Gleason— which, by the way, is the most absurd idea I ever heard of—the last thing he would do would be to make up such an unbelievable yarn as that of the man telephoning after he had been fatally shot."

"Doctor didn't quite say that."

"Circumstances say that. Gleason called up the doctor's office and said he was shot. The fatal shot was fired first. Elucidate."

"I can't. That's the reason I'm here. We've got to find out about it. I'm the Lindsays' lawyer, and Mrs Lindsay is having hysterics and all that. She's of a revengeful temperament and wants the murderer of her brother punished. This is not an unnatural feeling, and I want to do all I can to push matters along. I don't want the case to drift on and on, until it's laid on the shelf with lots of other unsolved mysteries."

"I don't either, Lane," Belknap said, earnestly, "and we're working on it night and day. Any news, Prescott?"

The query was addressed to the detective, who entered at the moment.

"No, Mr Belknap. But what you folks talking about? Doctor Davenport?"

Guardedly, Lane spoke of the strange story the doctor had told and Prescott caught the drift at once.

"Where'd you get that dope?" he asked, his shrewd eyes scanning Lane's face.

"It isn't dope—if you mean evidence; it's merely scouting for possible clews."

"Yes, and it may be a boomerang clew! It may rebound against the man that started it. Who did?"

"Nobody in particular," and Lane looked stubborn.

"Yes, they did, now," persisted Prescott. "Somebody started that lead, and did it on purpose. Who made the suggestion? Manning Pollard?"

"No," said Lane. "I'm not sure I know who spoke about it first."

"Well, *I'm* sure you know, and you'd better tell. Unless you're shielding somebody yourself. Better speak up, Mr Lane."

"All right, then, it was Philip Barry. I believe it's wiser to say so than to conceal it. You can't suspect him."

"Why can't I? I can suspect anybody that can't prove his innocence. And I've been thinking about Mr Barry myself. Isn't he in love with the heiress?"

"What heiress?"

"Miss Lindsay—half heiress of Mr Gleason's big fortune."

"What if he is? I could name a dozen young men in love with Miss Lindsay. She's a belle and has numberless admirers."

"Yes, but Philip Barry's a favored one, I've heard. Now, didn't he know Miss Lindsay would inherit?"

"I don't know whether he did or not."

"You knew it—you drew up the will."

"Yes."

"Did you tell anybody?"

Lane stared at him. "I'm not in the habit of babbling about my clients' affairs!" he said, coldly.

"Of course not. But did it leak out in any way—say, in general conversation? Such things often do. It was no real secret, I suppose."

"I treated it as one," said Lane. "Of course, I considered it confidential."

"Of course," put in Belknap. "Lawyers have to be close-mouthed people, Prescott."

But Prescott would not be downed.

"I know all that, Mr Belknap, but listen here. The news of that inheritance might have leaked out in a dozen ways. Not purposely, of course, but by chance. Wasn't anybody ever in your office, Mr Lane, when Mr Gleason was there, talking about it, or didn't you ever mention it in conversation with some intimate friend, say?"

Lane thought back.

"No," he said, decidedly. "Unless—yes, one day, I remember, Manning Pollard was in my office when Gleason came in. Gleason only stayed a few minutes, but he did refer to his will, and after he went, I think I did speak of it to Pollard."

"Did he ask you about it?"

"No, I'm sure he didn't. I think I volunteered an observation on the queerness of the Western man, and, as Pollard didn't like him, anyway, very little was said."

"But the terms of his will were spoken of?"

"Yes, incidentally. Pollard is a close friend of mine, and I may have been a bit confidential."

"There you are, then," and Prescott nodded his sagacious head.

"Manning Pollard is a babbling sort of chap. I mean, he says things to make a sensation—to shock or astound his audience. Ten chances to one, he implied a knowledge of Gleason's intentions just to appear importantly wise."

"No," Lane demurred. "Pollard isn't that sort, exactly. He does like to make startling speeches, but they're usually about himself, not gossip about others."

"Well, anyway, say Barry got an idea Pollard knew of Gleason's will, and got at the truth somehow. Or, maybe

Barry found out from some one else. Didn't Miss Lindsay know of her inheritance?"

"I think not."

"It doesn't matter how he found out; say, Barry knew Miss Lindsay would inherit, say, also, he was jealous of Gleason—which he was—and say—just for the moment— he did kill Gleason. Wouldn't he be likely to try to turn suspicion on some one else—and who could he select better than Doctor Davenport himself?"

Prescott beamed with an air of triumph at his conclusion, and looked at the others for concurrence.

"Rubbish!" Lane scoffed. "You surely have built up a mountain out of a silly molehill. Try again, Prescott."

"I will try again, but it will be along these same lines," and the detective shook his head doggedly. "What say, Mr Belknap?"

Belknap looked thoughtful.

"I don't see much in it," he declared, "yet there may be. All you can do, Prescott, is to investigate. Check up the doctor's story, the nurse's story, and keep a watch on Barry. Your evidence is *nil*, your suspicion has but slight foundation, and yet, it's true Philip Barry is a favored admirer of Miss Lindsay, he was jealous of Robert Gleason, and whether he knew of the will or not, his name can't be ignored in this connection."

"Go ahead," said Lane, "investigate Barry thoroughly, but for heaven's sake, don't be misled. Don't assume his guilt merely because he admires Miss Lindsay and was jealous of Gleason! Get some real evidence."

"I wasn't born yesterday, Mr Lane," Prescott said, looking at the lawyer with some irritation. "I must find a direction in which to look, mustn't I? I must look in every direction that seems likely, mustn't I? I happen to know that there was bad blood between Doctor Davenport and Mr Barry—"

"What do you mean by bad blood?" asked Lane.

"I mean they didn't like each other—weren't friendly—never chummed. And the reason was that they were in love with the same girl."

"Natural enough state of affairs," commented Belknap. "Go ahead, Prescott, look up the doctor's yarn, look up Barry's alibi, but, as Mr Lane says, go carefully. I fancy, that though you may not get anything on either of these men, you can't help turning up something in the way of evidence against somebody! Get all the facts you can, all the information you can, and then see how it affects the individuals. Of course, you must see the nurse that took the message from Gleason. I'm surprised that hasn't been done."

"We simply accepted the doctor's story," said Prescott. "Now, I'll verify it."

But before the detective began his promised verification, he elected to go again to the Gleason apartments.

Here he visited Miss Adams, whose story, told him by Belknap, interested him.

He used his best powers of persuasion on the spinster, and his wheedlesome ways, and pleasant smile made her affable and loquacious.

By roundabout talk, he drew from her at last some descriptions of the callers or visitors at the Gleason apartment.

She was loath to admit her curiosity, but she finally confessed that she occasionally hung over the stairway to watch matters below.

She defended her deed by explaining that she was lonely, and a little diversion of any sort was welcome.

"And, indeed, why shouldn't I?" she asked; "it's no crime to watch a body going or coming along the street, or into a house!"

"Of course it isn't," agreed Prescott, sympathetically. "Now, whom did you see go into Mr Gleason's apartment on the day of the murder?"

"Two people."

"Two! Both at once?"

"No; the lady came first."

"Oh, she did. Wait a minute—did you see Mr Gleason himself come in?"

"I heard him."

"What time?"

"After five. I don't know any nearer than that."

"Go on, then. A lady came? When?"

"Quite soon after Mr Gleason himself. I heard a light step on the stairs and I looked out."

"Describe her."

"She was a gay little piece. Big eyes, tomato-colored cheeks and a nose powdered like a marshmallow."

"Small? Young?"

"Both; that is, very slim, but about average height. I looked mainly at her clothes."

"What were they?"

"Mostly fur, and long gray stockings and a little round cap of gray fur."

"Squirrel fur?"

"Yes, I guess so. Gray, anyway. A pert little thing she was, and yet pretty too, in a sort of way."

"What sort of way?"

"Oh, fly, flippant—flirtatious."

"I don't know—she just gave me that impression."

"Would you know her if you saw her again?"

"I'm not sure—those little trots all look alike. But I'd know the clothes."

"Don't squirrel furs all look alike?"

"Perhaps—yet I think I'd know her. You don't think she killed Mr Gleason, do you?"

"Gracious, no! Do you?"

"Well, I never saw her come out."

"But you weren't on watch all the time, were you?"

"No; of course not." Miss Adams turned thoughtful. "But I didn't hear her go out—funny."

"Who was the other caller?"

"A man."

"After the girl came?"

"Yes; soon after. He was a swagger, well-dressed chap; not very large, but tallish."

"Derby hat?"

"No, sort of soft felt—"

"Gray?"

"Maybe—but more like olive green—dull olive."

"Overcoat?"

"Yes, of course. Dark, plain, but with an air."

Prescott looked at the old maid interestedly. How should she know when men's clothes had an air?

"I'm very observant," she said, catching his expression.

"I'm fond of clothes, though I never had a smart gown in my life. But I know when people are well-dressed."

"The man went in then, before the girl came out?"

"Why, yes; but I never saw or heard the girl come out."

"Did you see or hear the man come out?"

"No; but that's not so strange. I wasn't interested in him."

"And you were in the girl?"

"Yes, I was. She's no right to be calling at a man's apartment! I'd no thought of the man visitor, but I'd like to catch hold of that silly young thing and give her a talking to."

"Do you think she'd listen?"

"I know she wouldn't! But I'd like the satisfaction of giving her a piece of my mind!"

"You may get it. I'm going to try to find her."

"Can you?"

"I don't know. Well, now, see here; we are assuming that Mr Gleason died at about quarter to seven. Do you think either or both of those people stayed as long as that?"

"How on earth can I tell? I didn't see them leave, you know."

"And you saw no one else enter?"

"No."

"Nor heard any one?"

"Not that I know of. After six o'clock, there's more or less trafficking on the stairs anyway. The tenants come home, you know."

"Yes; now, you're sure about these two, and that they came about five o'clock?"

"I'm sure they came, but I can't say certain about the time. It was quite some after five, but I've no idea just how much after." Concluding he could learn no more from Miss Adams, Prescott went to Doctor Davenport's office to interview Nurse Jordan.

He found a calm, placid-faced woman, who, being interrogated, told the story just as the doctor had told it.

"Describe the voice that came to you over the telephone," said Prescott.

"Well, it was gasping and faint—just what you would expect a man's voice to be after he had been shot."

"Fatally shot?"

"Of course not! But I heard it, and I know what he said. Now if he spoke, he must have been alive, and if he was alive, he hadn't yet been fatally shot. Had he?"

"Not likely. Then you assume the second shot was the fatal one?"

"How can I, when the doctors say otherwise?"

"What, then, do you think about it?"

"I don't know what to think. If any other nurse had taken that message I'd say she dreamed the thing. But I took it myself, and I know. The only possible explanation I can think of, is that the murderer stood there ready to shoot, but hadn't yet fired. The victim somehow managed to get the telephone call—"

"How could he? Why would the murderer let him?"

"I don't know, I'm sure. But, say the murderer threatened him, and say the victim made some plausible plea that made the murderer grant him a moment's respite to telephone—"

"Oh, I see. Or, say, the murderer was threatening Gleason's life unless he telephoned a certain party—not the doctor. Then say, Gleason called this number as a last hope—and shouted that he was already shot, when he was merely anticipating the deed, and in his frenzy of fear, hoped that to tell the doctor that, would be to stay the murderer's hand."

"That's a way out," Nurse Jordan said, musingly. "And that's all I can think of—that it was something of that sort. As I say, the voice was husky and scared, but it would be that if he was threatened. Still, it certainly sounded like the voice of a suffering, dying man. It was short, gasping—as if strangling."

"In that case, if he were already shot when he called up, I mean—the death shot was not instantaneous, as is supposed, but the victim lived a few moments. Might that be so?"

"I can't say. I've never known Doctor Davenport to make a false diagnosis and, too, the other doctors agree the shot in the shoulder was fired after the man was dead."

"That seems to be inexplicable."

"It's all inexplicable. There's Doctor Davenport himself—talk to him."

Prescott blessed his luck that the doctor came in just then, and eagerly began to question him.

"I was at Mrs Ballard's," the doctor said; "up on Ninetieth Street, near Fifth Avenue. After I got the nurse's message, I hurried down to the Gleason place as fast as I could. I didn't know the exact number—"

"You didn't!" Prescott felt sure this was meant as a blind, to indicate the doctor's slight acquaintance with Gleason.

"No; I didn't. I had to telephone some one to find out. I tried the Lindsays first, but the wire was busy, so I called up Manning Pollard."

"And he told you?"

"Yes, I didn't get the call, but the Ballards' butler did, and Pollard gave him the address. Of course, the man told Pollard I wanted it."

"I see. Then you went right down there?"

"Yes; and the rest is public knowledge. Look here, Prescott, what are you getting at?"

"Only the truth. Go on, tell the story. I have to get these details."

"What details?"

"Of what happened before the police came."

"Oh, you know it all. How I got help and broke in the door, and found Gleason on the floor, dead."

"He was dead when you entered?"

"Of course he was."

"With two shots in his body."

"Yes; why go over these things with me? I've made my report."

"I know! but I want to find out about the telephoning. How do you account for a man telling of his own death?"

"That's the puzzle. It's the queerest thing I ever knew, Prescott, but it isn't my province to ferret out the truth. My duty in the case is done, and you know it. Now good-by."

"One minute, Doctor. Will you tell me where you were that afternoon—the afternoon of the murder?"

Davenport stared at him.

"Meaning that you suspect me of the crime?"

"I haven't said so. Are you one of those people who think every question a detective asks implies an accusation? There might be a dozen reasons for my asking you that besides suspicion of you as Gleason's murderer."

"Well, of course, I've no reason for not telling. I left the Club with Dean Monroe. I set him down at his home, in West Fifty-sixth Street, and then I made a short round of calls. Not more than three or four, special cases. And while I was at Mrs Ballard's the message came from Nurse Jordan. Satisfied of my alibi?"

Davenport's tone was sarcastic, and his smile was not pleasant. But, as Prescott reflected, nobody likes to be wrongfully suspected.

A fleeting thought went through the detective's mind that if Doctor Davenport had killed Gleason he might have done so when he went down there at seven o'clock. But that would mean that Nurse Jordan told a string of falsehoods, and the whole affair would have been a most complicated proceeding. No, if the doctor were the murderer, he would not have called up Pollard to get that address.

But did he do that? Prescott went away and went straight to a telephone booth and called Pollard.

"What?" Pollard said as he heard the query. "Called me up to ask Gleason's address? Why, no—oh, yes, he did. I remember now. He did, and I gave it to him. Why?"

"Tell you some other time," said Prescott. "Good-by."

Chapter 9: Ivy Hayes

"I've no faith in the police, no faith in detectives and no faith in anybody!"

This wholesale skepticism was voiced by Millicent Lindsay, and addressed to her small audience of friends gathered in her library.

"It's outrageous," she went on, "nearly a week has passed since my brother's murder, and no real step has been taken to find his murderer."

"Steps have been taken," said Louis, "but they all seem to have been taken in the wrong direction."

"At any rate they led nowhere," Millicent went on. "Nobody knows anything; nobody can explain the mystery of the two shots. Nobody knows of any motive for the crime."

"You've ceased to suspect Phyllis, then," Philip Barry said, his smile a little forced as he eagerly awaited the answer.

"I have and I haven't," Millicent returned, speaking slowly. "Of course, it seems absurd to think a young girl like Phyllis would do such a dreadful thing—but—she won't tell where she was, and, too, she didn't like my brother—at least, she didn't welcome his offer of marriage, and if she knew of his will, and I think she did, why shouldn't I suspect her?"

"Well, quit suspecting her," Louis growled. "Phyllis is as innocent as a baby. You're off your head, Millicent, to dream of such a thing."

"All right, why won't she tell where she was at the time of the crime, then?"

"She doesn't have to. Nobody really suspects her, and her affairs have no reason to be inquired into. That right, Barry?"

"Yes, of course. I think Phyllis would be wise to say where she was at the time. But, I say, Millicent, I'm going to get busy myself, and do a little detective work. Like you, I feel the investigations so far have led nowhere."

"Have you a suspicion—" began Louis.

"Not a suspicion, exactly, but a pretty strong notion of which way to look. I won't say what it is, for I had another hunch, that pretty much fell through; but now I'm going to work on a new line, and I think I may unearth something."

"You won't," said Millicent, despondently. "You're all alike—dig up a lot of evidence and then never prove anything from it. Do tell me, Phil, what way your suspicions turn."

"Why, yes, I'll tell you, for I think you ought to be kept informed. I can't help leaning to the chorus girl theory. I feel sure that fur collar was left by the girl at that time, and as I see it, she could have gone there with some man, a friend of hers who either was jealous of Mr Gleason, or who had it in for him for some other reason. Then suppose, in a quarrel, the man shot Gleason—perhaps Gleason threatened him—anyway, you can't tell what occurred, but I'm going to find the girl."

"You're all wrong," said Louis, and his voice was so full of concentrated passion that Barry looked up quickly.

"You're all wrong," Louis repeated; "the idea of a man shooting another man before a girl! Do have a little sense of probability, Barry."

"I have, and it's not an impossibility that the deed should have been committed before the girl witness. I've thought it all out. I don't believe it was premeditated, but suppose the pair went there to settle a grievance and Mr Gleason lost his temper and threatened his visitor—the man—and in a quarrel, the pistol was flourished about, and the visitor grabbed it and shot, maybe in self-defense."

"All theory," scoffed Louis. "Nothing at all to back it up."

"I'm going to find out," Barry persisted. "I'm going to find the owner of that fur—"

"I wish you wouldn't, Phil." Louis' face was white and his voice trembled a little.

"Why, Louis," Millicent exclaimed; "what's the matter? Do you know anything about this business? Actually, from your agitation you might be unduly interested."

"No! I don't know anything about it, but I think it's awful to hunt down some poor little innocent girl—"

"I'm not hunting her—I'm hunting the man who was with her."

"A purely imaginary man!" Louis exclaimed.

"So far. But if he doesn't materialize, there's no harm done."

Just then, Phyllis came in with Manning Pollard.

"We've been for a walk," she said, and the roses in her cheeks proved the good effects of the exercise. "Mr Pollard said I needed more outdoor air, so we walked forty-five blocks. I wish you'd go out, Millicent, it would do you good."

"Come on, Mrs Lindsay," Pollard suggested; "I'll take you next."

"Thank you, I may go some other time. Now, we're discussing the case. Sit down, and tell us what you think, Mr Pollard."

"My opinion is no secret. I incline to some earlier acquaintance of Mr Gleason's. Perhaps some one from his Western home, or from anywhere. I've heard all the evidence that has been brought forward about any one of his New York acquaintances, and I must admit there's not a shred of it worth considering. Indeed, there's practically no evidence—do you know of any, Barry?"

"Only the fur collar," said Barry, with a decided nod of his head. "I think, as that is the only piece of real, tangible evidence, it ought to be run to earth. I believe Prescott tried to do so, but his effort fell through, somehow. At any rate, I'm going to take up that clew, and see if I can't get a line on the truth."

"All rubbish," Louis growled. "Tell him not to do it, Pollard."

"Why should I do that?" Pollard asked. "If Barry's sleuthing leads to anything, I'll be glad of it. Like Mrs Lindsay, I want to know who did this thing. I don't have much faith in the fur collar sign-board, myself, for I think the thing was left there by some little girl caller, who had no connection whatever with the crime."

"Maybe," Barry acquiesced. "But in that case, I'll do no harm. I promise not to bother the little girl—why do we all assume her to be little—if she knows nothing of interest to us."

"How are you going about your task?" Louis asked. He was still annoyed about it. His bent brows and frowning face showed a special interest and a dislike of Barry's plans. He moved uneasily in his chair, suddenly sitting bolt upright, and then falling back in careless relaxation.

"Do sit still, Louis," said Phyllis; "you make me quite nervous—acting like that. I wish you'd go out for a walk. You sit mewed up here, brooding, until you're in a perfect state of feverish excitement. Run out, dear; go for a brisk walk. The air is fine and bracing."

Phyllis looked anxiously after her brother.

He returned her gaze, seemed touched by her concern for him, and finally rose and followed her advice.

"I've always had the care of him," Phyllis said, as she looked fondly after him. "He's a darling, but he has moods. And the best thing for him is to get away from this eternal discussion of the 'case.'"

"Perhaps you'd like to get away, too," said Millicent, tartly. "I don't think you show any sympathy for me, Phyllis, in my trouble. But, why should you? You've got your inheritance and you're rid of a troublesome suitor—"

"Don't talk like that, Millicent," Phyllis begged, tears in her eyes. "Indeed, I do sympathize with you, and I'm ready and willing to do anything I can to help you."

"All right, then, turn your mind to thinking about who caused Robert's death. You're a bright girl, you have a really clever mind. Why can't you ferret out the truth as well as a man? As I've been saying, I don't think the police detectives get anywhere. I think friends know much more about the possibilities and probabilities—"

"We do," Barry agreed. "And to prove it, I'm going to start on my search at once. I'm going down to the Gleason apartment, I'm going to get that fur and take it with me, and I'll bet I'll find somebody in the house, some busybody or curious woman who has seen a girl there with that fur on. We all know Mr Gleason had friends among the younger members of the theatrical profession. There's no use blinking that fact, and I propose to find out something, at any rate."

"Well, go on, then," urged Millicent, impatiently; "don't sit there and talk about it! Start off, now."

"I go!" and with a smiling good-by, Barry departed.

"He won't do a thing," Pollard said, with an indulgent smile. "He's on a wild goose chase. I'd like to help you, Mrs Lindsay, but I confess I don't take any stock in the girls. Now, have you any old letters or papers of your brother's that you can look over. I feel that in those you might find a past acquaintance or some old quarrel or altercation that might show you a way to look. This is only a theory, but it's as plausible as any other I've heard put forth."

"It is, Mr Pollard," Millicent agreed. "I've none of Robert's papers here—they're all at his rooms still. And I suppose Mr Lane has charge of them. But I can get them, and I shall do just as you've advised. Of course, there may be something divulged that way, but I doubt if my brother had an enemy out West. He was a much-liked man—"

"I know that," Phyllis interrupted, "but you must admit, Millicent, that even well-liked men may have enemies. There's lots about a man's private life that would contradict the general impression of him."

"That's you all over, Phyllis! You never lose a chance to cast a slur on my brother's memory. I should think you would have a little gratitude to the man who left you a fortune."

"I have, Millicent. And you must not misconstrue my words as you do. I am anxious, too, to find your brother's murderer. And if, as Mr Pollard suggests, it may be some Western acquaintance, we must try to find him. And Mr Gleason's private letters and papers may reveal much."

"Yes, I suppose so. Now, with Phil Barry after the chorus girl, and Mr Pollard's suggestions of hunting among the letters, we, at least have something to do. I shall send word to Mr Lane at once that I want all the papers from Robert's desk."

She went away to telephone, leaving Phyllis and Manning Pollard alone.

"It's a mere chance," said Pollard, thoughtfully; "it may well be that Mr Gleason would destroy any letters that are indicative of the sort of thing we're looking for."

"I don't think so," the girl returned. "I imagine Mr Gleason would have kept such papers. You see, I knew the man better than you did. You hardly knew him at all, did you?"

"No; I never met him more than two or three times, and that in the most formal way."

"Yet you threatened to kill him!"

"Don't put it that way, Miss Lindsay—please. My idle words have been repeated till I'm tired of hearing them! I did say I disliked the man—and I did. That's all there was about it."

"I disliked him, too," said Phyllis, slowly. "I always had a nervous dread of him. I don't know why, but he always affected me unpleasantly, even when he was most kind."

"Then you know what I mean. That unreasonable, inexplicable detestation of his presence. So, of course, when the man was killed, they assumed it was my work. I left it to them to find out where I was at the time for I knew that would be a surer proof of my innocence than if I vehemently denied guilt and tried to prove an alibi. But you, too, I'm told, refuse to say where you were at the time of the crime."

"Yes," Phyllis whispered. "Don't ask me. I don't want to tell. I have good reasons for my silence, truly."

"And not connected with Mr Gleason's death."

Pollard did not voice this as a question, but merely as a statement of fact, and Phyllis gave him a glance of gratitude for his faith in her.

But she did not corroborate his assertion and his inquiring glance that followed met with no definite response.

"Now is there anything I can do?" Pollard asked, after a more or less desultory chat. "I'm at your command—"

"I thought you were a very busy man," and Phyllis smiled at him.

"Not when I can be of any assistance to you or Mrs Lindsay. Though now that you have come into a great fortune, perhaps an humble pen-pusher will cease to interest you."

"No," said Phyllis, seriously; "on the contrary, I shall have more need than ever of friends who can advise me in certain ways."

"Surely your lawyer will do that. Lane is a most capable legal adviser—"

"I don't mean that. I mean in other ways—things on which I wouldn't dream of discussing with Mr Lane. Oh, I have awful troubles—"

"I'm so sorry." Pollard's serious, kindly manner carried conviction. "I'd be glad to help you, but in important matters you'd better consult some one of sound judgment and special knowledge. If you don't care to confide in Lane, ask him for the type of adviser you do need."

"But, Mr Pollard," the girl hesitated, "it isn't a question of special knowledge at all. I just want advice from some man of the world—a man of our set, of our interests. Somebody who knows what to do in a crisis—"

"Please, Miss Phyllis—don't talk like that! If you do, I shall be tempted to offer my own services, and I'm sure there are many better fitted for the position."

"Oh, I wish you would help me—"

"Why not go to Barry?"

"Phil Barry? He's a dear, and a good friend to me, but he has what is known as the artistic temperament—and you know what that means. No—the weight on my mind—the awful quandary I'm in, couldn't be helped by him. He's the last man to help me. Oh, Mr Pollard—I oughtn't to ask you—in fact, I oughtn't to tell anybody— but I feel so helpless. Perhaps Mr Lane would be the best one after all. I don't know what I ought to do!"

Pollard looked at the lovely face, so full of grief and uncertainty. He wondered what it could be about. Was it the exaggerated fear of a young girl, that had little or no real foundation. Or—could it be possible that she had some knowledge, guilty or evidential, of the Gleason affair.

After a pause the man spoke.

"Miss Phyllis," he said, with a gentle courtesy, "I want to help you, more than I can tell you—more than I ought to tell you. But I'm not going to take advantage of what may be merely a mood of confidence. You think things over; you consider your other friends—or legal advisers— and after careful thought, if you want to make me your confidant, I shall be honored, and I will advise you to the best of my powers. But don't be hasty. Think it over well, and—may I see you to-morrow?"

"How kind you are!" the girl held out her hand with a pretty impulsive gesture. "That's just what I want; to think it over a little and decide whether I want to tell Mr Lane,—or whether I'd rather confide in a—a friend."

"Of course you do," was the hearty response. "And Lane, who has wide knowledge, is also a good friend.

Consider carefully, and decide slowly. But depend on me to the last ditch, if I can be of help."

Meantime Philip Barry was on his quest.

He had decided on straightforward measures, and, gaining an accurate description of the fur piece, had gone directly to the home of Ivy Hayes, whose picture, he knew, graced the Gleason apartment.

He found the young lady and obtained an interview without difficulty.

"Well?" she said, as she appeared before him.

He saw a slim young thing, who might have been any one of thousands of young girls one meets everywhere, in the street or on the streetcars.

Muffs of dark hair over her ears; hand-painted cheeks and lips; saucy, powdered nose, and a slender shape encased in a one-piece frock, both scant and short.

"Miss Hayes?" said Barry, bowing politely.

"The same. And you are—?"

"Philip Barry."

"Oh, are you? Hello, Phil, what's the big idea."

"Only to learn if you lost your fur collar?"

"H'm. My sable one—or my chinchilla?"

"Neither," Barry couldn't help smiling at the impertinent face; "your gray squirrel."

"Oh, that one. Now, s'pose I say no?"

"Then you're out one piece of fur."

"And s'pose I say yes?"

"Then you get your fur back, but you'll be asked a few questions."

"Guess it's worth it. Where's the pelt?"

"The police have it."

"Lordy!" Ivy dropped into a chair and pretended to faint. "Now how does that come about?" she asked, cocking one eye up at her caller.

"Oh, I fancy you know."

"Come on—let's put all the cards on the table. You don't think I had anything to do with the—the fatal deed, do you?"

"What fatal deed?"

"Don't be silly. I told you to be frank. Old Gleason's murder, to be sure."

"You left your fur there?"

"Yep, I did."

"The day of the murder?"

"Sure. I was there that afternoon."

"You admit this!"

"Why not? It'd be found out anyway, and, as I didn't have anything to do with the shooting, I don't see why I don't get my fur back. It's an awful nice little collar."

"You'll get it back, Miss Hayes; and now, instead of waiting for a police detective to interview you, suppose you tell me all you know about the matter."

"I don't know much, but what I have is yours. I went round there, that afternoon, on—an errand."

"What was the errand? You may as well tell as to have me drag it out of you."

"That's so. Well, our old gentleman friend said he'd give a party for me and a few friends. Oh, a nice, proper supper party—after the theater some night. I'm in the chorus now. Used to be in the movies. Anyway, he promised and promised, and never set the time. So I telephoned and telephoned and I couldn't get him to make a date, so I just went round there to try and persuade him."

"Did you see him?"

"Sure I did."

"Did he make the date?"

"No; the old fourflusher! He crawled out of it, and said if I'd let him off he'd give me a nice present. Said he'd take me to any jewelry shop I chose, to pick it out. Said he'd take me the next day. Now, you don't suppose I'd croak a guy that was about to give me a bracelet, do you?"

"I do not. And you were so excited you came away and left your fur there?"

"Just that! I wasn't sure I did leave it there, for I was at two or three other places that day. When do I get the squirly?"

"Oh, in a few days, I should say. I'll take your yarn to headquarters, and they'll do the rest. But, I say, when you came away from there, Mr Gleason was alive and well?"

"You bet he was! He fairly shooed me out—he was in a hurry to get ready to go to a party or something. Oh, my gracious!"

"What's that exclamation for?"

"Nothin'. A pin stuck into me."

Barry knew better. A sudden thought had come to the girl, a thought that filled her with dismay for some reason. But Philip Barry felt the matter was getting too serious for him, and he decided to put it in the hands of the police.

He went straight back to the Lindsays'.

"Come in, Mr Barry," was the first greeting he heard, as he entered the library, where several people were sitting in conclave. "You're just the man we want!"

The speaker was Prescott, the detective, and he held an open letter in his hand.

"We've nailed you," he said to Barry. "No use your saying much. This letter speaks for itself."

Mechanically, Barry took the paper the detective handed to him.

It was a letter, typewritten, on club paper. In ran thus:

Mr Robert Gleason: Sir:

There is small necessity of words between us. Unless you see fit to cease your attentions to a lady of our mutual acquaintance, I shall take matters into my own hands and shall so arrange things that it will be impossible for you to annoy her further.

Philip Barry.

The signature, pen signed, was undoubtedly Barry's own, and the date was the day before the murder.

CHAPTER 10: THE SIGNED LETTER

Philip Barry stood staring at the paper the detective had handed to him.

"What foolery is this?" he said, angrily. "I never saw this before."

"No?" said Prescott, a sarcastic smile on his face. "How'd you write it then? Blindfolded?"

"So it was you!" Millicent Lindsay cried. "I knew we'd get at the truth, but I didn't think you were the criminal, Philip! Oh, you may as well own up—the proof is positive!"

"Not positive," Phyllis said, looking at Barry, kindly. "It isn't sure that Mr Barry killed Mr Gleason, just because he wrote this note—is it, Mr Prescott?"

"Looks mighty like it," the detective returned. "But we'll listen to what he has to say. You wrote this?"

"I did not!" and Barry's eyes flashed ominously. "I tell you I never saw it before."

"That is your signature?"

"It looks like it, I admit, but it can't be, for I never wrote that letter. Where'd you get it?"

"In Mr Gleason's desk. At his apartment. As you see, it's dated the day before the murder took place, it's—to say the least—a bit incriminating. What's your explanation?"

"I haven't any—I—"

"Wait a minute, Mr Barry." Prescott spoke seriously. "Here's a threatening note, signed by yourself, written on your Club paper to Mr Gleason. Unless you can prove that signature forged, I think your denial of any knowledge of this document cannot be believed."

"Believe it or not," Barry stormed, "I tell you I never wrote that. I never saw it! I don't know anything about it!

I've been out investigating the case, getting evidence and all that, and I came back here with it and you thrust that thing at me! I tell you it's a forgery! Somebody's trying to get me into this thing—but the game can't be worked!"

"Will you sign your name, Mr Barry?" Prescott asked quietly.

"No, I won't! I deny your right to ask it!"

"But a refusal is a tacit admission—"

"No admission at all! I refuse to do a silly thing like that! The signature does resemble mine—but it can't be mine, for I didn't write it."

"Have you any of Mr Barry's signatures in your possession?" Prescott asked of Phyllis.

"No," she said, promptly, and though Prescott doubted her word, he didn't say so.

"How silly!" Louis exclaimed. "It's dead easy to get a signature of yours, Phil, why not write one now, and have it over with. Of course the thing is a forgery!"

Apparently seeing the sense of this, Barry went to the desk and dashed off his name on a sheet of paper.

"There!" he cried, angrily, as he flung it at Prescott.

The detective examined the two, and gave a short whistle.

"Well," he declared, "if I knew of anybody who could forge as well as that—I'd get him behind bars as quick as possible! Why, man, the signatures are identical! As to the typing, that is as personal as penmanship. Have you a typewriter?"

"No"; growled Barry, looking like a wild beast at bay. "I haven't."

"Do you ever use one?"

"No."

Louis looked up, with such a surprised air, that Prescott said, "Yes, you do. Whose?"

"Nobody's," repeated Barry, now furiously incensed. "You quit these absurd questions! I won't answer any more!"

"Why, Phil," said Phyllis, gently, "don't get so angry. Mr Prescott is only trying to find out about this letter."

"And an important letter it is," cried Millicent.

She was greatly excited, her eyes flashed and her lips trembled, as she fairly glared at Barry.

"So you're the criminal," she went on, "you killed my brother! Some need to ask why! Just because you're in love with Phyllis and you found Robert was cutting you out! A fine way to remedy matter—to kill your rival!"

"Oh, Millicent," Phyllis begged, "don't jump at conclusions like that! Even if Phil did write that letter it doesn't prove he killed Mr Gleason."

"No"; Barry said, as if struck with a new view of it all; "even if I did write that, it proves nothing further."

"Oho!" said Prescott, "you're admitting that you wrote it, then?"

"I admit nothing. I deny nothing. I only say—"

"Don't say anything, Phil," Louis warned him. "You say too much, anyway. Prescott's on the job, let him find out who wrote the letter, and who signed it."

"As if there was any doubt;" the detective scoffed. "But, laying aside the question for the moment, did you say, Mr Barry, that you have been doing some investigating on your own account?"

"On my own account, and on account of my friends here," Barry replied, but his tone and expression betrayed agitation. "I've found out who owns the fur collar."

"Who?" Prescott asked.

"Ivy Hayes."

The effect of his announcement was slight on all present, except Louis Lindsay. He started, looked frightened, began to speak and then checked himself.

"Well, Louis," Barry said, "out with it! I know you're interested in Miss Hayes—what's the word?"

"This is the word," said Louis, and his low voice was intense and incisive, "if you or anybody else undertakes to drag Ivy Hayes' name into this muddle, you'll have to reckon with me!"

"Oh, come, now," Prescott smiled, "in the first place, I won't have my case called a muddle—next, if Miss Hayes or anybody else is connected with it in any way, she's in it already, without having to be dragged in—as you call it. Go on, Mr Barry, what did you learn from or about Miss Hayes?"

"I learned that she was in Mr Gleason's apartment the afternoon of the murder—"

"She wasn't!" Louis exclaimed, "She wasn't!"

"Oh, hush, Louis," Barry said, contemptuously, "she told me herself she was."

"Go on," said Prescott.

"She left Mr Gleason alive and well, when she departed."

"At what time?"

"She doesn't remember exactly—it's the hardest thing in the world to make people assert a time. But I gathered it was not far from six o'clock when she left Gleason's rooms."

"That's getting pretty close to the time of the murder," Prescott said thoughtfully.

"Oh, she didn't kill Gleason," Barry put in, "He was planning to take her next day to buy a bracelet—as Ivy said, why would she kill a man who was about to do that?"

"You innocent!" exclaimed Millicent; "of course, she said that to pull the wool over your eyes! I don't believe you did it after all, Phil! I believe it was that Ivy person! A girl like that wouldn't leave her fur collar, unless she went away in a fearful hurry or trepidation."

"A point, Mrs Lindsay," and Prescott looked at her admiringly. "It would indeed denote a preoccupied mind, to leave a fur collar. And she was there about six, you say. But the man wasn't killed till nearly seven."

"Oh, she didn't tell the truth about the time," said Millicent, nodding her head sagaciously. "I'm surprised she admitted being there at all—but, I'm told they always slip up on some details."

"Well, at any rate, there are several matters to be looked into," Prescott said, rising to go. "I'm interested in your story of the Hayes girl, Mr Barry, but I'm even more interested in this letter you wrote."

"I didn't write it, I tell you!"

"I know you tell me so, but I can't take your word for that. I'm going to consult a penmanship expert. And, if you'll take my advice you won't try to leave town—for, you'd find it difficult."

"Meaning I'm to be under surveillance?"

"Oh, well, the matter has to be cleared up," Prescott shrugged.

"Perfectly ridiculous!" Barry stormed on, after the detective had gone; "you know, don't you, Phyllis, I had nothing to do with the matter?"

"Of course," Phyllis replied, but her voice was disinterested and her gaze was far off. "But, look here, Phil, tell me something. When can I get my money—or some of it?"

"How much?"

"Twenty thousand dollars."

"Whew! What do you want of all that? Are you mercenary, Phyllis?"

"No; but I want it—"

"Oh, she does!" cried Millicent. "She's been harping on that all day. I think it's disgraceful! She thinks of nothing but that."

"Oh, no, Millicent," and Phyllis' face flushed painfully—"I do want some ready cash, for an important purpose—"

"And sometimes I go back to my first idea that you killed my brother," Mrs Lindsay glared at her stepdaughter.

Millicent Lindsay was becoming more and more nervously unstrung about her brother's death. Hers was a super-emotional nature, and combined with a desperate spirit of revenge, she grew excited every time the subject was discussed. And as she never lost a possible chance to discuss it, the state of her nerves was becoming permanently affected. Not content to leave the matter to detectives, she continually discovered, or thought she did, new evidence, and promptly changed her suspicions to correspond. She transferred her accusations from one suspect to another with remarkable speed and often unjustifiable assurance.

At present she was quite willing to believe in the guilt of Ivy Hayes or Philip Barry, or, as she just stated, to turn back to her original suspicion of Phyllis.

"Oh, Lord," Barry groaned, "you're the limit, Millicent! You are quite capable of believing every one of us killed Gleason! Why do you except old Pollard from your mind? He said he was going to do it, you know."

"Yes; that's why I know he didn't! If he had intended it, he wouldn't have said so."

"I say, Mill, you do have flashes of insight," Louis said, "that's the way I look at it."

"But I saw Pollard down in the vicinity of Gleason's place today," said Barry. "Now, what was he doing down there?"

"Drawn back to the scene of his crime!" Louis chaffed. "They say that's always done. No; Phil, you can't hang anything on Pollard. Prescott checked up his movements at once. Also, I want you to drop Ivy Hayes' name. For my sake, old chap, do let up on that. Now, what about yourself? Explain that letter, boy."

"I can't," Barry looked troubled.

"Oh, bosh. Why not own up you wrote it, but you didn't mean murder and didn't commit murder. That's the truth, you know."

"No, Louis—I didn't write it."

"'Scuse me, but your tone and look are not those of a man telling the pure unvarnished. Now, I know that nobody on this green earth could have written that signature but Philip Barry himself. And I also recognize the typewriter you used. As Prescott says, typing is as traceable as penmanship, and that note was written on the machine in the writing room at the Club. It's been there for years, and we all write on it now and then. So you see, Phil, you'd better be careful what you say."

"Be quiet," Phyllis warned them; "here comes Mr Pollard; I don't suppose you want him to hear this."

"Why not?" said Louis, but Barry checked him with a look as Pollard came in.

"May I come?" he said, as he greeted the women. "I'm starving for a cup of tea, and you asked me to come informally and unbidden—"

"Of course we did," Phyllis smiled; "sit down, tea is imminent."

"I've been writing my head off all day," Pollard went on, as he took an easy chair. "Haven't even been out for a breath of air—"

"Why—" Phyllis was about to say that Barry had seen him down near the Gleason home, but she stopped herself in time. She had no wish to trip up Phil Barry—indeed, her feelings prompted her to shield him—but surely, surely, he had falsified in this instance! Why?

There was but one answer. Barry was trying to make Pollard again suspected. Notwithstanding Barry's insistence on Pollard's alibi, a stray hint, such as he had given about seeing him down town, made things questionable again.

Quickly changing the subject, Phyllis made the conversation general, and though the Gleason matter cropped up now and then, other topics were mentioned.

Also, Phyllis returned to her great desire to get some of her inheritance at once.

"Why, surely you can," Pollard said; "how much do you want? Can't I advance you some?"

"No; I want twenty thousand dollars, and I don't want to say what for."

Like a flash, Pollard's mind went back to that afternoon—the day of the murder—when he saw Phyllis pass him in a taxicab. He had been standing, he remembered, in the corner of Fifth Avenue and Forty-second Street, and he distinctly saw Phyllis, and a strange man with her. She had not seen him—of that he was sure—and now, as she voiced this strange desire, he wondered what in the world she had been up to.

"I'm not asking what you want all that for," he said, with a kindly smile, "but maybe you'd care to say."

"No; I wouldn't." Her face was pink, but her voice was calm and her glance at him steady. "I will say, however, that it is for a purpose which no one could disapprove of—"

"Then why not tell?" Millicent exclaimed. "That's Phyllis all over, Mr Pollard; she'd make a mystery out of nothing! If her purpose is a good one, why keep it so secret? I'll tell you why; only because Phyllis loves to create a sensation! She loves to be wondered at and thought important."

"Oh, Millicent, what nonsense!" Phyllis blushed painfully now.

"Let up, Mill," Louis said; "my sister is not like that. I can easily understand why she might want a round sum of money, for a perfectly good reason, yet not want to tell everybody all about it. And she ought to have it, too. Lane could give it to her, if he chose—"

"He says he can't," Phyllis said.

"I'll be glad to lend it to you," Pollard told her, "as soon as I can get it together. I've stocks I can sell—"

"Don't you do it, Mr Pollard," said Millicent. "Phyllis can wait. There's no such desperate haste—or, if there is—"

"Hush, Millicent!" Louis spoke sternly. "You're going to insinuate something about Phyllis and the—the affair—and I won't have it!"

"Oh, Mr Pollard," Millicent broke forth, "you haven't heard about Phil Barry's note, have you?"

"No, he hasn't," said Barry, looking daggers at Millicent; "but, of course, he soon will, so I'll tell it myself. Why, Pol, a note has been discovered among Gleason's papers, signed by me."

"Well, did you sign it?"

"Never! But—"

"If you didn't sign it, why bother? Experts nowadays can tell positively a forgery from a real signature. You're all right. But what was the note? Of any importance?"

"Oh, it contained what might be looked upon as a threat against Gleason's life."

Pollard smiled involuntarily.

"We're in the same boat, then, Phil. You know I'm accused of threatening the same thing."

"Yes, but you did threaten it—I heard you. And you were just talking foolishly. But this written matter is different. The thing said if Gleason didn't let Phyllis alone, I'd do for him."

"Why, internal evidence, then, proves you never wrote it. You wouldn't express yourself in that way in a thousand years."

"I haven't quoted it verbatim. That's only the gist of it."

"Oh, well; tell me more. Is it all written by you— apparently?"

"No; but it's on that typewriter—over at the Club— you know—"

"I know," Pollard looked serious now. "A note written on that old junk-heap, and signed by you—I don't get it, Phil."

"Of course you don't, Pol, I don't myself! There's a conspiracy against me, I believe! Somebody—"

"Oh, come, now, Barry, what sort of talk is that? You had no animosity against Gleason—"

"Oh, didn't I? Well, then, I did—very much so!"

"Phil, stop!" cried Phyllis. "Don't you see you oughtn't to say such things? Please don't."

"It doesn't matter, here among ourselves," said Pollard, "but speak out, Phil; say where you were at the time of the murder. Quash all possibility of suspicion at once. I used that bravado stunt, and though it's all right now—yet it made him a lot of bother. I wouldn't do it again, nor advise any one else to."

"Do what again?" asked Millicent.

"Oh, that smarty-cat business of not telling where I was at the hour of the crime. Of course, being right there at home, I knew they'd have to prove it, but it was sheer, silly bravado that made me refuse to speak plainly and tell my own story. And, now, that the case is farther along, I'll tell you, Phil, you make a mistake if you try that fool game. Speak up, man, where were you?"

"Why," Barry spoke slowly, "I left the Club with you."

"I know you did. We walked together down to your street, Forty-fourth—and then you turned off and I went on down home. What did you do next?"

"Nothing. Just dressed for dinner."

"Hold on, there was a long time in there. We parted about six, and dinner was at eight. Dressing all the time?"

"Yes—yes, I think so. Or in my room, anyway."

"Anybody see you?"

"Oh, I don't know. Let up Pollard, I won't be quizzed!"

"I'm not quizzing you, old chap, but I'm warning you that others will. What you tell me about this letter, doesn't sound good to me. I don't say you wrote it, but I do say the experts will know—and if they prove it on you— the letter I mean—you'll be questioned, and mighty closely, too."

"But I didn't do anything—I'm not afraid of being questioned."

"All right, son. Neither was I. And when they questioned my hotel people they were satisfied of my innocence. If you're fixed like that, you're all right, too."

Barry looked thoughtful. Pollard watched him, though not seeming to do so. This letter business sounded queer to them all.

Phyllis and Louis watched Barry in silence, but Millicent exclaimed:

"Did you do it, Phil? Oh, say you didn't. I can't stand suspense—tell me the truth."

"No, Millicent, of course, I didn't kill your brother," Barry said; "nor did I write him a letter saying I would do anything—"

"That's enough, Barry," Pollard said, cordially. "I wouldn't ask you myself, but since you make that statement, that's all I want to know. Now, about that money, Miss Phyllis. I'm sure I can get it for you inside of forty-eight hours. Will that do?"

"Yes," and Phyllis gave him a grateful look. "I hate to ask you, but Mr Lane only laughs when I talk to him, and tells me not to be impatient."

"Most girls are impatient," Pollard smiled. "Very well, then, I'll bring it to you day after tomorrow—or tomorrow, if possible."

And then, to their surprise, Prescott returned, and asked Barry to go with him to the District Attorney's office, which, perforce, and with a bad grace, Philip Barry did.

"Oh, say you think he is innocent," Phyllis begged of Pollard, after Barry's departure.

"I would say so," Pollard returned, "but if that note is proved to be from him, it looks a little dubious."

Chapter 11: Miss Adams Again

"Everything looks dubious!" Millicent exclaimed. "I do think it's a shame! Here the days are flying by and absolutely nothing done toward discovering who killed my brother! Unless the police achieve something soon, I shall get a private detective."

"Oh, they're no good," Louis advised her. "They're terribly expensive and they make a lot of trouble and never get any results, anyway."

"You speak largely, Louis," Pollard said, smiling at the boy. "Do you know all that from experience?"

"No, not exactly; but I've gathered some such convictions from what I've heard of private detectives as a class."

"What about Phil Barry and that letter?" Phyllis asked, her great eyes full of a troubled uncertainty.

"He must have written it," Louis declared. "Isn't that right, Pollard?"

"I don't see any way out of it. It is most surely his signature, and he often writes on that old machine. Also, he did have a grouch about Mr Gleason's attentions to Miss Lindsay—that I know. But, I don't for a minute think he meant to kill Gleason and I don't think he did. But the note will make him a lot of trouble."

"You still suspect some Western friend?" said Millicent, looking earnestly at Pollard.

"Scarcely a friend! But I do think that's a reasonable supposition, for I can't see any real indication anywhere else."

At this point Lane arrived, and joined in the wonderment about Barry.

"It's most surely his signature," Lane said, "I know it as well as I know my own—and it's no forgery. Why

should it be a forgery, anyway? Supposing the murderer
to be a Western man, or a chorus girl, or even Doctor
Davenport, who has most foolishly been mentioned in this
connection, why should he write a note and forge Barry's
name to it?"

"To throw suspicion on Phil," said Louis, simply.

"Yes, of course, but, I mean, how could it be done?
Your Western stranger or your chorus girl can't get into
the Club to use that machine—"

"Are you positive the note was written on that
typewriter?" asked Pollard, thoughtfully.

"Yes; I looked it up. There are some broken letters
that don't print well, and that makes it unmistakable.
Now Davenport could get access to the typewriter, of
course, but I can't see old Doc sitting down and writing
that note and forging Barry's name! Can you?"

"No"; and Pollard smiled at the idea. "But Davenport
and Barry hate each other like poison."

"Yes, they've an old quarrel, something about a
Picture Exhibition where Doc is a director, and didn't fall
down and worship Barry's pictures. But that's not enough
to make a man kill."

"No. Yet it was a deep full-fledged quarrel—rather
more than you represent it. However, I say, grant Barry
wrote the note—which he must have done, but don't hold
it as proof positive of murder."

"What else could he have meant by it?" Millicent
asked, her eager face demanding reply.

"Well, as we are assuming he meant Miss Lindsay—
and we've no real right to assume that," Pollard smiled at
the girl, "we may say he only meant to cut Gleason out,
and gaining the lady's hand himself, make it impossible
for Gleason to hope any more."

"That's an idea," Lane said, "but you'd hardly think if
that was in Barry's mind he would have worded his note
just as he did."

"Yes he would," put in Louis. "Barry's a temperamental chap, and he'd say anything. I know him—I like him, but he does do and say queer things."

"All artists do," Pollard observed.

Millicent and Lane went off to another room to discuss some business matters and Louis followed.

"I'm glad you didn't mention that money before Lane," Pollard said; "it's wiser not to."

"Why?" and Phyllis looked at him curiously. But her eyes fell before his gaze, and a faint blush rose to her cheek.

"Because—forgive me if I seem intrusive—because I think you want it for a purpose you don't care to talk about. And if so, the least said the better."

"You're right, Mr Pollard," and Phyllis looked troubled, "I don't want anything said about it. Also, I don't want it in a check—that I should have to endorse. Can't I have cash?"

"Why, yes—if necessary. But it is wiser to have a check for your own safety and security. Shall you get a receipt?"

"I—I suppose so—I never thought of that." The lovely face was so anxious and worried that Pollard's deepest sympathy was roused.

"Let me help you further," he said, impulsively. "Oh, Phyllis, confide the whole story to me. I'm sure I can help—and you can trust me."

The frank glance that accompanied these words was also tender and appealing. Phyllis knew at once that here was a friend—even more than a friend—but at any rate, a man she could trust.

"I can't tell you," she said, hesitatingly, "for it isn't all my secret. I wish I could speak plainly—but—"

"That's all right; don't tell me anything you're in honor bound not to. But let me know what you can of the circumstances and let me advise you. Can't I pay the money whenever it is due, and bring you a receipt—and so save you unnecessary embarrassment?"

"Oh, if you could do that!" Phyllis' eyes shone with gratitude and pleasure at the thought of thus having her burden shared.

But Lane's return to the room precluded further planning just then.

"Pollard," Lane said, "I'm beginning to think things look a bit dark for Phil Barry."

"As how?"

"Not only that letter business, which is, to my mind very serious, but other things. Merely straws, perhaps, but they show the direction of the wind. Mrs Lindsay told me that Barry said he saw you, Pollard, to-day, down in the vicinity of the Gleason house. Then, Mrs Lindsay said, you came in here and said you had been at home all day."

"So I have," Pollard returned, staring at Lane.

"Well, here's the funny thing. Only yesterday, Barry told me that he had seen you over in Brooklyn—"

"Brooklyn! I never go there!"

"Well, Barry said he saw you there. Now, it's quite evident to me, Barry is lying, and it must be in some endeavor to get you mixed up in the Gleason matter."

"It looks a little like that—but, how absurd! Why should he say he saw me in Brooklyn?"

"I don't know. You weren't there?"

"No; I almost never go to Brooklyn, and I certainly was not there yesterday. I haven't been there for a year, at least!"

"I'm not quite on to Barry's game, but there's two cases where he falsified in the matter of seeing you. Now, why?"

"I say why, too. I can't see any reason for the Brooklyn yarn. I suppose I can see a reason for his saying he saw me down in Washington Square, if he means to try to fasten the crime on me. But, the Brooklyn story I see no sense in. What do you think, Lane?"

"I begin to think Barry's the guilty man, though up to now, I had quite another suspicion."

"A definite one? A person?"

"Yes, decidedly so. And I've no reason to give up my suspicion—except that Barry has loomed up more prominently than my suspect."

"Speak out—who's your man?"

"Yes, Mr Lane, tell us," Phyllis urged.

"No; not at present. It's some one whose name has not even been breathed in connection with the case, and if I suspect him wrongly it would be a fearful thing to say so."

"All right, if that's the way of it, better keep it quiet." Pollard nodded his head. "Been all through Gleason's papers?"

"Yes; and I can't find any letters from any one out West or anywhere else who would seem a likely suspect. No old time feuds, or present-day quarrels. If we except Barry."

"And me."

"You haven't a quarrel with him, Pollard—or had you?"

"I had not. I never saw him more than three times, I think. And when I said—"

"Yes, I know what you said, and why. Don't harp on that, Pol, but try to help me out in this Barry business. Can you see Barry going down there and shooting Gleason?"

Pollard was still for a minute; then he said:

"I suppose you mean, can I visualize Barry doing the thing. No, I can't. To begin with, he hasn't the nerve."

"Oh, some quiet, inoffensive men pick up nerve on occasion."

"Well, then, he hadn't sufficient motive."

"A lady in the case is frequently the motive."

"I daresay. Well, here's a final disclaimer. I was with Barry myself until about six o'clock that night. I hold he wouldn't have had time to go down to Gleason's after I left him, and get back and appear at Miss Lindsay's at dinner time, quite unruffled and correct in dress and demeanor."

"Are you sure he did do this?"

"Certainly; I was there myself."

"But he left you, say, at six. Dinner was at eight. Seems to me that was time for all."

"Yes, if he rushed matters. It would, of course, imply premeditation. He would have had to get down to Gleason's quickly—hold on, the telephone message was received at Doctor Davenport's office at about a quarter to seven—I remember the detective harped on that."

"All right. Say he did commit the crime at about six-thirty, or quarter to seven, that would give him time to get home and to the dinner at eight. It all fits in, I think."

"I suppose it does," Pollard agreed, slowly. "But, that would mean that when he left me that afternoon, or evening—about six o'clock, anyway, he had this thing all planned, and rushed it through. I submit that if that were so, he would have been excited, or preoccupied, or something. On the contrary, Lane, he was as calm and casual as we are this minute. I can't see it—as I said in the first place."

Then Phyllis spoke.

"It's this way, Mr Lane," she said; "I happen to know that Phil Barry told two untruths—or else, Mr Pollard did. I mean, Phil said, he saw Mr Pollard twice, in places where he himself says he was not. Now shall I believe the one or the other?"

"Choose," said Pollard, smiling at her.

"But, Miss Lindsay," Lane said, "don't choose because of your faith in one man or the other. Choose by rational deduction from circumstances."

"That's just what I want to do," Phyllis replied. "And here's how it looks to me. Phil Barry didn't tell the truth or else Mr Pollard didn't. Now, Mr Pollard has no reason to prevaricate, and Phil, if guilty, has. Therefore—and yet, I can't believe Phil shot Mr Gleason."

"I can," Millicent exclaimed. "I see it all now. Phil's madly in love with you, Phyllis—as who isn't? I don't know what it is, child, but you seem to set all men wild, and you so demure and sweet! Well, it's common knowledge that Phil adores you. And we all know my brother did. Now the theory or hypothesis or whatever you call it, that Phil was jealous of Robert and killed him—after sending him that warning letter—is, to my mind the only tenable theory and one that proves in every detail. For, granting Phil Barry is the criminal, the letter is explainable, the stories he told about Mr Pollard are explainable, and the whole thing becomes clear."

"Millicent," Phyllis said, looking at her seriously, "you are only too ready to assume the guilt of any one you suspect at the moment. I admit your theory, but—I can't believe Phil did it!"

"No," cried Millicent, "because you are in love with Phil! That's the reason you won't look facts in the face! I declare, Phyllis, you have more interest in your foolish love affairs than in discovering the murderer of my brother! But I am determined to find the villain who shot Robert Gleason! I shall find him—I promise you that! I am not mercenary, I shall devote every last cent of my money—or my brother's money to tracking down the murderer."

"Do you know," said Pollard, quietly, "it seems to me that we all look at this thing too close by. I mean, too much from a personal viewpoint. You, Mrs Lindsay, want to find your brother's murderer, but you, Phyllis, and you, Louis, are more interested in whether friends of yours are implicated or not. Isn't that so, Lane?"

"Yes," agreed Fred Lane. "But, see here, Pollard, I'm laying aside this personal interest you speak of, and I'm trying to go merely and solely by evidence. Now, I think that the evidence against Phil Barry is pretty positive."

"Well, I don't,'" Pollard disagreed with him. "It is, in a way—but, good Lord, man, lots of people may write to a person without intending to kill him."

"Not a letter like Barry's."

"Yes, just that. Oh, for Heaven's sake, use a little intelligence! If Barry had meant to kill Gleason, do you suppose he would have written that letter? Never!"

"Yes, I think he would." Lane spoke slowly and thoughtfully. "You see, Pol, you're tarred with the same brush—I mean the artistic temperament, and you ought to see that a man's mind works spasmodically. Barry had the impulse to kill, I hold, and he wrote that warning letter as—well, as a salve to his conscience, and there it is."

Meantime, Detective Prescott was on the job. He had taken Barry down to the Washington Square house, but not to Robert Gleason's apartment.

It was Miss Adams' doorbell he rang, and to her home he escorted Philip Barry.

Barry's anger had subsided from belligerent altercation to a subdued sullenness.

"You'll be sorry for this," he told Prescott, but as that worthy had often been similarly warned, he paid little attention.

"Now, Miss Adams," said Prescott, when they were in the presence of the spinster. "I want you to tell me whether this is the man whom you saw go into Mr Gleason's apartment that afternoon."

Miss Adams scanned Barry carefully.

They were all standing, and as the lady looked him over, Barry turned slowly round, as if to give her every opportunity for correct judgment.

"Thank you," she said, quite alive to his sarcastic intent. "No, Mr Prescott, this is not the man."

"Are you sure?" Prescott was disappointed, not because he wanted to prove Barry guilty of the crime, but because Miss Adams' negative made it imperative for him to hunt up another man. For the caller of that afternoon must be found.

"Why, I'm pretty sure. Though, of course, clothes might make a difference."

"You said the man who came wore a soft hat."

"Yes; but it was a different color from Mr Barry's. It was a dull green—olive, I think."

"It was after dark when he came, wasn't it?"

"Yes; but the hall was lighted and I saw him clearly. But a man may have two hats, I suppose."

"I haven't," said Barry, shortly. "That is, I haven't two hats that I wear in the afternoon. This is the only soft felt I possess."

The hat he wore was of a medium shade of gray, an inconspicuous soft hat of the latest, but in no way, extreme fashion.

"That's nothing," Prescott said. "A man can buy and give away a lot of hats in a week. Size him up carefully, Miss Adams; your opinion may mean a lot. Never mind the hat. How does Mr Barry's size and shape compare with the man you saw?"

"Mr Barry is a heavier man," the lady said, decidedly; "also I feel sure, an older man. The man I saw was slighter and younger."

"Did you see his face?"

"No."

"Yet you're sure he was younger?"

"Yes, I am. He was of slighter build, and a little taller, and he walked with a jauntier step, almost a run, as he came up the stairs."

"You are very observant, Miss Adams."

"Not so very. I took him in at a glance, and he impressed me as I have stated. I have a retentive memory, that's all. I can see him now—as he bounded up the stairs."

"In a merry mood?"

"I don't know as to that. But the impression he gave me was more that of a man in haste. He tapped impatiently at the door of Mr Gleason's apartment, and when it was not opened instantly, he rapped again."

"And then Mr Gleason opened it?"

"Then somebody opened it. I couldn't see who. The man went in quickly and the door was closed. That's all I know about it."

Miss Adams sat down then, and folded her hands in her lap. She was quite serene, and apparently not much interested in the matter.

A fleeting thought went through the detective's mind that possibly Barry had interviewed her before and had persuaded or bribed her to say all this. But it seemed improbable.

Barry, too, was serene. He seemed satisfied at the turn events had taken, and appeared to think that Miss Adams' decision had cleared him from suspicion.

Not so the detective.

"Well, Mr Barry," he said, "we've got to find another man to fit that olive green hat, it appears. But that doesn't preclude the possibility of your having been here that day, too. You didn't hang over the balusters all the afternoon, I suppose, Miss Adams."

Offended at his mode of expression, the lady drew herself up haughtily, and said, "I did not."

"But you saw no one come in who might have been Mr Barry?"

"No."

"Could he have come and you not have known it?"

Miss Adams was about to make a short reply, and then thought better of it.

"I want to help you all I can," she said, "and I am answering your questions carefully. I suppose any one could have gone into Mr Gleason's apartment that day without my knowing it, but it is not likely. For I was listening for the arrival of my niece, who, however, did not come. I kept watch, therefore, until about six o'clock, or a little after, then as I gave up all hope of my niece's coming, I also ceased to watch or listen. Anybody may have come after that. I don't know, I'm sure."

Prescott ruminated. Whoever killed Robert Gleason may well have arrived after six o'clock. For the telephone call didn't reach the doctor until about quarter of seven, and if it were Barry, it must be remembered he didn't part company with Pollard until six or after.

It would seem then, that Miss Adams' testimony amounted to little, after all. However, the man with the green hat ought to be found.

"Tell us again of the young man," Prescott said. "See if you can describe him so we can recognize some one we know."

Miss Adams thought a moment, and then said: "No, I can't. He just seemed to me like a young chap, an impulsive sort, who ran in to see a friend. He came upstairs hastily, yet not in any merriment—of that I'm sure. Rather, he gave me the effect of a man anxious for the interview—whatever it might be about."

"Didn't he ring the lower bell? Why wasn't Mr Gleason at his own door when the chap came up?"

"I don't know. I think he must have rung Mr Gleason's bell down stairs, for the front door opened to admit him. But Mr Gleason didn't open his own door until the visitor had rapped twice. Of that I'm certain."

"Do you think the girl who came before the young man did was still in Mr Gleason's apartment?"

"Why, I don't know." Miss Adams seemed suddenly more interested. "Maybe she was. Maybe she didn't want to be seen there. Maybe—"

She paused, and sat silent. Prescott gave her a minute or two, to collect herself, for he felt sure there would be some further disclosure.

Meantime Barry had taken an envelope from his pocket, and was rapidly sketching on it. A very few lines gave a distinct picture of a young man.

"Does that look like the man you saw?" he asked, holding it so that Miss Adams could see it, but Prescott could not.

"That's the man himself!" she exclaimed, her eyes wide with astonishment.

CHAPTER 12: LOUIS' CONFESSION

Before Prescott could snatch at the paper picture to do so, Barry had torn the paper into bits and thrown them into the fire in the old-fashioned grate.

He laughed at the detective's chagrin, and said, "Nothing doing, Prescott. If the man I sketched is the criminal, you must find it out for yourself. If not, I'd be mighty sorry to drag his name into it."

"I deduce, then, that his name is not already in it," Prescott returned; "in that case, I can guess who it is."

"Guess away," Barry said, not believing the statement. "I'll only tell you the man I drew on that paper bore no ill will toward Gleason, so far as I know. And, moreover, the fact of his coming here, and running upstairs, doesn't necessarily prove him a murderer."

"Tell me more of his appearance, Miss Adams," urged Prescott, hoping Barry's sketch had refreshed her memory.

For Philip Barry had a knack of characterization, and with a few lines could give an unmistakable likeness.

But the spinster could tell no more in words than she had already done and Prescott was forced to be content with a vague idea of a young man who ran lightly upstairs.

"Was it Louis Lindsay?" he asked, suddenly, but the non-committal smile on Barry's face gave him an impression that this was a wrong assumption.

At Prescott's request, Barry accompanied him to Gleason's rooms.

The detective had a key and they went in. Except for some tidying up, nothing had been disturbed since the day of the crime. The rather commonplace furnishings were in direct contrast to the personal belongings which were still in evidence.

There were pictures and ornaments, books and smoking paraphernalia that had been selected with taste and good judgment.

The desk, too, was a valuable piece of furniture, and fitted with the best of writing appointments.

"Any more letters from you here?" Prescott said, as if casually, while he took a bundle of papers.

"Probably," Barry returned, shortly; "if one could be forged, more could be."

"Look here, Mr Barry," the detective said, seriously, "just explain, will you, how that letter could have been forged? Experts have concluded that the signature is yours. They say it is impossible that your very distinctive autograph could have been written freehand, as it evidently is, by any one but yourself. If it were traced or copied, some deviation would appear. Now, granting that, there is still a possibility that some one, evilly disposed, might have written the typed message above your signature. But how do you explain that? Did you ever sign a blank sheet of paper? Club paper?"

"Never!" Barry declared. "Why should I do such a thing?"

"Why, indeed! Yet, if you didn't, the letter must be all yours. Why not admit it? The admission, to my mind, would be less incriminating than the denial."

"But I didn't write it," Barry insisted. "I didn't type it, or sign it."

"Then the murderer did," Prescott nodded his head, sagaciously. "Can you make it out? I mean, can you suggest how it could be done? If you had ever signed a blank sheet, it would be easy for him to write on it, you see—"

"Of course I never did! If I had done such an inexplicable thing I should remember it! No; I can't suggest how it was done. It is to me an insoluble problem, and I admit I'm curious. But I never saw that letter until you showed it to me."

Barry's straightforward gaze went far toward convincing Prescott of his truthfulness, but he only said:

"If you're the criminal, you'd be smart enough to throw that very bluff. I don't believe you are—but—I don't know. You see, if you'd admit the letter, you could more easily establish your innocence—"

"No; Prescott, I couldn't establish my innocence by telling a lie. I am innocent, and I know nothing about that letter. Now, work from those facts and see where you come out."

"Just here," and Prescott faced him. "If those are facts, then the murderer forged that letter to hang the crime on you. Never mind now, how he forged it, merely assume he did so. Then, we must infer, the murderer is one who has access to the Club typewriter—"

"Well," Barry was thinking quickly, "here's a suggestion—if, as you say, the impossible was accomplished, and that letter was forged by some one with Club privileges, why not Gleason himself?"

Prescott stared. "Robert Gleason? Forge the letter?"

"As well as any one else. He hated me—suppose it was suicide—"

"Oh, bah! it wasn't suicide! That man had all there is of it to live for! He had wealth, and he hoped to win Miss Lindsay for his bride. Don't tell me he thought of suicide! Absurd!"

"That's so," and Barry dismissed the idea, "But say he knew he was doomed and wrote the letter to get me in bad."

"Flubdub! Though, wait—if Mr Pollard's idea is correct, and the murderer should be some Western friend—or foe—and, just suppose, say, that he threatened Gleason's life so definitely that Gleason knew he was doomed, and so—"

"And so he manufactured evidence that he hoped would incriminate me?" Barry spoke thoughtfully.

"Ingenious, on your part, Prescott, but I can't think it. The letter is too elaborate, too difficult of achievement. In fact, I can't see how anybody did it!"

"Nor can I!" Prescott turned on him. "And nobody could do it, Mr Barry, except yourself. You've overreached the mark in denying it. The forgery of that letter is an impossibility! Therefore, you wrote it."

"Does that argue me the criminal?"

"Not positively. But your denial of the letter helps to do so! If you wrote it, and denied it at first, through fear, you are now, of course, obliged to stick to your denial. But, criminal or not, that letter was written and sent by yourself."

"You're wrong, Mr Prescott; but as I can't even imagine who did it or who could have done it, there's small use in our arguing the subject."

And there was something in his tone of finality that helped to convince Prescott of his entire innocence.

The poor detective was at his wits' end. Every way he looked, he seemed to be peering into a blind alley. Conferences with his colleagues or his superiors helped him not at all. Lack of evidence brought all their theories to naught. Unless something more could be discovered the case seemed likely to go unsolved. Or, and this troubled Prescott, unless something was discovered soon, the impulsive and impatient Mrs Lindsay would employ a private detective. And that would be small credit to the work of the force. So Prescott worked away at his job. He went over the letters and papers in the desk, but these gave him no further clew. There was no other communication from Barry, though that, in itself, proved nothing. Yet had there been another it would have been edifying to compare the two.

"No clews," Prescott lamented, looking hopelessly about the room.

"No," Barry agreed. "This detective work is queer, isn't it?— Now in story-books, the obliging criminals leave all sorts of interesting bits of evidence or indications of their presence."

"Yes, but real criminals are too canny for that. Not even a fingerprint on the telephone or revolver, except Gleason's own. And that, though meant to indicate a suicide, proved only a diabolically clever criminal!"

"How do you explain the telephone call after the man was fatally shot?"

Prescott grunted. "An impossibility like that can be explained only by the discovery of facts not yet known. Maybe the doctors diagnosed wrong—"

"No, not Ely Davenport!" Barry declared.

"Well, then, maybe the man telephoned before he was shot, but was positive the shot was coming."

"Telephoned in the presence of the murderer?"

"Oh, I don't know! Didn't I tell you nothing could explain that but to discover some *new* facts? I haven't got 'em yet!"

"Do you expect to?"

"Honest, Mr Barry, I don't know. A case like this—so full of queer and unexplainable conditions may suddenly become clear—or, it may never do so!"

"Isn't that true of every case?"

"Well, I mean some unexpected clew may drop from the skies and clear it all up at once, or it may never be solved at all. Most cases can be worked out piece by piece, and require only patience and perseverance; but when you strike the work of a super-criminal, as this certainly is, then you have to wait for chance to help you. And that's mighty uncertain!"

"Well, I'll help you, Prescott, to this extent. I won't leave town and I'll always be where you can find me. If you believe me, you can call off your shadowers—if you don't, let them keep on my trail. But as to any startling clew or evidence I can't promise to give you any."

"Even if you get it yourself?" said the detective, quickly.

"You have uncanny intuition!" exclaimed Barry. "I didn't say that."

"Be careful about compounding a felony, sir."

"Be careful about suspecting an innocent man," returned Barry, and went away.

The artist went to the Lindsay home, but not finding Louis there, followed his trail to the Club.

Getting him into a secluded corner, Barry asked him abruptly: "Were you at Gleason's the afternoon of the murder?"

"No; why?" was the reply, but the nervous agitation the boy showed seemed not to corroborate his statement.

"Because I've been told you were. Come across, Louis. Take my advice—there's nothing to be gained from falsification. Own up, now. You were there."

"Yes, Phil, I was. But don't let it be known—for I didn't do for old Gleason—truly I didn't! Any more than you did!"

"Of course, Louis—neither of us killed that man. But I tell you it's better to tell the truth."

"But I won't be believed—" Louis whimpered like a child. "Don't tell on me, Phil. Who said I was there?"

"You were seen to go in."

"By whom?"

"A tenant on another floor. Better come clean, boy. What were you there for?"

"The old reason. I wanted money." Louis spoke sullenly, and his dark eyes showed a smoldering fire. "I was in bad—"

"Oh, Louis, gambling again?"

"Quit that tone, Barry. You're not my father confessor!"

"You'd better have one. Don't you see you're ruining your life—and breaking your sister's heart—not that you'd care! You are a selfish little beast, Louis! I've no use for you! But, listen, unless you tell the truth when you're questioned, I warn you, it'll go hard with you. Promise me this; if you're asked, admit you were there. If you're not asked, do as you like about withholding the information."

"I'll do as I like, anyway," and young Lindsay's eyes showed an ugly light, though his glance at Barry was furtive rather than belligerent.

"Of course you will, pighead!" Barry was thoroughly angry. "Now, tell me this; were you at Gleason's at the time Ivy Hayes was there?"

"No! What do you mean?" the astonishment was real. "When was she there?"

"Oh, she didn't kill Gleason. Don't worry about that. But it does seem as if a great many people chose that day to call on the Western millionaire."

"And all for the same purpose!" Louis shot out, with a sudden incisive perception.

"Of course," Barry said, contemptuously; "I dare say I'm the only suspect who can't be accused of killing the old man for lucre."

"He wasn't so awful old—and, I say, Barry, who else is suspected *but* you?"

"You!" Barry flashed back. "Or you will be! I meant to warn you in kindness, Louis, but you're so ungrateful, I'll let you alone. Better be careful, though."

Louis sulked, so Barry left him, and went away. He went to Fred Lane's office, and demanded an interview alone with the lawyer.

"What's up?" Lane asked him.

"Oh, nothing. That's the worst of it. I don't believe, Lane, that they'll ever get at the truth of the Gleason murder."

"Then they'll railroad you to the chair," said Lane, cheerfully.

"What about the letter, Lane? Can you see through it?"

"No, I can't. You wrote that signature, Phil; now think back and see how or when you could have done it?"

"Don't be absurd! I couldn't have done it, except as a signature to that very letter, and I didn't do that."

"But—"

"But, look here, Lane—just supposing somebody wanted to blacken my name—in this connection. What a roundabout way to take! Imagine some one writing that screed on the Club typewriter, and managing somehow to get my signature on it—could it be done with a transfer paper, or something of that sort?"

"Don't think so—it would be backward, then, wouldn't it?"

"Why, yes—"

"But did nobody ever persuade you to sign a sheet of blank paper? Wanted your autograph, or that sort of thing?"

"Never! I'm not a celebrity!"

"Well, here's an idea! Did anybody ever get you to sign a paper written in pencil? Then, he could rub out the pencil marks and type in the letter?"

"No, smarty! Why, that has been suggested by some one. But the expert said that the pencil marks would show, even if carefully erased."

"You mean the erasure would leave its traces. That's right, it would. And if ever there was a genuine looking letter that's one."

"On the surface, yes. But if I were a detective, I would note at once that the letter itself is not in a phraseology that I would use—"

"And if I were a detective, I should note that, too, and set it down as a further proof of your cleverness!"

"Hello, Lane, are *you* convinced of my guilt?"

"Not a bit of it, but I am frankly puzzled about that letter. It's so positively Club paper, Club typewriter, your signature—what's the answer?"

"I'll find out—I swear I will!"

"If you don't, old chap, it'll go hard with you, I fear."

"As a starter, I'm going to see that Hayes girl. No, I don't think she's implicated, but I may be able to get something new."

"Go ahead. Sound her and you may, at least, find some new way to look. Louis Lindsay never did it—"

"Oh, no, I know that! He'd hardly have nerve to kill a fly!"

To the home of Ivy Hayes Barry went next.

The girl willingly saw him, and seemed glad to discuss the matter.

After some preliminary conversation and as Barry grew more definite in his queries, she began to be a little frightened, and was less frank in her responses.

"You came to see me before, Mr Barry," she said, "and I told you then all I knew about this thing. Now, I've no more to tell."

"I think you have. I remember the other time I was here, you had a sudden recollection, or thought, and you gave a startled exclamation. What was that thought?"

"As if I could recall! I suppose I was nervous—I often jump like that. It's—it's temperament, you know."

"It was more than that. You did think of something that gave you a new idea regarding Mr Gleason's murder or murderer. Now, don't say you didn't, for I know it. Come across, Ivy, tell me what it was—or you may get in deep yourself."

"Tell me this, Mr Barry," and the girl spoke quietly and earnestly; "is there any danger of my being suspected? For, if so, I'll tell something. It's awful mean to tell it—but I've got myself to look out for—oh, no—no! I don't know anything! Not anything!"

"You do. You've already proved it. Now, Ivy, I won't exaggerate your danger, but I'll tell you that I think the only real suspects they have, as yet, are you and me. As I'm not the criminal, and as I shall do my very best to prove that, suspicion may come back on you. I don't say this to frighten you. I merely state the fact. So, don't you think yourself that you'd better tell me what you know, and I assure you that I will use the knowledge with discretion."

"Oh, I can't tell," and the girl burst into tears. "I can't tell anybody, and you least of all!"

Barry stared. What could such a speech mean?

"Please go away," Ivy moaned. "Go away now, and come tomorrow. Then I'll decide what to do."

"No," Barry said sternly; "you know something, and you must tell me. If you refuse I'll go away, but I'll send Mr Prescott here—and I'm sure you'd rather tell me—wouldn't you, Ivy?"

Barry's tone was ingratiating, and too, his words carried conviction. Ivy wiped her eyes and looked at him dolefully.

"I don't know what to do. You see, for me to tell what I know would be mean—oh, worse than mean—it would be too low down for words! And yet—I don't want to be arrested!"

"Then tell—tell me, my girl—you'll feel better to tell it."

Barry sensed the psychological moment, and knew he must get the story out of Ivy, while she was frightened. If she really knew how little she was suspected, she might never tell. And Barry felt it imperative that her knowledge be revealed.

Persuaded by his urgency, Ivy began.

"Well, you see, I went there about half past five—"

"How do you know the time so well—most people don't."

"Oh, I don't know how I know it, but I just happen to. I was due home at six, so I went there at five-thirty, or within a few minutes of that time. Does it matter?"

"No; go on."

"Well, I rang the bell, you know, and the door clicked open and I went up and Mr Gleason let me in."

"Yes."

"Well, I hadn't been there hardly any time at all—not ten minutes, anyhow, when Mr Gleason's bell rang again. And I said, 'Who is it?'"

"What made you think he would know who it was?"

"Don't know as I did. Guess I just said it—but, anyway—he said—'It's Miss Lindsay—I expect her—she mustn't see you here!'"

"What did you do?"

"Why, he pushed me through into the dining-room—"

"He never used the dining-room—"

"Oh, he did sometimes. Well, anyway, the room was there—and he pushed me in, and told me to go through the pantry and down the back stairs and out that way."

"Why did he push you? Weren't you willing to go?"

"Yes, but I was rattled—bewildered. And, I've never seen Miss Lindsay, and I was curious to see her. I didn't mind being found in Mr Gleason's rooms, but he minded very much. And so he hurried me off, and that's when he told me he'd give me the bracelet, if I'd sneak off without making a sound."

"And did you?"

"Yes; but I waited a minute to try to see Miss Lindsay."

"Did you see her?"

"No; the door opened the wrong way. I peaked through the crack, but I couldn't see her. I heard her, though."

"You did?" Barry's nerves were pounding, his heart beat fast, as he listened for, yet dreaded her further speech.

"Yes, and I couldn't make out a word she said, her voice was so low. But they were quarreling—or at least discussing something on which they didn't agree."

"What was it?" Barry controlled himself.

"I don't know. Mr Gleason walked up and down the room as he talked—he often did that—but it kept me from pushing the door a speck wider open. In fact, he pushed it tight shut as he passed it."

"Did he suspect you were there listening?"

"Oh, I don't think so. He just closed it on general principles. Maybe he thought I was there. But after that I couldn't hear a word, so I went through the pantry and down the back way."

"Anybody see you?"

"I don't think so."

"You're sure it was Miss Lindsay who was there?"

"Yes. I heard Mr Gleason say 'my sister is your stepmother, I know,' and again he said, 'Yes, you're Lindsay—you're both Lindsays—but I've made my will—' that's all I heard."

"What time did you leave there?"

"It must have been about quarter to six, for I was home at six."

"And Miss Lindsay was there when you left."

"Oh, yes, she was there when I left."

And then, Philip Barry's secret fear was confirmed.

CHAPTER 13: PHILIP AND PHYLLIS

Philip Barry, though of the artistic temperament common to his calling, had also a businesslike instinct that prompted him to straight-forward measures in any case where he was specially interested.

And he was deeply interested in learning that Phyllis had been at Gleason's rooms the afternoon of the murder, and he wanted the matter cleared up to his own satisfaction.

Wherefore, he went to Phyllis herself and inquired concerning it.

"Were you at Mr Gleason's that day?" was his somewhat direct way of opening the conversation.

They were alone, in the Lindsays' library, and Phyllis, looking demure enough in a little white house gown, was in perverse mood.

"Good gracious, Phil, are *you* beginning to suspect me? Go to Millicent with your theories? She has thought from the first that I shot her brother. Go over to her side, if you like."

"I don't like! It isn't a question of 'sides'! And if it is, of course, I'm on your side. You know that, don't you, Phyllis? You know I'm for you, first, last and all the time."

"Then help me, Phil, and sympathize, and don't come rushing in here and screaming out, 'Was I at Mr Gleason's when he was killed?'"

"I didn't say that!"

"You did, practically. Now, what do you mean by it?"

"Why," Barry hesitated, "why, I've been to see that—"

"Ivy Hayes?"

"Yes. And she said you were there."

"Ivy Hayes said I was there! She must be crazy!"

"Weren't you? Tell me you weren't, Phyllis. I'll be so glad to know it. Where were you that afternoon, late? You never would say."

"Why should I? I won't say now, either, but I was not at Mr Gleason's."

"Oh, then that's all right." Barry's tense expression relaxed, and he smiled. "Then that youngster made it all up. I fancied she did—just to make a sensation."

"Why—what did she say, exactly?" Phyllis looked ill at ease.

Barry couldn't suspect her sincerity, but he watched her as he told of his interview with Miss Hayes.

"She said I was there! That she was hidden in another room while I was there! Why, I wasn't there at all!"

"You didn't go to Mr Gleason's the day of—the day he died?"

"No, I've never been there! Why should I go? It isn't my custom to go to the homes of men I know. They call on me."

"Of course, Phyllis—don't get angry, dear. I didn't think you'd go there—but there might have been a reason—an errand, you know."

"Well, there wasn't. I wish you'd all stop trying to find out who killed that man! What difference does it make? He's dead, and it won't bring him to life to punish his murderer. I think Millicent is foolish about it."

"It's natural, Phyllis, dear. It isn't exactly revenge, but more an avenging spirit. It's human nature to demand a life for a life."

"But it can't be found out. If they do arrest somebody, it'll most likely be the wrong person."

Phyllis looked very lovely as she drew her brows together in a perplexed frown and then smiled.

"Oh, make them stop, Phil. If you advise Millicent, she'll stop."

"I'm afraid my sense of justice is too strong—" Barry began, but Phyllis interrupted him:

"It *is* too strong if it's stronger than your wish to please me," and she pouted like a scolded child.

"Nothing in my heart is stronger than my wish to please you," Barry said, gravely, "and you know it, Phyllis. If you make it a condition, I will most certainly suggest to Mrs Lindsay that she give up her quest. But, such advice would be against my own better judgment."

"But why, Phil?" Phyllis was coaxing now. "Don't you feel sure they'll never find the murderer?"

"If they don't, Phyllis, they'll always suspect me."

"What do you care—since you are innocent?"

"I care very much! Why, my dear girl, do you suppose I could carry that burden all my life? Always go about, knowing that many people—or even a few people suspected me of Robert Gleason's murder? No; when I think about it, I'm ready to move heaven and earth, if that were possible, to find the true criminal!"

Phyllis shuddered and her face went white.

"Couldn't you forget in time?" she said, bravely struggling to speak steadily.

"Never! Why, Phyllis, that letter is enough to condemn me—only I didn't write it."

"Didn't you, really, Phil?"

The girl leaned forward, and looked into his eyes so earnestly that Barry recoiled in amazement. Did she suspect him? Phyllis!

"Don't!" he cried out, "don't look as if you thought me guilty! You, of all people!"

"Oh, I don't," she said, quickly, "but I thought you might have written the letter, meaning something else. The fact of your writing it doesn't make you the criminal."

"But I didn't. Listen, Phyllis—I love you—oh, sweetheart, how I love you! but I've resolved not to ask you for love, until I can offer you an unstained name—"

"Your name isn't stained! I won't have you say such things!"

Her sweet smile was encouraging, but Barry shook his head:

"No, dear, you mustn't even be kind to me. I can't stand it! You know my name *is* affected until the mystery of that letter is explained. It's the most inexplicable thing! Why, look at it! We fellows all discussed murder, and discussed Gleason and that very day he was killed and that letter was found in his desk! It was a piece of diabolical cleverness on somebody's part!"

"But, Phil, just as an argument. How could anybody write that letter but you?"

"I don't see, myself. But somebody did do it. I've thought it over and over. I've looked at this letter through a lens, but there's no trace of erased writing, nor any possibility of my signature having been pasted into another sheet, or anything like that."

"I've seen wonderful inlay work, where one piece of paper is joined to another actually invisibly."

"So have I, and I thought of that. But it wasn't done in this case. That sheet of paper—Club paper, is absolutely intact, it is typed just as I type things-a little carelessly—and the signature is like mine. I would say it is mine, only—I didn't write it!"

"Maybe somebody hypnotized you."

"No; I've never been hypnotized—nor has any one ever attempted such a thing with me. It's diabolical, as I said. But I'll find out if it takes my life time! Now, you see, dear, why I don't want you to urge me to stop investigation on the part of anybody. Besides, Mrs Lindsay isn't the only one eager to solve the mystery. The detectives, the police, are as anxious as she is."

"I don't think so. I think they're getting tired of having no results. I think, if Millicent gave up the search, they soon would do so."

"But why? Why, Phyllis, are you desirous of having it given up?"

"Oh, I don't know! I'm tired of it, that's all. And now, you're dragging me into it—"

"Phyllis, as you said to me—if you're innocent, your name can't be harmed."

"Well—suppose I'm not innocent—would you stop then?"

Barry stared at her. He thought at first her speech was merely an outburst of the perversity which now and then showed in her volatile nature. But her face was drawn and white and her eyes dark with a sort of terror he had never before seen her show.

However, he saw no choice but to treat her speech lightly.

"Oh, yes, of course! But until you tell me you're the villain of the piece, I shan't be able to believe it."

"I didn't like Mr Gleason."

"Who did? Check up, now. If we're to suspect all who didn't like the man, there's Pollard, Davenport, you, me—"

"And Mr Pollard's mythical Westerner. Oh, Phil, I wish *he* could be found!"

"Who? Pollard?"

"No; the man he thinks came from the West—an old acquaintance of Mr Gleason's."

"Yes, he's a fine suspect, but a bit intangible. Perhaps he wrote the note I signed!"

"Don't jest, Philip. I'm—I'm so miserable."

Phyllis bowed her face in her hands and cried softly.

"Don't—don't, Phyllis, darling. For heaven's sake, keep out of the muddle."

"But you dragged me into it! You came here checking up on my movements. Why did you do that?"

"I told you why. Because Ivy Hayes said you were there."

"Oh, yes—so she did. I forgot that. Well—maybe I was—maybe I was—"

"Phyllis, hush. You're talking wildly. And here's another thing. Where was Louis that afternoon?"

"Phil Barry, you stop! Are you going to accuse the whole family? Why don't you ask where Millicent was?"

"I ask about Louis because I've been told he was there."

"And I was there! And Ivy Hayes was there! And the man from the West was there! Quite a party!"

Phyllis laughed shrilly—not at all like her usual gentle laugh, and Barry watched her in alarm, lest she grow hysterical.

"I won't," she said, divining his fear. "I'm not hysterical, but I'm distracted. Oh, Phil, do help me!"

"Of course I will, little girl," Barry held out his arms. "Come to me, Phyllis, let's forget all the horrible things of life and just love each other—and belong."

"No," she drew away from him. "Not yet. If your name must be cleared—so must mine."

"But your name isn't even mentioned."

"Yes, it is," Phyllis said, speaking in a dull, slow way, "yes, it is—and the worst of it is, my name can't be cleared."

"Hush," Barry cautioned, "somebody's coming in."

The street door closed, and a moment later, Manning Pollard made an appearance.

The conversation, though general, was not spontaneous, and after a short time, Barry took his leave. Though he did not consider Pollard an actual rival of his in Phyllis' favor, yet he felt disgruntled when the other was present. And, too, he wanted to go off by himself to think over what Phyllis had said.

He knew her too well to imagine for a moment that she was merely upset by the whole situation and wanted the investigation to be stopped.

He knew she had some definite and imperative reason for begging him to quit searching and also that she meant something when she said her own name could not be cleared.

That remark, of course, could not be taken at its face value, but all the same, it meant something—and he must find out what.

Manning Pollard was confronted with the same question.

Apparently unable to control her nervous fear, Phyllis said, at once:

"Oh, Mr Pollard, can't you help me? I'm in such trouble. That Miss Hayes says I was at Mr Gleason's the day of the murder!"

"And were you?"

"No!—or, well, maybe I was. But that has nothing to do with it. Can't you hush up the Hayes girl? Must she tell of it, if I *was* there?"

"It would be a pretty difficult matter to stop her mouth."

"But if I paid her?"

"Ah, then you would get yourself in trouble! Don't do anything of that sort, I beg of you! Tell me all about it, Miss Lindsay. I'm sure I can help—and if not, won't it relieve you to talk it over? What is the new development?"

"Oh, only that probably I shall next be suspected of the Gleason murder!"

"Yes?" Manning Pollard didn't look so intensely surprised as Phyllis had anticipated.

"Oh, I know Millicent has foolishly said that I did it—but she didn't mean it. She'd suspect anybody from the mayor to the cook! But, now, that little chorus girl—or whatever she is—has said that I was in the room with Mr Gleason, when he—"

"When he was killed! Oh, no!"

"Why, she practically says that. It seems she was there herself."

"She was there! When Mr Gleason was shot!"

"Oh, she couldn't have been—could she? But—you see I don't know exactly what she said—"

"Then don't try to quote her, but tell me what you do know. Did she try to implicate you?"

"Yes—I think she did."

"You're not sure—"

"No; only she said I was there—"

"Were you?"

"I—I don't want to tell you—"

"Miss Lindsay, don't tell me—don't tell anybody! If you were there keep it to yourself—and if not—there's no occasion to say so. I understand what you're trying to do. Keep it up. That's why I invented the Western man!"

"Invented him! You don't really believe in him?"

"Oh, I suppose invented isn't the right word. But—of course, I've no proof of his existence. He *may* well be a fact—or, again, he may not be. I only say that there's a possibility—even a probability that Gleason *may* have known somebody out there who came after him here and killed him. Nobody can deny the possibility, at least."

"No, of course not."

"You've no idea of the identity of any such person?"

"I? Oh, no."

"It would be a good thing if you could remember Mr Gleason's having told you of such a one."

Phyllis looked up suddenly, and caught Pollard's meaning glance. Could it be? Was he hinting that she should make up some such story. It couldn't be!

"Why?" she said, quietly.

"I think you know," he spoke gently, "but if you want me to put it into words, I will. The Hayes girl has told several people—Mr Prescott among them, that you were at the Gleason rooms about six o'clock that night. Now, you know, you have refused to say where you were at that time—and it is not surprising that their suspicions are aroused. For you to deny being there would not be half so efficacious as for you to turn the thoughts of the detectives in some other direction. Suppose, for instance, you were to remember some man Mr Gleason told you of. Some name—let us say—and suppose the detectives set themselves to work to find the individual. If they can't find him, you harm nobody, and—you divert attention from yourself."

Phyllis did not pretend to misunderstand. Nor did she treat the matter lightly.

"You think I am in danger, then?" she asked.

"Oh, don't say danger—I don't like the word. But, your name will be bandied about—will be in the papers—unless you quash the thing in the beginning. You haven't admitted you were there, but, suppose it is proved that you were, and suppose you tell of this man, of whom Mr Gleason spoke to you—spoke to you at that very time—and suppose your story is that you were there about six—that you left soon after—and that Mr Gleason was even then fearing the arrival of this enemy of his."

Again Phyllis looked him in the eyes.

Pollard was a magnetic man, his face inspired confidence, but more than that, the girl read in the deep, dark eyes a troubled care for herself—for her own safety and well-being.

She knew Pollard admired her—most of her men friends did, but only now was she aware of his passionate love.

"It's a terrible thing that I'm advising," he said, in a whisper, "but I realize the gravity of the situation. Phyllis—I care so much—so much—and I can't help seeing how things are tending. You know I have no shadow of suspicion of you—my beautiful—my darling—but others will—others will be swayed by the Hayes story, and—though you left the place before Mr Gleason was killed—yet it must have been only shortly before—and somebody did come in and kill him—so, why not say—"

"I see your point, I see how I am endangered—even if I'm innocent. If I'm innocent."

"Why do you say that?" Pollard looked at her wonderingly. "At least, don't say it to me! And forgive my abruptness, but I must tell you how I love you. I must ask you if you can't love me—oh, Phyllis, even a little? Do you, dear?"

"Please, Mr Pollard—please don't say those things now—I'm so-worried—" The soft eyes filled with unshed tears.

"I know it, my little girl—I know it—and that's why—
I want to be in a position to help you—I mean I want to
have a right—to let the world know I have the right, to
protect you. Will you give it to me—Phyllis—will you?"

The big man leaned toward her, his attitude
reverently affectionate, and Phyllis felt wonderfully
drawn to him. He was so capable, so efficient, and though
she felt a sense of potential mastery in his manner, she
did not resent it, but rather rejoiced in it.

"Oh," she breathed, looking at him, with startled,
shining eyes, "oh—I can't say—now. Don't ask me now."

"Yes, I shall—now—my beloved, my queen! Oh, you
beautiful girl, you may not love me yet, but I'll make
you—I'll make you!"

The smile that accompanied the words took away any
hint of tyranny, and the pleading in Manning Pollard's
eyes was hard to resist.

But Phyllis hesitated. She didn't know him so very
well, and, too, she had a feminine notion that to say yes
at once would make her seem too willing. Moreover, she
wanted to think it over, alone, by herself.

She had always thought she loved Phil Barry—but
somehow, in a moment this insistent wooer had pushed
Phil to the background.

"Not now," she said, softly, as she gave him her hand,
"I will think about what you've said—but I can't promise
now."

"No, dear, I understand," and as Pollard's strong
fingers closed over her own, Phyllis was almost certain
what her eventual answer to him would be. He was so
gentle in his strength, so tender in his manliness—and he
seemed a real refuge for her in her uncertainties.

"But, here's another thing," he went on; "I hate to tell
you, but the question of your having been in Gleason's
room is bound to be raised—and I want to say that I saw
you—that afternoon at about six o'clock. I tell you, so you
won't try any prevarication on me."

The last was said with a good-natured smile, that gave a feeling of camaraderie which delighted Phyllis' heart. She didn't want to give herself irrevocably to Pollard—yet—but she was glad to have him for a friend— and his frank, pleasant friendliness cheered her very soul.

"Where in the world did you see me?" she asked.

"At the crowded corner of Fifth Avenue and Forty-second Street. I had just left Phil Barry—we came down from the Club together—and I saw you, in a cab—with a strange man. Who was he, Phyllis?"

The assured manner of his query was not lost on the girl, but she did not resent it.

"Must I tell you?" she smiled.

"No—no, dear. But I wish you wanted to be frank with me—to confide in me."

"Oh, I will—I do—but—I can't."

"Then you needn't—and, don't look so distressed, my poor little girl. Tell me only what you want to—just let me help in any way that you want me to. And, Phyllis—I hate to make this proposition, but I must. If anything happens—if anything is said that frightens you, or troubles you deeply—will you—if you feel it would help you in any way—will you say that you are engaged to me?"

"When I'm not!"

"You may consider that you are or not, as you wish; but I have an idea that occasion might arise, when it would help you to announce the engagement—to assert that you have some one to look after you. If you want to break it later—that is, of course, your privilege."

"Oh," said Phyllis, looking at him, admiringly, "how good you are! Nobody else would have thought of that!"

"Don't misunderstand me. I want you—I want you to say yes to me for keeps, some day. But in the meantime, if it ever should serve your purpose, claim me as your fiance."

Chapter 14: Hester's Statement

Pollard and Lane, sitting talking in the Club Lounge, were joined by Dean Monroe.

"It's a queer thing," Monroe said, "that nobody gets any forrader in the Gleason matter. What are police for? What are detectives for? And most of all, what are we chaps for, if we can't solve a mystery right in our own set?"

"I don't know that it matters, being in our own set," Pollard began, but Monroe interrupted:

"Yes, it does. We know all the principals—"

"Hold on," Lane said; "what do you mean, principals? There's the principal character, the victim, himself, but further than that we know no 'principal.'"

"We don't! Well, I should say we know most of the suspects."

"Suspects don't amount to much," Pollard observed, "unless you can hang more evidence on them than has been attached to anybody so far."

"Evidence!" Monroe exclaimed; "what further evidence do you want than that letter of Phil Barry's?"

"Oho," said Lane; "you're out for Barry, are you? But, Pol, here threatened to kill Gleason. That's far more incriminating evidence to my mind than Barry's letter. For the letter may have been forged, but Pollard said his words himself."

"Oh, I know, but Manning was home in his rooms all the time, and nobody knows where Phil was. Why don't they find out?"

"Why don't they find out anything?" Lane smiled. "Because they don't go to work with any intelligence."

"You could solve the mystery, I suppose?" Monroe flung at him.

"I'd be afraid to try," and Lane looked serious.

"Meaning?" Pollard asked.

"That investigation of a determined sort might lead to awful conclusions."

"Don't say it!" Pollard cried. "I can't help knowing what you mean, but don't breathe it, Lane. You know how a word—a hint—may start suspicion. And there's not a word of truth in it!"

"Who? Miss Lindsay?" Monroe asked, bluntly.

"Hush up, Dean," Pollard growled.

"I won't. And it's silly to evade an issue. If there's nothing in it, drag it out into the light and prove there isn't."

"No," Lane said, thoughtfully, "it isn't wise to drag out anything concerning the Lindsays—any of them. Not even Mrs Lindsay. They're an emotional lot, and if they get excited, they say all sorts of things. If they must be questioned, it would better be by somebody with their interests at heart, and the thing should be done quietly and with few listeners."

"Well, you go and do it, Lane," Monroe suggested. "I feel sure unless you do, the police will get ahead of you, and they'll put Miss Lindsay through the third degree—"

"Oh, nonsense. The police are hot on Barry's trail. That chap'll be arrested very soon, I believe. Why, that letter is damning. How do you explain it, except at its face value?"

"But what is its face value?" asked Pollard. "The letter doesn't threaten violent measures at all—"

"It implies something of the sort. And Barry has no alibi."

"Of course not," Pollard said; "an innocent man doesn't have. I mean, an innocent man is very likely not to know where he was at any given time. It's your criminal who has his alibi at his tongue's end."

"I'm going over to the Lindsay house now," Lane said, rising. "Want to go along, Pol?"

"No, not this time. If you're going to quiz Miss Lindsay I'd rather not be there. And you said yourself you'd rather be alone."

"Right. But I'm going to ask Mrs Lindsay a few questions, too. After all, she and Miss Phyllis are the only heirs."

"Meaning one of them is doubtless the criminal!" Dean Monroe spoke scornfully.

"Oh, I don't say that," Lane returned, "but there's lots to see about."

Others than Lane were of this mind, for when the lawyer reached the Lindsay home, he found Belknap and Prescott both there, and the Lindsay ladies, as a result of their visitors' questions, both in a highly excited state.

"I'm glad to see you, Mr Lane," Millicent cried, as Lane entered; "do help Phyllis and me. These men are saying awful things to us!"

"To me," Phyllis corrected. "They've nothing against you, Millicent."

Phyllis looked exhausted. Apparently, she had had all she could stand of the detectives' grilling, and she was at the end of her self-control.

"You must excuse me a few minutes," she exclaimed, starting up, and without another word she left the room.

"You were rather blunt, Prescott," Belknap said. "You must remember Miss Lindsay is a delicate, sheltered young lady, and unaccustomed to hear such rough speech as you gave her."

"No matter," said Prescott, doggedly. "If she killed Gleason, such talk is none too bad for her. And if she didn't, it can't hurt her."

"What!" cried Lane. "Miss Lindsay kill Mr Gleason! Man, you must be crazy!"

"Oh, no, not that," Prescott said, quietly. "But when a young lady goes to a man's rooms half an hour before he is killed, when she at that interview learns for the first time that she is heiress to half his fortune, when she is overheard in altercation with the man a very short time before he is shot, when no other person is seen there at the time or anywhere near it, when the young lady doesn't care much for the man, when he wants to marry her—and she knows if she refuses she'll lose the inheritance—well, isn't that about enough?"

"First," asked Lane, "are your statements all proved facts?"

"Facts don't have to be proved," Prescott flared back. "But my statements are facts, as you mostly know, yourself. We have Miss Hayes' word for it that Miss Lindsay was at Mr Gleason's about six."

"She says she wasn't," Millicent broke in, angrily.

"Now, look here, Mrs Lindsay," said Belknap, "the very day of the crime you accused Miss Lindsay. Why do you now try to defend her?"

"Oh, she never did it," wailed Millicent. "Never! Never! When I said she did, I was out of my head. Just at first, you know, I was so stunned I scarcely knew what I was saying."

"Well, you know now. Was Miss Lindsay here at home at six o'clock that night?"

"I don't know—"

"You do know. Answer."

"Well, then, she wasn't—but that doesn't prove she was down in Washington Square!"

"Leave us to do the proving. You answer questions."

"Now, don't frighten the lady," Lane advised, frowning at the detective's manner. "She will answer your questions—or I will."

"All right, then, you answer. What does Miss Lindsay want twenty thousand dollars for—and in a hurry, too?"

"Does she want that sum?"

"She does; and she's bound to get it. Wants her inheritance right off. What for, I say?"

"And I say, I don't know," Lane replied. "But there are lots of things the modern young woman wants money for—"

"Yes, but if they're right and proper things, why won't she tell what they are? No matter if they're extravagances or foolish luxuries, why not say so? But if the destination of that twenty thousand can't be told—it's clear there's something wrong about it."

"Meaning?"

"Meaning nothing but that. Something wrong— something shady—something that must be covered up. Therefore, she had to have the money at once. Therefore, she went to Robert Gleason for it. Therefore, he told her he would give it to her on one condition—marriage."

"Hold on, Prescott, do you know this?" Lane demanded.

Prescott jerked a finger toward Millicent Lindsay.

"She knows it," he said. "She knows that for weeks Miss Lindsay had kept Gleason dangling—waiting for her answer. Then, when the young lady discovers she can get the money by the man's death—and as she really abhors him and doesn't want to marry him—and as the opportunity offers—"

"What opportunity?"

"The fact that she's there alone with him in his rooms, his pistol conveniently at hand, and nobody about—"

"Oh, you're romancing! That girl! She couldn't do it!"

"You know she could, Mr Lane," Belknap interposed. "You say that because you don't want to think it. But the only thing that would positively disprove it would be for Miss Lindsay to tell where she was at the time. This she refuses to do."

"Yes, and Manning Pollard refused to tell where he was——"

"But we found out where he was, without his telling us. To prove where a man was by outside witnesses, many of them, is proof, when his own statement is far from proof. Now if we could check up Miss Lindsay as we did Mr Pollard, that would settle her question. But we can't."

"Where was she?" Lane asked of Millicent.

"I don't know, I'm sure. She came home just in time to dress for the dinner-party. But I don't know what time it was."

"That's the trouble," Prescott said, despairingly. "Nobody ever knows what time anything happened. The only thing we are sure of is that Gleason was still alive and telephoning at quarter to seven, and even at that, that nurse may have been mistaken."

"Not she," said Lane. "She's most accurate."

"Then, we're fairly sure of Miss Hayes' evidence, for the simple reason that we've no cause for doubt in her case. She says she left the Gleason place, by the back entrance, at six o'clock. And, she says Miss Lindsay was with Gleason at that time. Now, the puzzle fits into place. Miss Lindsay remained for a time, trying to persuade Gleason to give her this large sum of money, and when he refused—that is, unless she would marry him, she became desperate, and the tragedy resulted."

"Straight story," said Lane, "but little to back it save your imagination. What's to prevent Miss Lindsay going away and somebody else coming and committing the deed? Plenty of time between six and quarter of seven."

"Not likely. The people of the house were coming in then, and an arriving man would have been noticed. Oh, I don't say it would have been impossible—but we've no shadow of evidence for it. And, if so, where did Miss Lindsay go from there at six o'clock, that she didn't get home until seven or thereabouts?"

"You don't know that it was as late as seven—"

"No! I tell you I can't fix the time of anything. Nobody seems to have had a timepiece going that night—which is suspicious in itself!"

"What about Philip Barry?" Lane asked this quietly. "I thought you were sure of his guilt."

"It all fits in," said Prescott, slowly. "Mr Barry and Miss Lindsay are in love with each other—"

"Now how do you know that?" and Lane looked at the detective sharply.

"I gathered it from lots of sources. Barry's letter to Gleason for one."

"But that only proves that Mr Barry admired Miss Lindsay. Not that his regard was returned."

"Oh, well, that doesn't matter. Say they were friends, then. Say they were in cahoots. Say the money was wanted by Mr Barry, and together they planned to get it from Gleason—in one way or another."

Lane laughed shortly, and again remarked on the detective's fertile imagination, but in truth he was decidedly uncomfortable. He had been afraid some one would evolve a theory that included Phyllis and Barry both, and this was the thought that had haunted Lane's mind. It was incredible, but it was at least possible, that Barry's threatening letter and Phyllis' desire for a large sum of money and the liking of the girl for the artist and her detestation of Robert Gleason, all tended toward a theory that included the two, and that had much to be said for it.

And then a strange thing happened. One of the maids employed in the Lindsay household came into the room.

"What is it, Hester?" asked Millicent, in surprise.

"Oh, please, madam—please, Mrs Lindsay, I think I know something I ought to tell."

"You do!" Prescott pounced on her. "Well, tell it, then."

"Why—you see—I heard you talking about where Miss Phyllis was—on the night of—of, you know—at six o'clock. And I can tell you where she was."

Belknap looked at the girl without much interest. She was as emotional as the people she worked for. Her fingers twisted nervously, and she picked at her apron, and swayed from side to side as she talked.

Probably, Belknap thought, she's devoted to Miss Lindsay, and is making up a yarn to save her.

But Hester went on, speaking softly, but steadily enough.

"Yes, sir. And this is what I know. At six o'clock, Miss Phyllis was in a taxicab with a man driving up Fifth Avenue. She was near Forty-second Street."

Prescott laughed outright.

"You've a kind heart, and doubtless you love Miss Lindsay, but your story is a little crude. Wants verisimilitude,—if you know what that means. You may go, Hester."

"No; wait a minute," directed Belknap. "Were you out that afternoon, Hester?"

"No, sir."

"Then how do you know this?"

"I heard Mr Pollard say so."

"Wait! This grows interesting. To whom did he say it?"

"To Miss Phyllis herself, sir."

"Oh, he did! And when?"

"I'm thinking it was yesterday or day before. Anyhow, he was here a talking to Miss Phyllis, and I heard him tell her he saw her then and there and he asked her who was the man with her."

"And who was it?"

"Miss Phyllis wouldn't tell him, sir."

"And so, Hester, you listen at doors, do you?"

"No, sir, that I don't. I came into the library to mend the fire and to turn on the lights as is my duty at twilight. And Miss Phyllis was talking with Mr Pollard, and they said what I've told you."

"And just why are you repeating it to us?"

"Because—to-day I *was* listening at the door. I love Miss Phyllis and when I saw her rush out of the room here, and run up to her own room and throw herself on the bed and cry as if her heart would break, I didn't know what to do! And she wouldn't let me do anything for her, but said she wanted to be alone. So I left her and I came down, and when I heard you gentleman talking against my young lady, I thought maybe if I told that, it might help."

Hester's honest blue eyes, tear-filled and sad, left no doubt of her sincerity and her loyalty to her beloved young mistress.

"I think you have helped, Hester," said Belknap, not unkindly. "Now will you go and tell Miss Lindsay that we wish to see her. That she must come at once."

Hester went, and it was several moments before she returned.

The group waited in silence.

Millicent wept softly, and though Lane spoke to her once or twice she paid no attention. The volatile little woman was deeply sorry now that she had accused Phyllis in the first place. As she said, and she did not really mean it—or at least, she was so stunned and bewildered that she scarcely knew what she did mean. But when she became calmer, she knew she didn't suspect Phyllis—and yet, so susceptible is human nature to suggestion that when the detectives put the matter as they did, she began to think they might be right.

While they were waiting for Phyllis' reappearance, Barry came.

He was surprised at the presence of the Assistant District Attorney and the detective, but as he noted their reception of himself he was even more surprised. For they did not regard him as hostilely as usual, and he immediately concluded they were on another track.

But conversation was a bit constrained, and finally Barry blurted out:

"What's the idea? Why are you all sitting here as if looking for something or somebody?"

"We are," and Belknap looked grave. "We are waiting for Miss Lindsay to reappear."

"What about her?" Barry asked, suddenly alert.

"We want her to answer a few questions." Belknap kept a wary eye on the artist, for he was becoming more and more convinced that the secret of the murder was in the keeping of the two. His theory strengthened in his mind every moment and he wished Phyllis would come. Yet, something might be gained from Barry in the meantime.

"Were you in a taxicab with Miss Lindsay on the day of Mr Gleason's death?" Belknap sprang suddenly.

"What do you mean?" cried Barry, angrily. "Of course I wasn't."

"Who was, then?"

"I don't know, I'm sure. I don't know that anybody was."

"Well, some man was. At about six o'clock. At Fifth Avenue and Forty-second Street. Where were you at that hour?"

"Why, I was almost right there myself. I walked down from the Club with Pollard about that time, and I left him at Forty-fourth and he went on down."

"Very good," Belknap nodded.

Barry's air had been honest, his thinking back evidently real and his statement quite in accordance with the known facts. Pollard had said Barry walked down with him, and had left him at Forty-fourth. Now, from that time, Pollard's every movement had been checked up, but not so Barry's. Nobody seemed to have seen him from that moment until he arrived at the Lindsay dinner party.

To ask him as to this was sure to anger him, yet Belknap tried it.

"No!" Barry stormed, in answer to his query, "I haven't an alibi. I mean I've nobody who can swear to one. As a matter of fact, I went directly home after leaving Pollard. I went into my hotel, a small one on West Forty-fourth Street, and I went to my rooms."

"Meeting nobody?"

"Of course, I passed the doorman and the desk people. I don't remember whether I spoke to them or not. I usually nod if they're looking my way. But I can't remember what happens every single night! I'm not trying to establish an alibi, because I didn't kill Mr Gleason. But I'm ready to help you find out who did. I've not done much so far, because I thought the matter was in capable hands. But those capable hands have accomplished just nothing—nothing at all! Now, I'm going to put my finger in this pie—and I'm going to discover something!"

"Wait, Mr Barry," Belknap said, "what about that letter signed by you, yet which you say you didn't write. Suppose you explain that first."

"Just what I intend to do! I haven't quite proved it, but I have found out a possible solution of that matter. If I can prove I didn't write it, and can show who did and how and why, it'll help some—won't it?"

"You bet it will!" cried Prescott. "That's the kind of talk. But have you some real information, or merely a supposition that doesn't mean anything definite?"

"We'll see," and Barry shook his head. "I'm not telling it all now. But I came to see Miss Lindsay. Where is she?"

"She'll be here in a minute," Millicent said, eyeing Barry closely.

But in a minute, instead of Phyllis, Hester returned.

Excitedly, she exclaimed, "Miss Phyllis is gone. Nobody saw her go and nobody knows where she is!"

"Gone!" said Millicent contemptuously; "how absurd! If you mean she has run away! Phyllis wouldn't do that."

"Well, madam, she's not in the apartment. Her moleskin coat is gone from her wardrobe, and her little taupe hat. She has certainly gone out, ma'am."

And gone Phyllis surely had. It was foolish to look for her in the rooms, for her hat and coat were missing, of course she had gone out into the street; whether for some ordinary errand, or to disappear who could tell?

"I'll find her," said Prescott, and clapping on his hat he hurried away.

CHAPTER 15: PHYLLIS AND IVY

And where *was* Phyllis?

Why, sitting in the small, but pretty, little bedroom of Ivy Hayes, in that young woman's boarding-house home.

"And so you're Phyllis Lindsay," said the other girl, looking admiringly at Phyllis' smart, inconspicuous costume. "I'm jolly glad to see you. What can I do for you?"

The frank, pleasant manner of the hostess pleased the guest and Phyllis said, impulsively, "Oh, I hope you can help me. I'm in a quandary. Will you tell me frankly just why you said I was at Mr Gleason's the day he died?"

"Now, how did you know I said that? I declare those detectives tell everything!"

"I thought it was Mr Barry whom you told."

"Well, it's all the same. Why, I said you were there, because you were there."

"No, I wasn't."

"All right, then, you weren't. I like you, Miss Lindsay, and I'll stand by you. Now, you tell me what you want me to say, and I'll say it."

"Oh, dear, I don't want you to say anything that isn't true. Why did you think I was there, if you didn't see me?"

"I heard you."

"Heard me talking?"

"Yes."

"What did I say?"

"You were asking Mr Gleason for money—a big sum."

"And you heard me ask him?"

"I didn't exactly hear you, you spoke very low, and I was behind a closed door. But I heard all Mr Gleason said—so I could tell."

"What did he say?"

"He said, 'twenty thousand dollars! I should say not! Not unless—well, you know my conditions.' That's exactly what he said. And then you murmured something, and he said, 'You're a Lindsay—you're both Lindsays,' but I don't know whether he meant you and his sister, or you and your brother."

"What has my brother to do with it?"

"I don't know—but when he spoke of the two of you together, like that, I thought he meant you and Louis. But afterward, I thought he might have meant you and his sister, Mrs Lindsay."

"You know my brother? You call him Louis!"

"Yes, I know him—not awfully well, but enough to call him anything I like. You don't have to know anybody so very long to call him pet names."

"Pet names!"

"Oh, come now, Miss Lindsay, don't be so shocked. You're probably more conventional than I am, but you must know a few things. Well, anyhow, I didn't hear any more, because Mr Gleason shut the door, and I just scooted down the back way and home. I never knew whether you got the money you wanted or not. Did you?"

Phyllis gasped. She was annoyed at the girl's rudeness, but, after all, Ivy Hayes had a charm of her own, and it was impossible to feel deep resentment toward the flippant little thing.

"I didn't get it from Mr Gleason, because I didn't ask him for it. I didn't ask him for it, because I wasn't there. I've never been there."

"All right, Miss Lindsay—what you say goes. You've never been there. Is that what you came to tell me?"

Ivy cocked her foolish little curly head on one side, and gave Phyllis such a humorous wink that she couldn't help smiling.

"I don't wonder Louis likes you," she said, impulsively. "You're an adorable little piece."

"That's right," said Ivy, gravely. "Pile it on thick. I just lap it up. Do you think I'm pretty?"

"Yes," Phyllis returned, simply. "Now, tell me again, why did you think the—the person Mr Gleason said those things to was myself, when you never had seen me—and you say you couldn't hear me."

"Well, when the bell rang, Mr Gleason said it was you. That he expected you."

Phyllis turned pale. "Go on," she said.

"That's all. He said, 'That's Miss Lindsay coming up. You go.' So I went. I hung around a few moments, trying to get a glimpse of you, but I couldn't. I heard you speak, but you spoke so low, and the door was almost shut, so I couldn't hear a word you said."

"Well," Phyllis drew a long breath. "If I was there—I didn't kill Mr Gleason."

"Of course you didn't!" Ivy exclaimed. Then, with a look deep into Phyllis' eyes, she added, "And you weren't there. I know it now!"

"How do you know it?"

"Oh, it's come to me. You were not there that day at all, Miss Lindsay. As you say, you've never been there."

Ivy looked very grave. She gazed at Phyllis with a strange look of divination, and added, "I know you haven't."

"Oh, yes, I have," Phyllis cried quickly. "I *was* there that day—I was, really. I just said I wasn't—because—"

"Oh, come now," Ivy smiled a little but she did not laugh. "What am I to think? You were there and you weren't there! You've never been there and you were there that day! My goodness gracious!"

"I was there," Phyllis said, looking at her coldly. "I said at first I wasn't, for—for reasons of my own—"

"Yes, I know," and Ivy nodded a sagacious head. "What are we going to do about it?"

Phyllis stared. "About what?"

"About the—the reason you said—you know—"

"Don't! Don't look like that! You're uncanny. What do you know?"

"I don't know anything. Do you?"

"About what?"

"About who killed Mr Gleason."

This time Ivy looked directly at Phyllis, and that with a meaning glance.

Phyllis covered her face with her hands, and at once Ivy ran to her side and threw her arms around her.

"Now, don't cry," she begged. "It's no time for that. Let's see what we can do."

"Do about what? What are you talking about?"

"Shall I speak out? Shall I put it into words?"

"Yes," said Phyllis, but she shrank as from a sudden blow.

"Then, here's how I dope it out. It wasn't you who were there—but it was Louis."

"Oh, no, no! It was I. It wasn't Buddy."

"Yes it was. You're trying to shield him. I see it. Now, don't take that tack with me. Own up—tell me all you know—and I'll help you." Phyllis thought a moment.

"Might as well," Ivy urged. "I know too much to be ignored, and I truly think it would be better for you in every way, to take me into your confidence. Let me help you."

"How can you?"

"I don't know, quite. But I do know that if you stick to your story of having been there yourself, when you were not, you'll get a whole lot of unpleasant notoriety, if nothing worse."

"Meaning?"

"Suspicion. Accusation. Maybe arrest."

Phyllis jumped. "Arrest!" she whispered, and her eyes stared in horror.

"Well, maybe not that," Ivy soothed her, "but, you tell me all about it. Look here, Miss Lindsay, I'm a better detective than half the men on the force. And, say, I know a little girl—well, I don't suppose you'd want her—but start straight now—tell me everything you know. Let me be your father confessor."

"But I've nothing to confess."

"You haven't! How about that story—fib you just told about going to Mr Gleason's house—when you didn't go."

"You don't know that I didn't."

"Yes, I do, and I'll tell you how I know. It was Louis who went there—not you!"

"You didn't see him."

"No, and I didn't hear him—or I should have known at once. But it was Louis, of course, and when Mr Gleason said 'You're both Lindsays,' and referred to the stepmother, of course it fitted Louis as well as you. Louis wanted money—you know that?"

"Yes, I know that."

"Has he got it—yet?"

"He will have it to-morrow. A—a friend is going to let me have it for him."

"Who?"

"Mr Pollard."

"You seem to be able to get money easily!"

"Mr Pollard is my fiance."

Phyllis remembered suddenly that Pollard had told her she might want to say that, and just now, in the presence of this girl of a lower class and of a lesser degree of refinement, Phyllis felt a sudden impulse to justify her position. To her mind, to take money from one's fiance made correct what would otherwise be a questionable thing to do.

"Oho! I see! Why, I thought you and Mr Barry were pals."

"We are. Good pals. But I am engaged to Mr Pollard."

"And you're to get the money for Louis—in time?"

"Yes—in time. You know?"

"I know he'll be jailed if he doesn't fork over about twenty thousand to that old shark!"

"Never mind details. Now, truly, Ivy, do you think Buddy was at Mr Gleason's that day?"

"I don't think it, I know it. And, Phyllis—he—he killed him."

In the gravity of the moment neither noticed the intimate use of the name. Phyllis looked at the other, her eyes full of a dumb agony.

"Don't!" she begged, "don't say it!"

"Better face it, dear. I am positive. You see it all hangs together. That old maid person on the floor above, saw a young man come in, and I know it was Louis. Where was he at that time? I mean, where does he say he was?"

"I don't know. I haven't asked him. Oh, Ivy, he didn't?—he couldn't—"

"Maybe he could. Louis is not much on the strong-arm work, but he has desperate determination, and if he went there to get that money—and if Mr Gleason wouldn't give it to him—let me see—I suppose Gleason must have said that his condition was your acceptance of his suit!"

"I suppose so," Phyllis agreed. "He knew how I love Louis, and he often tried to get him to persuade me to do various things. Louis is my idol. I've always adored him. I really brought him up, for mother died when he was so little. We're far closer to one another than most brothers and sisters. Oh, Ivy, what can I do?"

"Hush, let me think. I wish I wasn't so sure Louis did the thing. But, you see, he was right there—johnny-on-the-spot! And he was mad—and he was desperate—and Mr Gleason's pistol was handy-by—and he was at the end of his rope—alone with him there—oh, of course, it was inevitable. How has he acted since?"

"Queerly," Phyllis admitted. "He's nervous and jumpy, and afraid of everybody."

"Of course he is. Well, Phyllis, he'll have to run away."

"Oh, no!"

"Yes, he will. It's all very well to be shocked at the idea, and to prefer to have him face the music—but the risk is too great! Even if he should be innocent—and he can't be—they'd put him through with bells on!"

"What do you mean?"

"I mean as soon as the police get Louis in their mind as a suspect, they'll pounce on him, and they'll fasten it on him, no matter what he says."

"Railroad him—"

"That's not quite the word. You don't know much about these things, do you? Railroad is a term they use about innocent suspects, and Louis—"

"Oh, Ivy, how can you? Stop! Don't you love him, too?"

"Oh, in a way. But it's enough of a way to want him to get off! I tell you he must vanish—disappear. And that big money must be paid, or those people will be after him. You know all about that deal?"

"Yes; and I may as well tell you, I was out that afternoon, in a taxicab with—with Bill Halsey."

"Halsey! You! Oh, you poor dear."

"Oh, he was respectful—very decent, in fact. He was to go with me to Mr Gleason—I was expected, you see—and I was to try to persuade Mr Gleason to pay that debt and free Louis from the sharks. I knew Mr Gleason's price would be my promise to marry him—and—I expected to pay."

"Well, why didn't you go to Gleason's?"

"Because—as we neared there, we saw Louis going in!"

"What time was that?"

"Oh, I don't know. It's all a horrid nightmare. I turned around and went right home. No, not right home; we drove around a bit, trying to decide what to do. Mr Halsey was nice; he said for me to follow up my brother or to wait developments, just as I chose. Of course, I said I'd wait and learn the result of Louis' visit—I knew what he went for."

"And since—since we know the result of Louis' visit, has Mr Halsey been after you?"

"Yes; but I told him that now the inheritance was mine, I'd pay him all Louis owes him just as soon as I could arrange it. He seemed satisfied, only he wants the money at once. So Mr Pollard is getting it for me."

"Well, anyway, Bill Halsey won't bother Louis about that. Now, I tell you, Phyllis, it's necessary that we get the boy away—smuggle him out of the country—"

"Out of the country!"

"Yes—Canada, Europe—anywhere. Or maybe it would be easier to hide him. Do you know of any country place—some friend's house—no, they'd find him. Oh, what can we do?"

"It's too big a question for us to handle. Two girls can't take care of a case like this. I'll ask Mr Pollard what to do."

"Yes, that's good. Mr Barry wouldn't be very capable—but Mr Pollard is."

"You know him?"

"Not personally. But I know he's a powerful and a wise man. He'll know just what to do. And as you're engaged to him—you'll want to tell him about Louis—or, won't you?"

"Why, yes—I suppose so. But how you take things for granted! I must see Louis first of all. Oh, Buddy, Buddy dear!"

In the meantime, Phyllis' mysterious disappearance was causing dismay and consternation in many hearts and minds.

Prescott, who had started out to find her, was looking everywhere, except in the home of Ivy Hayes.

Belknap, still at the Lindsay house, talked it over with Mrs Lindsay and Philip Barry and concluded that at last they were on the right track. He had no fears about finding the girl, for she could not disappear permanently. But it was a shock, and he was a little bewildered.

"Of course," he said, "disappearance is practically confession. Miss Lindsay must be found—can, probably, easily be found. But I am sorry."

"Sorry!" cried Millicent, "how you talk! You don't mean you think Phyllis killed my brother, do you?"

"You said that yourself, at first, Mrs Lindsay," Belknap reminded her.

"Only in the excitement of my first shock. Really, I was not quite responsible for what I said that night. Now, I know Phyllis couldn't have done it—"

"Why not?"

"A girl like that! Incredible."

"It has been done. It may be she was under great provocation."

"But, hold on, Belknap," Barry cried; "don't go too fast. What have you by way of evidence? Only that Miss Lindsay was seen in a taxicab with some man. What does that prove?"

"That there are some questions for Miss Lindsay to answer. I am not accusing her unheard. I want to hear her, to see her, to question her. And she has run away— which is, to say the least, a strange thing for her to do."

"Oh, she hasn't run away. There are dozens of plausible reasons for her sudden departure. And see here, Belknap, don't let your suspicions turn toward that girl. It's too ridiculous."

"It will bear investigation."

"Not even that. Since you've taken this attitude, I've decided to come through myself. I killed Robert Gleason."

Belknap looked at him. "Now, Mr Barry, that's too transparent. You're saying that to shield Miss Lindsay."

"Seems to me you'd better not jump at conclusions too continuously. And are you logical? You suspect Miss Lindsay with no evidence—only because she chanced to go out when you wanted to see her. Yet when I come and give myself up, you refuse to believe my confession. Can you not say, at least, that it needs investigation? Isn't it your habit to look into the matter of a serious confession?"

Belknap stared at him.

But Millicent Lindsay cried out: "Oh, Phil, I'm so sorry! Do you know, I felt it was you all along. And I like you so much! But when I learned about the letter you wrote to Robert—you did write it, didn't you?"

"Yes," said Barry.

"Well, as soon as I heard about that, I knew you did it. You never liked Robert, but that was mostly because you thought he would get Phyllis away from you. But to kill him! I can hardly believe it—and yet, I've felt sure of it for some time!"

The doorbell rang, and in a flurry of tears and agitation Millicent ran away to her own room.

The newcomer was Pollard, and as he entered he observed the serious attitude of the two men.

"What is it?" he asked, simply.

"I've just confessed to the Gleason murder," said Barry.

"What did you confess for?"

"Because I did it. What does any one confess for?"

"Usually because he didn't do it. The real murderer rarely confesses."

"Just what I think," Belknap said; "Mr Barry has an idea that Miss Lindsay will be accused, and he has confessed to prevent it."

"That it, Phil?" and Manning Pollard looked Barry squarely in the eyes.

"Take it any way you like, Pol," Barry said. "I make my confession, I give myself up—now let the law—if such a thing exists—take its course. And there's that letter. You know I wrote it, Pollard. You know I must have written it. There's no other possible theory. You know I left you about six—or a little before. You know I've no alibi—and there was time enough for me to go down to the Gleason place and get back for the dinner party."

"You rattle it off like a lesson, Phil. How did you go down there?"

Barry stared, but quickly said, "Taxi."

"Did no one see you go in?"

"Not that I know of. Shut up, Pollard."

Pollard shut up, and Belknap asked a long string of questions. These Barry answered, but even then, Belknap did not arrest him. The attorney went away, leaving the matter in abeyance, for, as a matter of fact, he had no idea Barry was telling the truth.

"Shielding somebody?" Pollard asked as soon as Belknap had gone.

Barry look at him. "I confessed," he said.

"Yes; I know. To shield Phyllis—or Louis?"

"Don't, Pol."

"Own up, old chap. Or perhaps you suspect them both."

"I do! How did you know? They were there together. There was trouble. Louis sent that telephone message— after the shooting—and he muddled it. It's all been a muddle ever since!"

"It surely has," agreed Pollard. "But I'm not sure you've chosen the best way to clear it up."

"Well, I had to. I can't see Phyllis dragged through a trial—and she would say or do anything to shield Louis. So I thought I'd throw myself into the breach."

"You've certainly done so—whether for good or ill."

CHAPTER 16: BUDDY

"Now that the money is paid, Phyllis, dear, and the whole matter is hushed up, Louis will never be suspected of having had anything to do with that Bill Halsey gang. It was a narrow escape—if the story had come out, it would have stained the boy's reputation badly. But, thanks to your quick action and watchful care, your brother is released from their clutches and you need worry about that no more."

"Thanks, too, to your kindness in letting me have the money. I will repay you just as soon as Mr Lane settles financial matters enough to give it to me out of my inheritance."

"No hurry about it. Instead of that, let's talk about ourselves. When are you going to let me give you a ring?"

"Oh, not yet," and Phyllis looked distressed. "Wait till this awful matter of the Gleason death is explained."

"Will it ever be?" Pollard spoke gravely, and added, "Do you want it to be?"

"Oh," she cried, "don't look like that! Do *you* suspect Louis, too? Buddy never did it! Never!"

"No, of course he didn't. Do you sometimes think Phil—"

"Philip Barry! No! He says he did, to shield my brother—"

"And you."

"Me!"

"Yes. Let's speak frankly, Phyllis. I can't bear to fence or quibble with you. Now, you know, you and Louis were there—"

"Oh, no, we weren't—well—maybe we were—oh, I don't know what I'm saying."

"Poor little girl. Don't try to make up stories to me. Tell me just how it was—or, don't tell me anything—as you wish, but don't tell me what isn't so. I can't help you if you do that."

Phyllis looked at him searchingly. She trusted him— and yet, she hesitated to put into words her own suspicions of Louis.

"I'm sure Phil Barry is shielding some one else," she began.

"But, dear, that letter—how could that have been written, except by Barry?"

"Now, don't you prevaricate to me!" she cried; "you know whatever is the explanation of the letter, Phil Barry isn't guilty!"

"I don't know any such thing! If Barry wrote the letter, he must have meant something by it, and until he is proved innocent, there's good reason for suspecting him."

"Don't you suspect Louis?" Phyllis asked directly, facing Pollard with a straightforward gaze.

"Don't ask me, dear. If I did—if I do—I wouldn't say so, because—because I love you. Confide in me—please do, darling. If you suspect your brother, tell me so, and I'll do all I can to divert suspicion from him."

"Even if you think him guilty?"

"Certainly. If Louis did it—he was blinded by rage, or, moved by a sudden homicidal impulse born of desperation—"

"But that doesn't excuse him."

"Not to the law—but to me, he is excused because he is your brother—"

"Yes, my brother—my little Buddy—oh, Manning, I can't face it!"

"You weren't there, too—at the time?"

"At the time of the murder? Oh, no!" Phyllis' eyes were wide with horror.

"Do you know that Louis was there?"

Pollard pressed the question, glad that Phyllis had abandoned pretense, and was telling truths.

"Yes, I do." The pained eyes looked beseechingly into his. "I have the evidence of an eye-witness—or, nearly."

"What do you mean by nearly?"

"Why, somebody else was there, who didn't see Louis, but who heard him—or, rather, heard Mr Gleason talking to him."

"Is that all? Phyllis, that isn't enough to convict Louis!"

"Isn't it? But, if they accuse him—he'll break down and confess. I know Buddy; as soon as a breath of suspicion touches him he'll go all to pieces—"

"Whether he's guilty or not?"

Phyllis stared. "Why, no, of course not if he isn't guilty. Oh, Manning, do you think he isn't? Tell me you do!"

"I wish I could, darling. But, I do say, there's no real evidence and we may be able to prevent any from coming to light. Even if Louis was there, didn't he leave before the time of the attack?"

"I don't know. I can't find out. I daren't mention it to him. Oh, Buddy, dear—I'm sure you never did it!"

"I'm sure, too," said Pollard, decidedly, and, whatever was in his mind there was conviction in his tone. "Now, see here, Phyllis, let's do nothing in the matter. As near as I can make out, Barry's confession is not believed at all by the police. They are sure he's shielding some one, but they don't know who it is. Of course, Barry won't tell, so Louis is safe."

"But suppose they do come to believe Phil, and he is arrested!"

"Not a chance."

"But if they should?"

"Would you care so much?" Pollard spoke softly, and tenderly. "If it should mean Louis' safety—"

"At the expense of an innocent man? Oh, impossible!"

"But you love Buddy—"

"I do, yes—but if he is guilty—nobody else can be allowed to suffer in his place. Least of all, Phil Barry."

Phyllis said the name, with a gentler light in her eyes, a softer inflection of her voice, and Pollard felt a sudden chill at his heart.

"What do you mean by that?" he asked, quietly, "anything especial?"

"No—oh, no," but Phyllis blushed.

"Remember, dear, you're engaged to me," Pollard said, smiling at her. "I resent such implications of any other interest of yours."

"You resent my interest in Phil Barry! Why, I thought he was your best friend."

"He is. But he can't be yours. Not your best friend—only second-best."

"Well, he's too dear a friend for me to let any undeserved suspicion fall on him," and Phyllis' eyes shone with righteous indignation.

"First, we must be sure it is undeserved."

"Very well, I will make sure!"

With a determined gesture, Phyllis pushed a bell button and a maid responded.

"Ask Mr Lindsay to come here," Phyllis directed, and then turning to Pollard with a pretty gesture of confidence, she said:

"Let's work together, Manning. You see what you think of the way Louis meets my questions. I've decided to meet the issue straight."

"What is it, Sis?" asked Louis, coming into the room. "What do you want of me? Hello, Pollard, how are you?"

"Buddy, dear," Phyllis began, "where were you the day Mr Gleason died?"

"Out with it Phyl. Do you think I killed him?"

Louis looked at his sister. The boy was haggard, pale and worried looking, but he met her eye and awaited her answer to his question.

"No, Louis, I can't think so—but there are circumstances that make it appear possible, and I want your word."

"Well, then, Phyllis, I didn't do it."

Calmly the brother gazed at the sister. Anxiously, Phyllis scanned the well-known face, the affectionate eyes, the sensitive, quivering mouth, but though agitated, Louis had himself well in hand, and his frank speech carried conviction.

Phyllis drew a long breath.

"I believe you, Buddy," she said.

Pollard was quiet for a moment, and then observed, "All right, Lindsay. And, in that case, you're probably willing to tell all about your presence there that afternoon. Why haven't you done so?"

Pollard's tone was not accusing so much as one of friendly inquiry, and Louis, after a moment's hesitation, replied:

"Why, Pol, I suppose I was a coward. I was afraid, if I admitted I was in Gleason's place that afternoon, I might be suspected of the crime—and I'm innocent—before God, I am."

The solemn voice rang true, and Phyllis clasped his hand as she said, "I know it, Buddy, I know you never did it!"

"But, if it comes out I was there, I can't help being suspected," Louis went on, a look of terror coming to his face. "I—oh, I hate to confess it, but I *am* afraid. Not afraid of justice—but afraid I'll be accused of something I didn't do!"

"You would, too, Louis," Pollard said. "Better keep still about the whole matter, I think. You see, Louis, except for the murderer, you are probably the last one who saw Gleason alive. Now, that, in itself is troublesome evidence, especially if the murderer doesn't turn up. That is why, I think, my theory of the stranger from the West is undoubtedly the true one. You see, none of the people hereabouts—I mean you, Barry, Davenport, myself, or any of us Club men could have been down there so late, and then turned up here for the dinner party. Of course, that would have been possible, but highly improbable. While an outsider, a man known to Gleason but not to any of use, could have come and gone at will."

"He had to reach the Gleason apartment soon after Buddy left," Phyllis mused, thinking it out. "Well, Manning, I'm convinced of Buddy's innocence. My boy can't lie to me! I know him too well. He is worried and anxious about the suspicions that may attach to him, but he's absolutely innocent of crime, aren't you, dear?"

And Louis looked into his sister's face, and quietly replied, "Yes, Phyllis," and she believed him.

"Now," she said, "I'm going to free Phil Barry."

"You!" exclaimed Pollard. "Are you going to turn detective?"

"I'm going to help the detectives work," she declared. "Or, rather, I'm going to get a detective that can work. I don't think much of what has been accomplished so far. I'm going to get another detective—"

"A private detective?" asked Pollard. "Better be careful, dear. Don't get mixed up in this thing too deeply."

"No, I won't. I'm not going to do anything myself. But, I want to tell you something. Ivy Hayes knows of a girl—"

"Ivy Hayes!" exclaimed Louis, while Pollard raising his eyebrows, murmured, "A girl!"

"I seem to have exploded two bombshells!" said Phyllis, smiling.

She was in better spirits now, since the assurance of Louis that he was not guilty.

"But it is the truth. Ivy Hayes knows of a girl detective—"

"Oh, Phyllis, don't!" begged Pollard. "A private detective is bad enough—but a girl one! Please don't."

"But she's a wonder—Ivy says so."

"Sister, for goodness' sake, don't tell me you know Ivy Hayes!"

"Certainly I do, Louis. If you may know her why can't I? And I like her, too. And she'll get this person for me, and I know Millicent will agree—"

"Quite a feminine bunch," Pollard laughed. "Do you think you and Mrs Lindsay and Miss Hayes and the girl sleuth can succeed where several men have failed?"

"That's just what I do think," cried Phyllis, triumphantly. "This is the era of feminine achievement, and why not in detection as well as in other lines?"

"Have it your own way," said Pollard, looking at her fondly. "I must go now, but if I can help you—though, being a mere man, I suppose I can't—"

"Oh, yes, you can," Phyllis smiled at him. "I'll be only too glad to call upon you for assistance." Pollard left, and Phyllis at once called Ivy on the telephone to get more information about the girl detective.

"Oh, it isn't a girl!" Ivy replied; "that is, it is a girl, but it's a man, too. They're associated, you see. Of course, the man is the head of the firm—but the girl, who is his assistant, does quite as much of the work as he does. And, she's my friend, that's why I spoke of her as the detective. But he's the one to call on. He's Pennington Wise—they call him Penny Wise—how could they help it! Well, he's your man, and she's your girl. I used to know her, when we were both kids, and I don't see her often nowadays, but we're good friends, and she's a wonder."

"You're a wonder, too, Ivy," Phyllis said; "thank you lots and heaps. Give me the address, and I'll excuse you."

Ivy gave the number, and Phyllis went at once and told the story to Millicent.

"Oh, do get him!" cried Mrs Lindsay. "I've heard of Penny Wise—he's a wizard! I don't know anything about his girl assistant—but that doesn't matter. Penny Wise is great! I've often heard of him. He's frightfully expensive, but they say he never loses a case. But, Phyllis, I never suspected Louis! How could you think I did! But—don't faint now—I do suspect Phil Barry!"

"It doesn't matter much whom you suspect to-day, Millicent, it will be somebody else to-morrow! Aren't you about due to suspect me again?"

"You! oh, Phyllis, don't remind me of the foolish things I said, when I was hysterical and almost crazy! You know how you'd feel if Louis had been killed! You'd suspect anybody!"

"All right, Millicent, I'll forget it. But I don't believe for one minute that Philip Barry is the guilty man."

"You don't! Why, Phyllis, I thought you did!"

"Oh, I don't know what I think," and Phyllis broke down and sobbed.

"There, there, dear child," Millicent soothed her. "Don't cry. You're all worried to pieces. Now, let's get the Wise man, and then you shift all care and anxiety on to him."

"But, Millicent, suppose he should prove it to be Phil!"

"If it is Phil, he ought to be shown up. We can't stop now, for sentiment or preference. We must go ahead and prove positively who is the criminal."

When Millicent took the tone of an avenging justice, she was almost humorous, so ill did the role fit her. But she was in earnest, and she immediately set to work to engage the services of Pennington Wise.

Her efforts were vain, however, as the detective politely informed her that his press of business would not permit him to take on another case at present.

Greatly disappointed, she told Phyllis, who at once told Ivy Hayes, over the telephone, of her defeat.

"Huh," said the young woman, "won't come, won't he? Well, I guess he will. Expect him this evening, to talk over the preliminaries."

For the sanguine Ivy felt sure her childhood friend could somehow persuade the great detective to meet the engagement she had just committed him to.

"Zizi," Miss Hayes later remarked, to her friend, "You just simply got to take on the Gleason case. You hear me?"

"Hear you perfectly," Zizi's engaging little voice replied. "But—"

"No buts. You just do it. Why, Ziz, it's all mixed up with friends of mine. And say, dearie, I want you to do it for old times' sake."

"But, Ivy, truly—"

"Truly you will? All right, Ziz. You make Penny Wise stand around—you fix it somehow—and you send him or go yourself to the Lindsay home this evening at eight o'clock. Love and kisses. Your own Ivy."

Ivy hung up the receiver, satisfied that if her friend didn't or couldn't meet her wishes, she would call her up and tell her so. Not hearing from Zizi, Ivy concluded all was going well.

And it was. Zizi, the wonderful little assistant of the great detective, coaxed and finally persuaded him to take the case, assuring him that she, herself, would do most of the work. She put it on the grounds of a personal favor to herself, and as this was so unusual a condition as to be almost unique, Pennington Wise gave in.

And so, promptly at eight, he presented himself at the Lindsays' and was received with welcome.

For an hour Wise listened to the accounts of the case from the three Lindsays. No one else was present, and Wise asked them to tell him all they could, both of direct evidence or their own leanings or suspicions.

The detective was a man of great personal magnetism. Tall and strong, his very bearing inspired confidence and hope. His face was fine and mobile, his wavy chestnut hair, brushed over back, was fine and thick, and his keen blue eyes took in everything without any undue curiosity.

He was both receptive and responsive, and in an hour he had the history of the case, clearly and definitely in his mind.

"Now, then," he said, "we can admit of several suspects already. There was a motive, let us say, for any one who benefited by Mr Gleason's will. That includes Mr and Miss as well as Mrs Lindsay."

Millicent frowned at him. "Me!" she cried, explosively.

"I only say you benefited by the will," said Wise, mildly. "I have as much right to mention your name as those of the other two."

"Louis didn't get anything from the will," said Phyllis.

"He did, in a way," the detective returned. "You're so fond of your brother, that whatever is yours, is pretty much the same as belonging to him. Now, I'm not going to consider you two ladies as suspects at all. But Mr Lindsay's cause I shall look into."

Louis colored, angrily, and was about to make a sharp retort, when the kindness of Wise's expression caught his notice, and he suddenly decided he'd like to be friends with the detective.

"Look into it all you like," he said, with an air of relief at giving his troubles over to this capable person. "I'm glad to have you. You see, Mr Wise, I was there so fearfully close to the time of the crime, that I've been afraid to have it known how close."

"Don't be afraid, my boy. If you're guilty I'll find it out, anyway; and if not, you've more to gain than lose by being frank and honest."

"Who are your other suspects?" Phyllis asked, anxiously.

"Everybody," said Wise, smiling at her. "First, Doctor Davenport—"

"Oh, no!"

"First, Doctor Davenport, because, he first raised the alarm. Next, Mr Pollard, because he declared an intention of killing Mr Gleason. Next, Mr Monroe, because—"

"Dean Monroe!" exclaimed Louis, "why he has never been thought of!"

"That's the answer!" said Wise. "He was in that group who discussed murder that afternoon, he went away, his subsequent movements have not been traced, and, as you say, he's never been questioned or even thought of in the matter. Therefore, I investigate his case."

"And Philip Barry?" Phyllis could hold back the question no longer.

"Ah, yes, Mr Barry." Pennington Wise looked at her. "You are interested in him? Especially? Forgive me if I seem intrusive. I am not really, but I have to know some things to know how to go about others."

"Miss Lindsay is engaged to Mr Pollard," Millicent informed the inquirer. "She's a firm friend of Mr Barry's, but, I think you ought to know that Manning Pollard is her fiance."

"Yes," Phyllis said, as Wise asked the question by a glance. "I am engaged to Mr Pollard, but I don't want Mr Barry suspected."

"Not if he did it?"

"He didn't do it."

"But the letter? He wrote that?"

"No; he did not."

"He says he did. It is signed by him. It is in keeping with his nature and his attitude toward Mr Gleason. Why do you say he didn't write it?"

"I don't know, Mr Wise. I have a feeling, a conviction that somebody forged that letter."

"But how would that be possible?"

"I don't know. I can't tell you. But I'm sure."

"I haven't seen the letter yet, Miss Lindsay," Pennington Wise looked at her reflectively. "And until I do, I can't speak positively. But I've read up this case, more or less, and I can't see how a forgery could pass the experts as this has done. I incline to think it is genuine. But it need not have implied murder at all."

"No," repeated Phyllis, "he didn't write it. I know he didn't."

"If he didn't, trust me to find it out," Wise reassured her. And, as they heard the bell ring, "I dare say that's my little assistant. She agreed to come later. I want you to like her."

"I know I shall," said Phyllis, enthusiastically; "I've heard about her from Miss Hayes."

And in another moment Zizi appeared in the doorway.

Chapter 17: Zizi

"Mrs Lindsay?" Zizi said, by way of interrogative greeting, and, with a second nod to Louis, she crossed the room and sat down by Phyllis.

"Miss Lindsay," and the visitor took both Phyllis' hands in her own. "I am so glad to know you. May I help you?"

"Oh, I hope you can," Phyllis said, fascinated by the strange child.

For Zizi looked like a child. Little, slim, and of a lithe, nervous personality, her big, dark eyes gazed into Phyllis' with an expression of intense interest in her and her affairs.

"You're troubled," she went on, as Phyllis responded to her evident friendliness. "But it will be all right; Pennington Wise will clear up the mystery and you will be glad again."

"You queer little thing!" Millicent exclaimed. "Turn around here and let me look at you."

Zizi, turned, smiling, her white teeth just showing between her scarlet lips, her eyes dancing, cheeks glowing, and her black hair muffed over her ears—a highly-colored picture of vivid, restless vitality.

"Yes, Mrs Lindsay," she responded in her low, yet clear voice, "and please like me, for I'm going to stay here."

"Stay here!"

"Yes, please, during the investigation. Mr Wise will come and go, but I have to be here all the time."

"Why, certainly—of course, if you wish—"

"Good!" Louis cried; "glad to have you stay, Miss—"

"Zizi," she said, "just Zizi." And the smile she flashed on Louis was the complete undoing of that impressionable young man.

"And now to business," Zizi went on, her manner changing subtly from the witch-like, fascinating child to the energetic young woman. "Tell me things."

"We've already told Mr Wise about the case—" Millicent began.

"Not the kind of things you tell him—other things. About this Mr Barry, now. Has he a high temper?"

Phyllis stared-What had Phil Barry's temper to do with the murder of Robert Gleason?

"You see," Zizi explained, "if he had, the note might have meant he'd kill his rival—if not it might have meant a lesser threat."

"He has a high temper," Phyllis admitted, reluctantly; "I may as well say so, for others would tell you that. He's a mild, equable nature as long as things go his way. But if he's thwarted or crossed, even in trifles, he flies in a rage at once. I oughtn't to say this—"

"Because it seems to incriminate him," Zizi nodded her little head; "but I compel the truth—don't I?" she smiled at Phyllis. "I'll bet you wouldn't have said that to any other detective. Well, now, with the knowledge that Mr Barry is quick tempered, that he was jealous of Mr Gleason and that he wrote the threatening letter, and that he has given no positive account of what he was doing at the critical moment—shall we suspect him? Answer, no."

"Why?" Phyllis spoke breathlessly, relieved but anxious to know more.

"Well, principally for the reason that he has confessed."

"Don't murderers ever confess?" Louis asked, his eyes on the beautiful young thing that was of a type hitherto unknown in his experience.

Zizi was not really beautiful, but her magnetic charm was so great, her ways so winsome, and her mysterious eyes so full of changing expression and half-veiled witchery that she enthralled them all.

Wise watched her. He was accustomed to have his clients surprised at his strange little assistant, but oftener they were critical than wholly admiring. Tonight, however, Zizi was at her best—she was more than usually attractive, and her manner was gentler than she often chose to make it.

"Oh, yes," she said, in reply to Louis' query, "but you have to know why they confess. You see Mr Barry confessed to shield some one else."

"Who?" Louis asked, but he flushed and looked embarrassed.

"You know who," Zizi returned, "and maybe it wasn't only yourself, but Phyllis, too. You see—you must see, all of you, that the situation is serious. Louis was there very shortly before the crime took place. Phyllis is said to have been there—whether she was or not—no one can be found who saw or spoke to Mr Gleason after that—so it would be just like the detectives to fasten the crime on one or both of the Lindsays. Anyway, that's the way it looked to Mr Barry, and in his quick tempered—which means impulsive way—he gave himself up. Although he is as innocent of the crime as you two are."

"My goodness!" Millicent exclaimed, "you start out by clearing all those who have been suspected!"

"Not all. There still remain several of the Club men— also the possibility of a stranger—I mean a stranger to you people who are interested. Mrs Lindsay, where did your brother live before he went to Seattle?"

"In a little village in New Hampshire—Coggs' Hollow."

"Lovely name! Did you live there, too?"

"No; I lived in Ohio with my parents. An uncle, my mother's brother, took Robert to live with him, in New Hampshire, when the boy was quite small. That's why Robert and I never saw much of each other. We were affectionate enough when we met, but living apart, we

were not really intimate. I was surprised when he came
East, and we renewed our family relations. Then—"

"Then he fell in love with Phyllis"—Zizi interrupted.
"And it wasn't reciprocated."

"Quite true," Phyllis said, calmly.

"Yes," Millicent agreed, "it was really love at first
sight. And as Phyllis had any number of suitors, Robert
tried to cut them out by promises of such luxuries and
dazzling prospects as his wealth could offer. But Phyllis
couldn't seem to bring herself to say yes—"

"But she had, hadn't she?" Zizi didn't look at Phyllis.
"Wasn't the dinner party to be an announcement?"

Millicent shrugged her shoulders.

"I don't know," she said: "ask her."

Zizi turned. "How about it, Phyllis?"

"I don't know, either," Phyllis said, slowly. "I had half
promised—because—oh, why not tell? because Mr
Gleason had promised me a lot of money—which I very
much needed—at once—if I would make the
announcement that night."

"Go on, tell it all," Pennington Wise put in; "you
wanted that money—"

"To pull me out of a desperate hole," Louis burst forth.
"I got in bad—very bad—with some gamblers and some
loan sharks—and Sis was good enough to try to get me
out of it. She—she didn't have to marry old Gleason—
even if she did announce an engagement."

"Hush, Buddy," said Phyllis, looking at him
reprovingly; "I never thought of saying yes to him, and
backing out afterward. I wouldn't do such a thing. But I
planned to go there that afternoon and try once more to
persuade him to give me the money, without a definite
promise on my part. I hoped that for the sake of Louis'
good name I could persuade him. But—I didn't go."

"Never mind all that," Zizi said, impatiently, "it won't
get us anywhere to mull over that. Now, Penny Wise,
here's where I stand. All people here present are innocent
of this crime. Philip Barry—I think—is also innocent. I've

no reason to suspect a stranger—an acquaintance of Mr Gleason's—and I think if there were such an individual, there must have been some trace of him. People don't glide in and out of a situation like shadows."

"Go slow, Ziz," cautioned the detective, looking at her thoughtfully. "Keep your imagination in leash."

"Yes, sir," and she bowed with mock docility. "Now, if you'll excuse me, I have to go to Coggs' Hollow."

"To-night!" gasped Millicent, as Zizi rose, and began pulling on her gloves.

"Yes; there's a train at midnight, I can easily catch it. Good-by, all."

She drew her cloak together and fastened it, and held out her hand to Wise with a demanding gesture.

Understandingly, he took out his pocketbook, and gave it to her without a word.

She tucked it into her roomy handbag, and turned to the door.

"I'll go with you," Louis cried, already in the hall, and getting into his overcoat.

"To the station? Thank you," Zizi smiled.

"No; all the way. To New Hampshire."

"Nixy!" she laughed, flashing her white teeth. "He travels the fastest who travels alone. But I'll be glad to have you entrain me."

The two went out together, and hailing a taxicab, Louis delightedly put Zizi in.

"Anyway, I'll have you to myself for an hour," he exulted. "What are you, I can't make you out. A sprite, a witch, an elf?"

"Oh, yes, all those things, and a girl beside. And you needn't fall in love with me—it would be a foolishness."

"But I've already fallen."

"Oh, well, all right. It doesn't matter." Zizi was absorbed in thought, and seemed really to care nothing at all for Louis' state of mind.

Meantime, Millicent was demanding of Pennington Wise an explanation of the astonishing Zizi.

"Don't worry about her," he said, smiling. "Don't think about her. She never does a wrong thing—in detective work, I mean. She will some day—I daresay—and it may be she has now. But she acts on impulse, on intuition, on what some people call a hunch. And I've never known her to slip up. She is a wonder—but don't try to understand her—for you can't."

"But will she go to New Hampshire—all alone by herself? At night!"

"Oh, yes, and she'll take care of herself."

"Louis will go with her," Phyllis said, "I know he will."

"No, Miss Lindsay, you're mistaken there. Zizi won't let your brother accompany her."

"I'm sure it would be all right," Millicent observed; "at work on a case, you know."

"Right enough, but Zizi won't let him go because she doesn't want him to. Now, as to Mr Gleason's will. Did you two ladies know about its terms?"

"We weren't certain," Millicent said, "for my brother changed it quite often. He was ready to settle a large amount on Phyllis at once if she would consent to marry him, but he had already made a will leaving his fortune equally divided between us two. He never liked Louis, rather, he disapproved of him. Of late, Louis has run wild—"

"It isn't his fault," Phyllis defended; "he has been duped and deluded by a lot of men with whom he had no business to associate at all. But let's leave Louis out of it, for Mr Wise has declared he doesn't suspect him, and he is in no other way concerned in this business."

"That's true, Miss Lindsay. Now, tell me, did Mr Gleason contemplate changing his will again in case Miss Lindsay refused him definitely?"

"Yes, he did," Phyllis stated; "he told me unless I made the announcement at the dinner party, he would change his will and cut me out of it entirely."

"Did he, then, assume that you could be bought in that fashion."

Phyllis colored, but she replied, "Yes, he did. But, mostly because he knew how desperately I wanted money for my brother. And, too, it isn't a gracious thing to say— but Mr Gleason was not such an attractive man that he had much reason for being accepted outside of his wealth."

"I see; and he had made the existing will recently?"

"Within a month or so."

"Who knew of it?"

"No one, I believe," Millicent said, "but Phyllis and Louis and myself—except, of course, the lawyer who drew it."

"Mr Fred Lane?"

"Yes."

"Wasn't he one of that group of men who were discussing murder at the Club that day?"

"Yes," Millicent looked inquiringly at him; "but you don't dream that Mr Lane—"

"Why not?"

"Oh, nonsense, Fred Lane and my brother were good friends."

"At any rate, it is to the men of that group that I shall first direct my investigations. Few of them really liked Mr Gleason. Forgive me, if I seem unkind, Mrs Lindsay, but I cannot work if trammeled by too great consideration for your feelings."

"Don't stop for that, Mr Wise. I quite understand. And I know my brother was not a favorite with the Club men. He was too different. He was out of the picture. They had little in common. Now, in so far as that is of assistance to you in forming your theories, use it, for it is quite true. My brother was a far better and worthier man than most of them, but his ways were different and he did not show to advantage when among them. If Phyllis could have cared for Robert he could have made her very happy, I know. But that's all past. What I want now, is to avenge my brother's death. To discover and punish his murderer, no matter who he may be. I beg of you, Mr Wise, spare no time, pains or expense to ferret him out."

"Indeed I shall not. Can you think of any grievance or reason for enmity toward Mr Gleason on the part of those men I refer to?"

"Only one reason, Mr Wise, and that applies to several. They were jealous of his attentions to Miss Lindsay."

"Oh, Millicent!" Phyllis cried, in protest.

"It is true. Miss Lindsay is a belle, and all the men of that group were her admirers—or almost all. Doctor Davenport, is, of course, excepted, and Mr Lane. They are married men."

"Leaving Mr Barry, Mr Pollard and Mr Monroe."

"Yes; and they surely cannot be suspected. You have declared Mr Barry innocent, Mr Pollard was in his own home at the time of the crime, and Dean Monroe—why, he hasn't even been thought of."

"Has he been inquired of as to his whereabouts at the time?"

"I don't know, I'm sure. Has he, Phyllis?"

"I don't know. But it's silly to think of Dean! Why, he scarcely knew Mr Gleason."

"But he is devoted to you?" Wise asked the question so casually that Phyllis answered, frankly, "Yes, he is. That is, he has asked me to marry him."

"And you refused?"

"I did. But, Mr Wise, is it necessary to tell you such things?"

"It is, Miss Lindsay. I fully believe that you are the innocent cause of this murder. This attaches no blame to you, in any way, but it makes it imperative for me to learn these details. Probably nine crimes out of ten are committed because of a woman—so don't let it disturb you."

"Not disturb me!" Phyllis cried; "of course it disturbs me! If there are women so foolishly vain as to enjoy

stirring up strife among their admirers, I am not of that
sort. I wish I were dead!"

"There, now, Phyllis," Millicent said, "don't act like
that. I, too, believe the murderer was somebody who was
jealous of Robert because of you, but you can't help that.
I'm sure my brother had no enemy who would come from
the West to kill him."

"You can't be sure of such a thing as that, but we can
prove up where the people were who might be suspected
here."

Methodically Wise went about the job.

Although he had told the Lindsays he was sure of
Philip Barry's innocence, none the less did he look into
his alibi.

And it seemed to be all right. The doorman and the
desk clerk at the small hotel where he lived were almost
certain that he had came in that afternoon, just about six,
as he said he did. They were not willing to swear to it, but
they were reasonably certain, and Wise felt pretty sure
they were right.

Next he went to the nearby hotel where Pollard lived.

"Yes, sir," declared the doorman there, "I saw Mr
Pollard come in—he nodded to me just like he always
does. And later, I saw him when he went out again. I put
him into his taxi myself."

"At what time, about?"

"No about about it. It was just twenty-five minutes to
seven—"

"How do you know?"

"I'll tell you how I know. Mr Pollard glanced at his
wrist watch as he got into the cab. It had a radium dial,
and I saw it plain."

"Mr Pollard wears a wrist watch, then?"

"Yes, he's worn it ever since the war. Got used to it
over there, I s'pose. Well, anyway, that's what happened,
so—if the watch was correct—it was seven-twenty-five."

"Good," said Wise. "And, as I understand it, one or two people saw Mr Pollard in his room, or heard him telephone during the hour or so he was here?"

"Yes, sir," the desk clerk rehearsed the story a little wearily. The employees of the hotel had told the tale often, for owing to Manning Pollard's threat—which had passed into history—he was frequently being suspected by somebody, detective or amateur, and the hotel people had been called upon to rehearse the story until they were letter perfect in their parts.

Next, Pennington Wise investigated the doings of Dean Monroe.

And the result was that he learned that Monroe had gone from the Club that day straight to the home of his mother, and had remained with her until so late that he had to make great haste dressing for dinner in order to reach the Lindsay house on time.

"H'm," said Penny Wise, profoundly, to himself; "h'm."

Three days later, Zizi returned. She went to Wise's apartment before going to the Lindsay house.

"Find out much?" he asked her, as she flung off her wraps, and deposited her small person in a very large easy chair.

"I sure did! But I'm glad to get back! New England is no paradise in winter. Get me something to eat, there's a bright Penny."

"All right," and Wise rang a bell. "Take your time, Ziz, but have a little pity on a mere man, consumed with curiosity."

"I will. Coggs' Hollow is exactly what its name sounds like. A tiny, primitive village, just the same now as it was a quarter of a century ago, when Robert Gleason lived there, with his uncle."

"You found people who knew him, then?"

"I did."

"Could they throw any light on the murder—or its cause?"

"Not light—but a sort of a glimmer of a glow of a hint of dawn."

"Good! That's enough. You succeeded, then!"

"Oh, yes; and, Penny Wise, whom do you suppose I saw up there, also nosing about?"

"Who?"

"Mr Manning Pollard."

"Ziz, you're crazy. He wasn't there. I've seen him myself every day you've been gone."

"Seen him! Seen Manning Pollard? Penny, *you're* crazy!"

CHAPTER 18: THE LUMINOUS FACE

"No, Zizi, my child, I'm not crazy. And, as a matter of fact, I suppose you're not, either. Now, what do you mean by thinking you saw Pollard in New Hampshire when I know he was here in New York?"

"First, you tell me what you mean by thinking he was here in New York when I saw him in Coggs' Hollow?"

"Saw him? and talked with him?"

"No; I didn't see him to speak to—but I saw him."

"Where was he?"

"Walking along the street."

"Did he see you?"

"Yes."

"Did he speak to you, or bow?"

"Oh, no; he doesn't know me!"

"How do you know him?"

"I don't. But I've seen his picture—both in the paper and at Miss Lindsay's, and, as you know yourself, he's unmistakable. Nobody could take any one else for Manning Pollard! Why, that face is of a type not often seen. And his physique, and his big, square shoulders— why, Penny, I know it was he."

"Well, Ziz, I don't say it wasn't, but we must puzzle out how he got up there and why he went."

"What have you done here while I was away?"

"I've found out all about the Barry letter for one thing."

"Tell me."

"A cleverly contrived thing. It was originally written in vanishing ink and Barry signed it in real ink. Then, when the vanishing ink vanished, the perpetrator of the precious scheme filled in the typed letter above the signature."

"Clever! What was the original document?"

"It was a testimonial or something of the sort to a Club servant. Head Steward, or somebody, and this testimonial was arranged for him. Barry remembers being asked to sign and remembers signing. Then he forgot all about it."

"Weren't others to sign?"

"Barry thought so, but the matter was never carried on."

"H'm. Who asked Barry to sign?"

"Dean Monroe."

"How he continues to crop up! Is he the murderer?"

"Now, look here, Zizi, we're up against an enormously interesting case. It's simple up to a certain point, and then it's inexplicable. The murderer is one of the cleverest men on this planet. For, look. He arranged that letter deliberately, fixed up the Club servant scheme, to get Philip Barry's signature on a blank sheet of paper. Having that, he later wrote in whatever he chose. His cleverness consisted, at this point, in not overdoing. Had he made the letter a threat of murder, it would have looked false on the face of it, for Barry is not like that. Well, he had this letter ready to plant in Gleason's desk after he had committed his crime—and he did so. Next, he left no fingerprints on the telephone or on the revolver, save those of Gleason himself. Was that clever?"

"Oh, Penny, it was! And he made the prints on the telephone with Mr Gleason's fingers after Mr Gleason was dead! And he did the telephoning himself!"

"Yes; how quick you are, Zizi! That's exactly what happened, because that's the only way it could have been. Now, a man clever enough for all that is clever enough for anything. Yet I can't see how he did it. Nor do I grasp his motive."

"Jealous of Phyllis?"

"That isn't enough to account for the crime."

"No, it isn't! He had another motive, and I've found it out. I found out up in Coggs' Hollow."

"Going to tell me?"

"You bet I am! Right away. How did you guess the man?"

"I didn't guess. I deduced from his alibi. Such a clever villain—what would he naturally choose by way of alibi?"

"Just what he did do. Pretend not to have any—but when they investigate, they find he has a cast-iron one!"

"Exactly, and Manning Pollard's was all that. But I can't see how he managed it."

"There's only one way. He must have had a confederate who did the killing."

"No; a clever criminal doesn't have a confederate. No; Pollard killed Gleason himself. By the way, Zizi, I found Pollard's fingerprints on the Barry letter."

"But Dean Monroe did that."

"Dean Monroe asked Barry to sign it, but—he told me himself—Pollard gave him the paper and asked him to get Barry's signature. This, Monroe did, and gave the paper back to Pollard. Later, Pollard told Monroe the plan had been given up. I dug that all out, without speaking to Barry about it. I don't want Pollard to imagine we suspect him. Now, my child, what was his motive?"

"A pretty strong one. It seems that Manning Pollard is an illegitimate child. He was born in Coggs' Hollow, of unmarried parents. Later, his father and mother married, so he was legally legitimized. But of course, a stigma remains. Now, Mr Pollard is several years younger than Robert Gleason, so the assumption is that Robert Gleason, who lived all his boyhood in Coggs' Hollow, knew this secret of Pollard's birth, and had threatened to expose him, unless he desisted from trying to win Phyllis away from Gleason."

Pennington Wise thought a few moments.

"That's it," he said, at last; "that's it, Zizi. You're a wonderful child for sure! How did you get it?"

"I went straight to the town clerk, and he not only showed me his books, but he told me the story. He knows nothing of the Gleason murder, and I didn't tell him. Up in that little dot of a village they don't know the news of New York."

"But they must know of Gleason's death. He was a foremost citizen, wasn't he?"

"Of Seattle, yes. But when he left Coggs' Hollow he was a young man of twenty-five or so, and I suppose they've forgotten all about him. Anyway, the town clerk didn't remember him very clearly, but he remembered all about the Pollard family. Of course, it was a celebrated case up there.

"The fact of the couple's marriage, five or six years after Manning Pollard's birth, was a sensational affair, and though nobody could blame Mr Pollard, the fact remains that he was really an illegitimate child."

"And, knowing this, Gleason probably was quite ready to tell it, and so—"

"And so, Pollard made it impossible for him to tell. Now, Penny Wise, that's a fine theory, a noble deduction—but, how did Pollard commit that murder when he was at home in his hotel? Like you, I can't see him employing a gunman. Rather, I see him going there to plead with Gleason to spare him. Then, when Gleason refused, in the heat of passion, Pollard shot him."

"But the carefully prepared letter from Barry proves premeditation."

"That's so. And, remember his threat to kill Gleason. Would he have said that, if he had really intended to kill him?"

"I think so. I've thought all along, that Pollard's bravado was his hope of escape. He would argue that a man who made such a threat would not be suspected. And, quite as he calculated, everybody said, 'oh, if he had meant to kill Gleason, he never would have advertised his intention.' That was a bold stroke, but an efficacious one. Yet, we can't be right, Zizi, for he was at home. I've been to the hotel again. I've tabulated all his movements. He did go home at six, he did go out again at seven-twenty-five, and during that time he was in his room, because he telephoned twice, and he talked to the bellboy. And these three circumstances were at intervals of twenty minutes or so, therefore, he couldn't have been down in Washington Square at all. After he got into his taxi, the driver accounts for his every movement until he reached the Lindsay house at dinner time. So, there's his alibi."

"Perfect."

"Yes, that's the trouble—"

"Now, don't say, 'distrust the perfect alibi,' Penny, for that's a platitude and a silly one, too. Your innocent man has a perfect alibi. He may or may not remember it, but it's perfect all the same. Now, this alibi of Pollard's is, to all appearances, the alibi of an innocent man. He has that secret of his past, Gleason did know it, that makes a motive. He did, as you say, fix up the Barry letter— though that may not be quite true—"

"What do you mean by that, Ziz?"

"I mean perhaps somebody else worked the vanishing ink, and all that—"

"But who would want to?"

"The murderer—if it turns out to be not Pollard. Look here, Penny, Pollard is either innocent or guilty. If guilty, all your deductions are correct, but if innocent they must be transferred to some one else."

"Surely. But to whom?"

"Dunno yet. Me, I think it is Pollard—but how, *how*, how did he manage it?"

"Only by a confederate who did the deed."

"Which is not the solution! I don't know how I know it, but I know that didn't happen. Why, a villain might get a gunman to shoot somebody, but not to put up all that elaboration. The fingerprints, the telephoning stunt—all that was the work of an artist in crime, the cleverest criminal in the world, as you've admitted. Not a hireling."

"A hireling might be clever."

"Not in that way. No, a wizard like that is not anybody's hireling. He's in business for himself."

"Have it your own way. And I think you're right. Well, then, how did Pollard get down there? Aeroplane?"

"No; there's a simple explanation, only we haven't got it yet. Incidentally, how did he get up to New Hampshire and back without being missed here in New York. Aeroplane?"

"He couldn't have done it at all. You're mistaken about seeing him there."

"Maybe." Zizi knitted her pretty brows. "What time did he leave the hotel in that taxi to go to Phyllis' dinner?"

"Seven twenty-five. He had two errands on the way. He stopped—"

"I know. For theater tickets and for flowers. How do they know so positively the exact time he left?"

"That's a coincidence. The doorman happened to catch sight of Pollard's wrist watch as he got into the cab. It has a luminous face—I've seen him wear it—and the doorman noticed it was just twenty-five minutes after seven."

"What! Oh, oh, Penny! That explains it all! Oh, me, oh, my! To think of the simple solution! Oh, what a tangled web we weave, when first we practise to deceive! Oh, gracious goodness sakes! Be sure your sin will find you out!"

"For heaven's sake, Zizi, don't act like a wild woman! When you begin to quote things I know you're luny! Sit down and tell me what you're talking about!"

"Is this a dagger that I see before me? Oh, what a noble mind was here o'erthrown!"

"Don't get your Shakespeare mixed up. That first quotation is from Macbeth, but the other is from Hamlet. You look more like one of the witches!"

"Oh, I am! I am! Double, double, toil and trouble!"

"Zizi, behave! Stop your foolishness!"

The girl was dancing up and down the room like a veritable witch-elf. She flung her long, thin arms about, and was really excited, her brain teeming with the sudden revelation that had come to her.

"Do you remember the Macbeth witches?" she demanded, pausing before him, poised on one foot, and looking like a Sibyl herself.

"Of course I do! Double, double, toil and trouble; fire burn and cauldron bubble!"

"That's it—that's the answer! Oh, Penny Wise, it's as plain as day—as Day! I see it all—all—*all*!"

"Might I inquire what enlightened you?"

"The radium watch! The luminous face! Oh, I'm onto the watch! I'm on the watch!"

"Zizi, you are crazy. I refuse to talk to you as long as you act so foolishly. Will you be quiet and tell me things?"

"Penny, I'm so excited. Yes, I'll tell you, after I prove my case to myself. I've got to go to the hotel—to Pollard's hotel—and see about something."

And in a moment she was gone, and in the shortest possible time she was at the hotel.

"Again?" groaned the telephone girl, as Zizi earnestly began to whisper her questions.

"Yes, again—and yet." Zizi said: "Now, listen, and tell me this. What did Mr Pollard say when he called his cab that night?"

"Why, that's a funny thing. Why do you ask that? He said 'Will you call me a cab, please.'"

"Why was that funny?"

"Because he always says, 'Call me a taxi.' I remember, because I'm afraid some time I'll say, 'You're a taxi!'"

"Funny girl! Well, I'm trying to prove that Mr Pollard was not himself that night!"

"Oh—Mr Pollard never drinks anything."

"How do you know?"

"I just happen to know. You're wrong, he was perfectly sober."

"Then why did he telephone to the cleaner's when he knew it was past their closing time?"

"I suppose he didn't think of that."

"Not like Manning Pollard's way. One more thing. Isn't Mr Pollard a careful dresser?"

"Is he! The finest ever. He's so particular, he's an old fuss."

"You know a lot about him, don't you?"

"I can't help it. A telephone operator gets side-lights on people who are continually discussing their affairs over her lines. I don't have to listen in, but I can't help knowing how often Mr Pollard telephones to cleaners and tailors and haberdashers and all that. Can I?"

"No, honey, of course you can't. Good-by."

And as Zizi left the hotel she met Manning Pollard coming in. He looked at her curiously, for though they had never met, Phyllis had told him of the queer girl, and he felt sure this was she.

To confirm it he went directly to the telephone girl and inquired of her, and the obliging young woman repeated to him the whole of her conversation with Zizi.

"H'm," Pollard observed to himself, "h'm—exactly so."

And he turned on his heel and went out again.

Absorbed in his thoughts, he paid no attention to a slim little figure that slipped out from a protecting doorway and followed him. Nor did he notice that the determined little person kept on following him as he boarded a Fifth Avenue Bus and went southward.

Zizi, who could make herself as inconspicuous as a schoolgirl when she chose, sat in the rear seat, looking out of the window.

Pollard got out at the Washington Square terminus, and walked briskly westward. This was away from the Gleason apartments, though Zizi had not expected him to go there.

She followed, unnoticed, until Pollard entered what seemed to be a second-rate boarding house.

Nodding her head contentedly, Zizi waited until her quarry again made an appearance.

Then as the man went over and took a North-bound Bus, Zizi found a taxicab and gave the order to fly back to Penny Wise.

It was after fifteen or twenty minutes of the excited girl's conversation and explanations that Wise was in possession of all the facts.

"Can we get him?" he asked, and then the telephone rang.

"Hello," said Wise, and received this astonishing response.

"Manning Pollard speaking. You have been too many for me, Mr Wise. I give myself up. I don't know how you discovered so much, but I see there's no use in further effort to hide my crime. I confess, and you may come and take me. I am in my rooms at the hotel."

"You are a bit astonishing, Mr Pollard," Wise said. "But I accept your invitation and I will go at once to you. Will you stay there till I come."

"Certainly. When I perceive the game is up, what else is there for me to do? Moreover, would I call you up and surrender, if I were not sincere about it?"

"I can't see why you should. At your hotel, then? All right."

"Heavens, Zizi, what a man! I'll start right off. You call Prescott, and tell him just what Pollard said, and tell him to go to the hotel with two policemen—or enough to take the prisoner."

Wise went and Zizi did as he had bade her.

"What?" Prescott cried, over the wire, "you don't say so! Well, wonders will never cease! I don't altogether believe in it, but I'll hurry to the hotel."

Then Zizi herself hurried to the hotel, more excited than ever.

She calmed herself a little on the way, for she knew she must be cool and collected to take her part in the scene.

She reached the hotel a moment or two before Prescott got there.

But he came, as she waited, and, seeing her, exclaimed, "Are you sure? Where's Mr Wise?"

"He isn't here," she said, a little unnecessarily. "I'll go up with you."

"Come if you like," said Prescott, carelessly, and with his two husky companions he entered the elevator.

At Pollard's door the group paused, and Prescott knocked.

"Come in," they heard, and went in.

The man sitting in an easy chair sprang up.

"What the devil!" he cried.

"Easy now, Mr Pollard," Prescott said, "you told us to come and get you, and we're here."

"Told you—come and get me— Get out, I say!"

Prescott stared. Was this Manning Pollard? Talking so unlike himself! Clearly, it was not!

"Who are you?" Prescott said, curiously; and then, illogically, "Mr Pollard, who are you?"

"I'm not Manning Pollard. If you've come to arrest him, you've got the wrong man." But though blustering, the speaker was white with fear. Overcome with surprise and terror, he fell back into his chair and began to swear fluently.

"None of that, now," said Prescott, dumfounded, but vigilant. "If you're not Manning Pollard you're his twin brother! Is that it?"

"No—oh, no."

"Well, then, who are you?"

"I'm—oh, hang it all—I'm Horace Taylor."

"And just what are you doing in Pollard's rooms? And why do you look so much like him? You're his very double!"

"Double, double, toil and trouble!" Zizi chanted softly, to herself, but no one noticed her.

"I am," said Taylor, bitterly, "and he has betrayed me. I'll make a clean breast of it. I've done nothing wrong— and I didn't know he was going to. I'm—well I'm his half-brother."

"You're the exact image of him in form and feature, but your manner is utterly different."

"Yes, because he has had education and culture—and I've had none."

"Well, out with your story."

"Manning Pollard is the son of the man who was also my father. We are exactly alike, though I'm a couple of years older."

"Are you a legitimate son?"

"I am not—but neither is Manning, though he was legally made so, by his parents' marriage some years after he was born."

"You know all that?" cried Zizi. "You were up in Coggs' Hollow day before yesterday."

"Yes, miss. I saw you there, at the clerk's office. I knew then there was trouble brewing for Manning."

"Double, double, toil and trouble—"

"Yes, miss, exactly that! Manning hired me to personate him here in his rooms the night of—well, you know that night, Mr Prescott. He—oh, thunder! shall I tell it all?"

"Yes, tell it all," Prescott was breathless with curiosity and interest.

"Well, he paid me heaps to meet him at a certain spot."

"Fifth Avenue and Forty-second Street?"

"Yes, in the crowd. He had supplied me with clothes just like his own, and given me full instructions."

"What were the instructions?" Prescott demanded.

"I was to meet him there, at about six, and I was to assume his identity for a time. I was to come here, come up to his rooms, here, dress for dinner, take a taxi and go away at exactly twenty-five past seven. While here I was to telephone once or twice, also to call a bellhop and see him."

"What a plot!" exclaimed Prescott, "oh, *what* a plot!"

"I did all this, and then, later, when I went into the Astor for the theater tickets, Manning met me there, and in the crowd, we changed identities again, he got into the cab I had got out of, and he went on to the dinner and I went home."

"You knew what his object in all this was?"

"I did not! Before God I never would have consented if I had. He told me it was to play a joke on some of his friends, and the price he offered was so great I consented."

"And you telephoned to the cleaner's and all that?"

"Yes; and called the bellboy to take the letter—which Manning had prepared. Then afterward, when I read the papers I felt sure that Manning had killed Robert Gleason. I never taxed him with it, for it was none of my business and if it was true I didn't want to know it."

"This explains Mr Barry seeing Pollard over in Brooklyn—it was you, I suppose."

"I suppose so. What are you going to do with me?"

"Hold you for the present, but if your story is true, you're merely a dupe. How come you here now?"

"Manning came down to my place about an hour ago, and said for me to come right up here and personate him again for an hour or so, and then he said he'd never trouble me again."

"You came willingly?"

"Oh, the poor chap was so upset, seemed in danger, and said I could save his life by doing this."

"You have. Of course he's miles away by now. What a mess—oh, *what* a mess!"

Prescott was disgusted. First that such a gigantic hoax had been put over on him, and second that he had utterly lost all chance to catch the perpetrator thereof.

"You put it over neatly enough," Prescott growled, looking at the man, Taylor.

"Yes, but I nearly muffed it. While I was dressing here that night, some guy called up to know Robert Gleason's address. I hadn't a notion, but I chanced to see a little address book on the desk, and I soon found it."

"Yes, that was the butler of Davenport's patient," Prescott remembered. "Well, it was one great game. And we've lost our man!"

And then Pennington Wise came.

"Taylor?" he said, looking curiously at the double. "Well, you *are* an exact duplicate!"

"What do you know about this?" cried Prescott, "Where's Pollard?"

"Dead," replied Wise, gravely. "I've just left your place, Taylor, and your precious half-brother shot himself there fifteen minutes ago."

"Spill it," commanded Prescott.

"I knew when I got the message from Pollard that the dupe would be here so I sent you, Prescott, while I went down to Taylor's home. As I expected, Pollard was there. He made a full confession, seeing the game was up, and then eluding my watchfulness, he shot himself. I called the police in and I came up here to tell you."

"I can't get over it," said Prescott, his eyes wide with wonder. "What a scheme!"

"Simple in the main," said Wise, "but elaborate as to details. He left nothing unprovided for. He foresaw every condition and met it. The only thing, and the thing that proved his undoing was his forgetting that Mr Taylor had not enjoyed the same social advantages that he himself had."

"What do you mean?" growled Taylor.

"He had evening clothes ready for you here. He planned for every item of your conduct, but he couldn't know that you would wear a wrist watch with evening dress! That little incident caught the attention of Zizi, and from that she instantly deduced that the man that got into that taxi with a wrist watch on in the evening, could not have been Manning Pollard himself! Moreover, he drew the attention of the doorman to the time on its illuminated dial, and so, the luminous face fixed the time, but Pollard would have had on no wrist watch."

"That's so," agreed Prescott, "Pollard's a perfect dresser, I happen to know."

"He confessed it all," went on Wise. "He was game, I'll say, and he told me frankly that Gleason had threatened to tell of his shameful birth. He was very sensitive about the matter. Gleason told him he would disclose the secret unless Pollard ceased his attentions to Miss Lindsay. Also, Pollard knew, from Lane, of Gleason's will. Therefore, rid of Gleason, Pollard figured he could win Miss Lindsay and the fortune. So he set about to get rid of Gleason—and did. His threat that day was, of course, with the idea that such a remark would tend to divert suspicion from him—which it did. His alibi, so perfectly prepared, he scorned to declare, knowing that when it was learned by inquiry it would be satisfactory, which it was. That's all, except to credit my assistant, Zizi, with the acumen which found out the truth. Her suspicion of a double was roused by the wrist watch episode. She came over here, and learned that the exact doings of the man here that fatal evening were not precisely in Pollard's usual manner. She watched Pollard come in and go out again. She followed him, and when he went into a house, she felt sure it was the home of his double. It was! She saw a man come out, and though it was like Pollard, her newly attentive eyes showed her it was not really he. Off guard, Taylor has many dissimilarities from his brother. She flew back to me with the story, not knowing how soon the denouncements was to come. And then, when Pollard telephoned he would give himself up, I knew at once he meant to have Taylor here in his place. So I went to Taylor's place, and a more surprised man than Manning Pollard I never saw!"

"As my reward," Zizi said quietly, "I want to be allowed to go and tell Phyllis Lindsay the truth. I love her so, and I don't want her shocked at hearing about it from a lot of policemen."

There was no objection on the part of anybody, and Zizi went on her errand.

An hour later, when all three of the Lindsays had been told, and had indeed been shocked and horrified, Philip Barry came in.

"Phyllis," he said, scarcely seeing any one else.

Phyllis rose and went straight to him. He held out his arms, and she clung to him as they closed round her.

"I never doubted you for a minute, Phil," she said, "but that man had a sort of power over me—a—oh, almost an hypnotic power, I think."

"Forget him," Zizi advised, smiling at the pair.

"Now, you two talk over things, while I go in the library and flirt with Louis, with Mrs Lindsay for chaperon. Forget everybody else, and think there are only you two in the whole wide world."

THE END

Other Resurrected Press Mysteries
From Carolyn Wells

Resurrected Press Mysteries From Louis Tracy

The Albert Gate Mystery

Four men murdered and a fortune in diamonds belonging to the Turkish Sultan stolen, while the Foreign Office official in charge has gone missing. Was it a common jewelry theft or was it a case of international intrigue? This is the question that barrister detective Reginald Brett must solve.

The Bartlett Mystery

When Ronald Tower is murdered on his way to a bridge game on the yacht Sans Souci it at first appears a common crime. But as Rex Carshaw finds, a tragic case of mistaken identity leads to political scandal among the rich and powerful of New York.

The Strange Case of Mortimer Fenley

When the wealthy Mortimer Fenley is struck down by a shot from an express rifle on the steps of his mansion, detectives Winter and Furneaux of Scotland Yard must find the culprit. Was it the artist who claimed he was painting a picture at the time of the shot? The disaffected younger son? Or is there another suspect?

The Stowmarket Mystery

For five generations the Fergus-Hume family has been cursed. Each of the baronets has met a violent end. When the fifth baronet is found slain by a ceremonial Japanese dagger, suspicion falls on his cousin David. It falls to barrister detective Reginald Brett to prove his innocence and find the real murder in a case that spans two continents and as many centuries.

Visit www.resurrectedpress.com

Resurrected Press Mysteries by J. S. Fletcher

The Orange-Yellow Diamond
When an elderly pawnbroker is murdered in the London parish of Paddington, a young, down on his luck writer is accused of the crime. But then it's found the pawnbroker had had in his possession an extraordinary South African diamond worth over eighty-thousand pounds —a diamond that's now missing. It falls to Melky Rubenstein to unravel the mystery and prove the young man's innocence.

The Middle Temple Murder
When an elderly man's body is found on the steps of chambers in the Midde Temple, one of the Inns of Court, it falls to newspaperman Frank Spargo and Detective-Sergeant Rathbury to solve the crime. The murdered man, for indeed it was murder, was found with no money or identification on his person except for a piece of paper with the name and address of a young barrister. Who is the victim? Why was he killed? Who is the murderer?

Scarhaven Keep
Bassett Oliver, the famed actor, has gone missing. When Oliver fails to show for a rehearsal, aspiring playwright Richard Copplestone finds himself sent to the small village of Scarhaven on the northern coast of England to track down the actors movements. What he finds is mystery. Find the answers as Copplestone unravels the mystery of Scarhaven Keep.

Visit www.resurrectedpress.com

Resurrected Press Mysteries by Fergus Hume

The Green Mummy

Professor Braddock hoped to compare the burial practices of the Egyptians with those of the ancient Peruvians with his latest acquisition, the mummy of the last Inca, Caxas. But on arrival, the packing case proved to hold not the mummy, but the body of his assistant Sidney Bolton. It falls to Archie Hope to discover the murderer if he is to marry the professors step-daughter, Lucy Kendal. Who killed Bolton and where is the mummy? Was it the sea captain Hervey? The mysterious Don Pedro? Cockatoo the Polynesian servant? The professor, himself? And what has become of the emeralds? These are the questions that Hope must answer amongst the secrets of the past in The Green Mummy.

The Mystery of a Hansom Cab

"Truth is said to be stranger than fiction, and certainly the extraordinary murder which took place in Melbourne Friday morning goes a long way towards verifying that saying." Thus opens The Mystery of a Hansom Cab, the best selling mystery of the nineteenth century. When a man is found dead in a hansom cab one of Melbourne's leading citizens is accused of the murder. He pleads his innocence, yet refuses to give an alibi. It falls to a determined lawyer and an intrepid detective to find the truth, revealing long kept secrets along the way. Fergus Hume's first and perhaps most famous mystery... The Mystery Of A Hansom Cab.

Visit www.resurrectedpress.com

Resurrected Press Mysteries from the Dr. John Thorndyke Series

Dr. John Thorndyke Lecturer on Medical Jurisprudence and Forensic Medicine. Before Bones, before CSI, before Quincy, M.E– there was Dr. John Thorndyke solving the most baffling cases of Edwardian London using the latest tools of medical science. Read about his cases in:

The Eye of Osiris
John Bellingham, noted Egyptologist has vanished not once but twice in the same day. Now Dr, Thorndyke must unravel the tangled claims on his estate, solve the riddle of the missing man and find the "Eye of Osiris".

The Mystery of 31 New Inn
When Dr. Jervis is whisked away in a coach with no windows to an unknown location to treat a man in a coma from undivulged causes it is Dr. Thorndyke who must come up with the solution.

The Red Thumb Mark
The first of Dr. Thorndyke's cases finds him trying to prove the innocence of a young man accused of being a diamond thief despite the fact that his finger print was found at the scene of the crime.

John Thorndyke's Cases
More cases of medical mysteries as told by his trusted assistant Jervis, M.D. Eight stories of crime and deduction in Edwardian London.

Visit www.resurrectedpress.com

Resurrected Press Mysteries by John R. Watson & Arthur J. Rees

The Hampstead Mystery

High Court Justice Sir Horace Fewbanks found shot dead in his Hampstead home, a butler with a criminal past, a scorned lover and a hint of scandal. These are the elements of the Hampstead Mystery that Detective Inspector Chippenfield of Scotland Yard must unravel with the assistance of the ambitious Detective Rolfe. But will he be able to sort out the tangled threads of this case and arrest the culprit before he is upstaged by the celebrated gentleman detective Crewe. Follow the details of this amazing case at it plays out across Hampstead, London and Scotland until it reaches a stunning conclusion in the courts of the Old Bailey.

The Mystery of the Downs

When Harry Marsland was caught in a sudden down pour he sought shelter at Cliff Farm. Met at the door by a young woman clearly expecting someone else he is only too glad to get inside to wait out the storm. When they hear a noise upstairs in the deserted house they investigate only to discover the body of the farm's owner, Frank Lumsden, dead of a gunshot wound. Who then, killed Lumsden, and why? Who was the woman expecting and did she have any roll in the murder? These are the questions that private detective Crewe must answer in The Mystery of the Downs.

Visit www.resurrectedpress.com

Other Resurrected Press Mysteries

Mysteries on a Train

Before the Orient Express there was:

The Rome Express by Arthur Griffiths
A man is found dead in his first class sleeping compartment on the express from Rome to Paris. Who was his murderer? The Countess? The English General? His brother the clergy man? The maid who has disappeared? Is the French justice system up to solving the crime? Read about it in The Rome Express.

The Passenger from Calais by Arthur Griffiths
Colonel Basil Annesley finds he is the only passenger on the train from Calais to Lucerne. That is until a mysterious woman shows up at the last minute to book a compartment. Who is after her? What is her secret? Is she a criminal or a victim? Read about it in The Passenger from Calais

Visit us at www.resurrectedpress.com

About Resurrected Press

A division of Intrepid Ink, LLC, Resurrected Press is dedicated to bringing high quality, vintage books back into publication. See our entire catalogue and find out more at www.ResurrectedPress.com.

About Intrepid Ink, LLC

Intrepid Ink, LLC provides full publishing services to authors of fiction and non-fiction books, eBooks and websites. From editing to formatting, from publishing to marketing, Intrepid Ink gets your creative works into the hands of the people who want to read them. Find out more at www.IntrepidInk.com.